CRIMINALLY
GOOD STORIES
VOLUME 5

CONNOR WHITELEY

DEDICATION

Thank you to all my readers without you I couldn't do what I love.

INTRODUCTION

Romantic suspense is a rather new genre for me and it is also possibly one of the most interesting genres for a few reasons. The first reason is that whilst it is a perfect blend of romance and mystery, not a lot of writers write it unfortunately, and it's even more interesting to see that the romantic suspense *subgenre* is only morphing into its own genre. Therefore, one day, romantic suspense could be a genre in its own right.

I would love that to happen.

Since I really enjoy a good romance and a good mystery so when you combine the two genres then that only makes things even better. Hence why I dedicated an entire collection to it.

Additionally, one of the things I wanted to achieve with this collection was how varied romantic suspense can be because in this collection you get to see romance spies, romantic assassins and lots of other different ways how romantic suspense can be done. And to be honest, I haven't even scratched the surface of the different romantic suspense stories you can possibly do.

That's another great reason why I love romantic suspense.

And please, don't worry, none of these stories are spicy or steamy or sexual in the slightest. I think there might be a few implied sex scenes at the end of stories but that is it.

So now we know why romantic suspense is so great, let's turn over the page and start reading the final twenty stories in this great five-volume collection.

AUTHOR OF THE BETTIE ENGLISH PRIVATE EYE MYSTERIES

CONNOR WHITELEY

DROP AT
THE BAR

A GAY SPY ROMANTIC SUSPENSE SHORT STORY

DROP AT THE BAR
22nd October 2022

Brighton, England

Arthur Jeffo might have been 24 years old and he might have once really, really loved the gayness, clubs and men of Brighton but for some reason he didn't really feel like he could enjoy it tonight.

Arthur stood next to a large fake wooden bar that was thankfully clean without a single drop of sticky alcohol on it, which was surprising considering how bad the rest of the bar or club looked.

The floors of the bar were smooth, white with a few black marks on them from shoes and boots and whatever else the clientele had decided to wear, and to be honest Arthur would have been very surprised if fighting in this bar was an alien concept to them.

All around the bar there were very tasteful and attractive square wooden tables of different heights to size the taller and shorter guests, and it really did help to add a little texture to the entire bar and even some depth. Arthur just smiled to himself as that was his interior designer training kicking in, something after a breakup with an awful boyfriend he had wanted to largely forget.

Clearly that wasn't happening.

The beautiful smell of hot sexy men's earthy, fruity and very manly aftershave filled the bar as Arthur subtly (and failed at that) watched the young hot men walking about in all their different sexualities, sex appeal and heights.

There was a group of guys in the far corner next to a dark

staircase that Arthur really didn't want to know what it led down to, and those men were all wearing tight black leather pants that really highlighted how hot they were with cowboy hats, checked shirts and even cowboy boots.

It was clear they were part of a stag do or something and they were really hot, and maybe if Arthur wasn't strictly here on business then he might have been tempted to have a go at one of the men.

They were definitely hot enough.

But he was here on business, working for a top national newspaper and he was meant to be meeting a source, a corporate spy, that was meant to be bringing him top secret files on how the company was abusing its staff. This was exactly the sort of information that Arthur had been dying to get his hands on so he could make a name for himself and prove himself worthy for a promotion or two.

And then hopefully, and Arthur was seriously hoping, then he might be able to breathe and actually slow down a fraction in his crazy life so he might be able to meet a man again.

He would love that.

"What's your poison sugar?" a young woman asked from behind the bar.

Arthur just smiled at her for a moment, she was good-looking with her smooth facial features, dark chocolate eyes and her long wavy brown hair. Arthur wouldn't have been surprised if she had gotten a lot of male attention here but then he realised that a large group of men were staring at her and trying to call her over.

"Oh I don't know," Arthur said. "It might take me a while to decide,"

Arthur was glad to see the young woman smile at him, at least he was right about the young woman wanting to get away from the large group of men.

The sound of the loud almost-deafening music (and Arthur seriously couldn't tell what music it was meant to be), people shouting at each other and Arthur could have sworn there were fights breaking out in the far corners of the bar, this definitely wasn't Arthur's sort of scene, he much preferred places were he could sit down, talk to a cute boy and actually be able to hear them properly.

This really wasn't that sort of place.

But he was here on business, he had to secure the information to get a job promotion and if needed he needed to make sure the corporate spy he was meeting was safe.

Arthur never ever wanted someone to get hurt for trying to do the right thing.

Arthur had never met a spy at all before so he didn't have a clue about what to expect, but if this company was onto the spy then Arthur wanted to protect them, because this spy was trying to improve the lives of their fellow workers and that was something that Arthur seriously admired.

But he just didn't have a clue what he was walking into.

Not a clue at all.

***

Professional Corporate Spy Noah Davis felt like such an amateur fool as he walked the narrow cobblestone streets of Brighton with its ancient bars and clubs forced into walls and spaces that he was surprised they actually fitted in. The bright lights and massive crowds of men and women and underage people were right in his face and this wasn't a controlled environment in the slightest.

The damn bar that Noah was meant to be meeting this reporter in might have been close but it was a mistake to choose somewhere in Brighton.

The cold crisp night was chilling Noah's skin down to the bone which wasn't a bad thing as it kept him alert and focused and ready to act, but this wasn't ideal.

Noah slowly walked through the cobblestone street, gliding through hot drunk men in their tight jeans and shirts and breathing in their sensational aftershave that made him really horny. It had been ages since Noah had been with a man, he had been too busy for the past two years going into companies, exposing their secrets and getting paid hundreds of thousands of pounds for doing it. It wasn't an easy job, but it was fun, exciting and Noah really felt like he was making a difference by doing it.

Yet Noah would have preferred to meet away from Brighton, the home city of the company he had been investigating, and the major problem was that too many of the higher-ups in the company partied on Saturday nights in this area.

If they saw him, which he just knew they would, then Noah could be exposed and blacklisted from the industry as a spy and never work in a corrupt company again. That was a massive risk and it was all because he had heard of some hot reporter.

It was stupid really that Noah had been reading a newspaper of all things (he was never going to let his phone die again) and he had been reading a great article written by an Arthur Jeffo and there was a cute little picture of him at the bottom of the article. A sensible person might have taken that as a sign that Noah wanted to do a man sooner and actually needed to get back out on the dating scene.

But nope.

Noah took it as a sign that he needed to meet up with this hottie, risk his entire career and he didn't even know if this Arthur person was gay or that way inclined. It was a hell of a lot to risk for no reason.

Noah just smiled to himself as he felt his body turn warm and excited and his stomach relaxed because it was this thrill that he lived for and this was exactly why he kept doing his spying job because it was dangerous and extremely fun.

After walking down the street a little more and gliding past some very drunk women, Noah hooked a left and went towards a little bar that looked like a tavern from Victorian times.

He went through the wooden door, nodded politely to the bouncer that really didn't look like he gave a toss about Noah's age and he went inside.

The bar was definitely too loud and ugly and chaotic for Noah's liking. There were at least three fighting at the far end of the bar but thankfully the bar that served drinks weren't in that direction and in all fairness there were plenty of hot men in the bar too.

Noah started to make his way through the surprisingly clean wooden floors over towards the bar when he just stopped.

Standing right next to the bar was possibly the most beautiful man he had ever seen. He instantly recognised it as Arthur Jeffo and bloody hell that little stupid photo didn't do him justice at all.

Arthur was a fucking hot man with a typical gym body, manly sexy broad shoulders and a very thin waist that Noah couldn't wait to wrap his arms around, and Noah just knew that Arthur had a solid stomach without a shred of fat on it.

And even Arthur's face was divine with his strong manly jawline, amazing smile as he spoke to the young woman behind the bar and his short brown hair was so perfect that Noah was rather pleased that his wayward parts were flaring to life and tenting.

His heart was beating faster and his head was going light and Noah wanted to talk with Arthur right now.

"Noah?" an elderly man said.

Noah turned around and just gave the elderly man a fake smile when he saw that his boss was standing only a few metres from him.

This wasn't going to end well at all.

***

"Have a good night," Arthur said to the pretty young woman behind the bar as she went off to deal with other customers.

Arthur had really liked talking to her and she was actually rather interesting with her only working in the bar because she needed the money to start her own beauty business that was already starting to seriously take off.

And with more and more coming into the bar now, the temperature was starting to increase, but not too much as the room was still comfortable.

Arthur looked away from the wonderful bar and the young woman and really focused on the incoming crowd. He noticed a lot of hot beautiful men come in and out of the bar with their friends with a good night of clubbing and partying and probably some more adult activity ahead.

But there was one guy that seriously caught his attention.

In amongst the sea of other hot men coming into the bar, there was a young cute man that made Arthur's face light up, his smile reached ear to ear and Arthur felt like the entire world had stopped.

The young man was extremely cute with his dark brown buzzcut, his smooth expensive white shirt and black jeans that made him look smart and even more beautiful without making him seem like a poser.

He was so beautiful and Arthur felt his throat dry up and for the first time in his entire life, Arthur honestly didn't know what to say, do or even write in his article. His mind was starting to go blank for a moment until he noticed an elderly man start talking to the cute man.

Arthur felt like that wasn't good.

For a moment Arthur was concerned that he was just being jealous and almost overprotective of the cute man, he had sadly felt that feeling before, and this one just felt different.

Arthur was feeling an instinct that he had honed in recent years from meeting with informants, the odd (amateur) corporate spy and other confidential sources. This was the type of feeling that Arthur only felt when he knew there was danger.

Arthur needed to get to that cute man, get the information and go.

Arthur quickly ordered a drink of cola and pretended to walk over to the cute man acting completely drunk.

"You shouldn't be here. We know what you're up to," the elderly man said to the cute man.

Arthur's stomach immediately tensed but he kept acting drunk and walking over to the cute man. If this elderly man did truly suspect the cute man as a spy then this could get very ugly very quickly.

"We know you're gay and you will never get a promotion in our company," the elderly man said.

Arthur felt totally relieved when the elderly man said that and he was so close to the cute man that hopefully he could save him sooner rather than later. But the only problem with acting drunk was that Arthur sadly couldn't move as quick as he wanted.

"And what do you know about spies and missing files in the company?" the elderly man asked.

Arthur pretended to trip over and fell upon the cute man. Arthur really loved feeling the cute man's hot, hard and slightly sweaty body as he acted to recover whilst drunk.

"Play along," Arthur whispered to the cute man as he breathed in his hot manly scent that was really exciting Arthur.

The cute man wrapped his arms around Arthur like he was helping a stupid drunk, said bye to the elderly man and pretended to help Arthur over to a bar stool in a dark corner on the opposite side of the bar.

"Nicely played," Arthur said as he sat on a very uncomfortable and very worn bar stool and pressed his back against the warm wall.

"You don't get to be as good of a spy as me without learning a few things. The corporate spy game is deadly, messy and very dangerous at times," the cute man said.

Arthur just focused on every single sexy little word that came out of the man's big beautiful lips.

"The name's Noah and it's good to meet you at last Arthur," the cute man said.

Arthur was so glad to finally have this cute man's name but it was a little weird that Noah knew his.

"Relax Arthur," Noah said. "I always research the peeps I'm meeting. It keeps me alive so I wanted to be sure I was safe and giving the info to a good journalist,"

Arthur instantly knew what Noah meant. He had met plenty of journalists that would happily give the corrupt information back to the corporation the spy or whistle-blower stole it from, for the right price of course.

Arthur wasn't one of those journalists. The people had a right to know what corruption and laws were being broken by these massive monster companies.

And Arthur had to admit it was really hot to meet someone so beautiful but also so knowledgeable about companies, journalism and how everything worked behind the scenes.

"Do you have the info?" Arthur asked.

Arthur loved seeing Noah mockingly smile at him.

"You're all business aren't you?" Noah asked. "And anyway look at your nine o'clock with the elderly man,"

Arthur subtly looked over and saw the elderly man that was presumably from the company beautiful Noah was trying to expose and he was watching them with a large group of other people.

There had to be at least ten men watching Arthur and Noah and that really unnerved him. This wasn't good in the slightest.

"They know I stole the information and files and I wasn't as careful as I normally am," Noah said. "They're watching us to see when I made a mistake, they're exposed us and we'll probably get arrested for stealing information or corporate espionage,"

As farfetched as some of that sounded Arthur was all too familiar with some of the lies that big companies told to discredit journalists and articles that attacked them.

"Then we need to exchange the information and get out of the bar and disappear without getting caught," Arthur said with a massive smile on his face.

This was going to be great fun.

Noah smiled too and Arthur was really struggling to focus on anything else but this beautiful sexy man in front of him.

"Care for a dance cutie?" Arthur asked gesturing Noah to take his hand.

As soon as Noah took Arthur's hand, Arthur loved how soft, sexy and smooth Noah's wonderful hands were. And that was all before Arthur realised how amazing it felt to hold Noah and the sheer attraction and passion he felt for this beautiful man was almost overwhelming.

Arthur liked Noah a damn sight more than he ever wanted to

admit. Even to himself.

***

As stunning Arthur pulled Noah onto the dance floor which was a very fancy term for a tableless section of the bar that allowed people to dance on the hard wooden floors, Noah was so amazed how horny he was and how much he just wanted Arthur in that moment.

Arthur wasn't only the hottest man he had ever seen but he was also smart, intelligent and very, very crafty.

Noah just hoped that their plan of exchanging the information, getting out of the club and disappearing into the night would work.

It was even harder with Noah's bosses and other people that he suspected were cops watching their every move. Noah was going to have to be very careful and very clever and he had to protect the hot stunning man that was dancing with him.

Noah was rather grateful that the current song playing had a very sexual and sensual rhythm to it and whilst the vast majority of the bar were focused on them. His bosses and the undercover cops really didn't want to watch two men dance against each other.

The great sound of people cheering, singing along and more gay and straight couples joining the dance floor echoed off the bright walls of the bar.

The wonderful smell of hot sweaty men and women and aftershave and alcohol filled the dance floor and as soon as a group of straight people obscured the view from the undercover cops Noah got to work.

"Show time," Noah whispered into Arthur's ear.

Noah carefully and subtly took the USB stick with the information out of his pocket and started moving his hand all over Arthur's amazing body.

Noah feeling up Arthur's wonderful chest, hard stomach and lower regions definitely wasn't needed for the mission but it was fun.

And it certainly made Noah know for certain that Arthur was very gay, aroused and into him. Exactly how Noah liked his jobs.

The straight couples moved away and Noah noticed that the elderly man and the group of cops had moved.

They were gone.

"Excuse me," a young man said.

Noah pretended to trip forward and grab Arthur's very firm ass. Slipping the USB stick into his back pocket in the process.

Then Noah broke away, wrapped his arms round Arthur's shoulders and smiled at the rather cute male cop that was standing there showing them his police badge.

"Can we help you officer?" Arthur asked, like he was scared but of course Noah just knew that he was far from that.

"Sir can you please show me your hands," the cop said to Noah.

Noah nodded and showed the cop his hands but of course they were empty.

"Sir I believe you are in the procession of stolen property including highly confidential files that would inhibit and damage national security," the cop said.

Noah really forced himself not to smile, he had to give it to his bosses at the corrupt and abusive company. They certainly knew what lies and fake evidence to show the police.

"Oh my god," Arthur said taking a few steps back and sounding really high-pitched.

Noah loved it how Arthur was going to play the dumb-stupid-gay card.

"You mean he's a criminal. Oh my, I couldn't have that. I knew I shouldn't have come to a straight bar," Arthur said.

Noah forced himself not to laugh.

The cop smiled at Arthur. "It's okay sir. I just need to ask Noah a few questions but you're free to go. Have a good night,"

Arthur weakly smiled at the cop and started to back away.

Noah was so glad that Arthur was going to be able to slip away from the bar without suspicion with the information needed to expose the company.

As Arthur started to walk away Noah had to admit he looked

stunning from the rear and Noah's horniest was seriously struggling to stay in check.

"Wait officer," the elderly man said. "He was acting drunk earlier and now he's fine. Something is dodgy with him too,"

Noah just frowned as his idiot bosses in their dark black suits surrounded Arthur and the cop too didn't look impressed.

Maybe their getaway wouldn't be as easy as he thought.

Noah just feared things were going to get very ugly for both of them.

And he had no clue how to save the cute stunning man he was really attracted to.

Not a clue at all.

***

Arthur was seriously starting to hate this absolutely stupid and pathetic and homophobic dick of an elderly man and the other men surrounding him on the dance floor. All Arthur wanted to do was expose a corrupt and abusive company but clearly there was no way that was going to happen for a little while.

Arthur had to escape from this mess.

"Sir," the male cop said, "I'll ask you once and then you're on your own. Do you have the stolen information on you?"

Arthur partly wanted to keep playing up the dumb-gay routine because it was so easy and it was the only thing working for him at the moment and sadly he just knew it was the only thing saving him for now.

Arthur looked over the wooden bar with the pretty young woman currently pouring a tray of drinks and she was watching him intensely.

He winked at her and she lowered her head and kept pouring the drinks.

Arthur doubted she was going to be worth any help but he had to try.

"Sir," the cop said.

"Listen mate," Arthur said in a very high pitched voice. "I ain't a criminal, I ain't even from Brighton I came here fun. I didn't know it was so criminal honest,"

"He's lying," the elderly man said.

The cop looked at the ground and then exchanged glances with Noah and Arthur. Arthur really loved how cool and collective and confident Noah looked given the situation.

Even now with them both about to be arrested Noah still looked so hot and beautiful.

The cop took out his handcuffs. "Both of you are coming with me. We can sort this out down at the station,"

Arthur took a few steps back as the cop came towards him. Why the cop was going to arrest him first he didn't know.

"Wait officer. I'm innocent. Please, believe me," Arthur said.

The young woman walked past holding a massive tray of shots and Arthur instantly took out the USB stick.

The young woman tripped and the entire tray of drinks went over the cop.

The woman fell to the floor but Arthur subtly passed her the USB stick.

Arthur saw her quickly stuff the stick in her bra.

"I'm so sorry officer," the young woman said.

"It's okay Miss. It was an accident," the officer said with a massive schoolboy smile.

"She's lying," the elderly man said. "She-"

"Silence," the cop said and he just looked at Arthur.

"Officer," Arthur said. "Pat me down right here and now and you'll see I have nothing to hide,"

The cop didn't seem convinced but with the spilt alcohol dripping off him he clearly wanted to go back to the station and get changed and probably just go home so he nodded.

Arthur parted his legs and held his legs sideways and the cop quickly patted him down. Arthur hated the rough feeling of the cop's touch-up but the cop was done.

The cop even remembered to search all of Arthur's pockets

which a lot of cops forget but of course there was nothing to find.

"You're free to go and-" the officer said before he realised that Noah was gone.

"Officer-" the elderly man said.

The cop shot the elderly man and the rest of his large group a warning finger and just stormed off. Clearly the cop was done with the elderly man's stupid games and he left the bar.

The young woman walked past Arthur again and she subtly slipped the USB stick into the back of his jeans. Arthur had to admit she was flat out amazing and he was going to pay her later for all of her wonderful help.

Arthur just walked out of the bar but now he was really curious about where in the world that hot beautiful man Noah had gone to.

And why had he left so quickly without even saying goodbye?

***

As bad as Noah felt for just abandoning sexy Arthur in the bar, it was needed and from years of experience that was the only way to confuse and make the cop angry enough to just leave the two of them alone.

Noah sat on Brighton beach in the darkness with the pitch black sea in front of him crashing into the cold sand. The coldness radiated up through his jeans but Noah didn't really mind too much, it was the chills had made him feel alive and okay and alert.

In the darkness of the sandy beach seemed to stretch on endlessly to his sides with the bright almost-fun-fair lights in the distance and the lights from the hotels and casinos on the seafront burning away some of the darkness.

But after the mission, Noah just really enjoyed the quiet sound of the crashing waves, the coldness of the sand and the lack of people. But Noah still couldn't believe he had actually left that stunning man in the bar.

It was so normal for Noah to leave people behind and just get out of situations with cops, companies and everything else that he had actually done it without thinking, but Arthur was different.

And it was that feeling that Arthur was special that annoyed him, in a good way.

Normally Noah loved being with so many men, having great sex with him and then leaving the relationship after a few weeks (or days more often than not) it was just easier with his corporate spy lifestyle. But after meeting someone as stunning, clever and cunning as Arthur, Noah wasn't sure if he wanted that life anymore.

Ever since Noah had been a little boy he had dreamed of coming home to a stunning man after a mission, kissing him and just talking about it, like his parents did. Noah's parents worked hard every single day of their life, came home and told each other everything. They were both so loving and caring to each other.

Noah just wanted to do that with a man.

As much as Noah didn't want to admit it, he was going to have to risk everything again by going back to that bar, showing his face and making sure that Arthur was okay.

And if there was a choice between Arthur getting arrested and charged with the corporate espionage instead of him, Noah was perfectly okay with changing places for the first time ever. Not that this had ever happened before anyway.

Noah stood up and started to walk towards the concrete stairs upwards to the seafront when he just stopped and smiled when he saw stunning Arthur was walking down towards him.

And he wouldn't have blamed Arthur for leaving him, hating him or even exposing his corporate spying activities for almost getting him arrested, but Arthur honestly did look happy to see him.

It was in that moment that Noah knew that if Arthur wanted a relationship then there was a great chance that everything was going to be okay, wonderful and even magical.

And there wasn't a single man Noah would rather spend his time with. Arthur was wonderfully stunning, clever and cunning and that was exactly the sort of man Noah wanted.

He just hoped that Arthur felt the exact same way.

***

A month later, Arthur was sitting up on his massive Queen-size bed looking at his tablet early on a Sunday morning reading the news headlines when he learnt that his article had caused shockwaves throughout the UK.

Arthur pulled the very beautiful and sexy and seriously hot Noah closer to him as he slept in only his tight black boxers that thankfully left very little to the imagination. The bright morning sunlight shone through Arthur's large windows and the bright blue walls of his bedroom amplified the sunlight to make the bedroom feel even more perfect and spacious and airy.

Some other interior designer tricks that he had learnt from that damn ex-boyfriend.

Arthur really loved how his article had exposed the entire string of abusive, corrupt and illegal practices that not only Noah's company used but a ton of other companies in the same industry. Arthur's article had even become so major that it had made international news and Arthur had received ten job offers from all over the world.

Arthur would be lying if he wasn't considering travelling to New Zealand, Canada or mainland Europe to tackle some corrupt companies in these countries.

But as Noah woke up and kissed him, Arthur just savoured the passionate, soft kisses that he had really loved waking up to every single morning for the past month. He had even helped Noah on another corporate espionage case that was surprisingly tense, and that had only made him love Noah even more.

And then it dawned on Arthur that for the first time in maybe ever, he actually realised that there was more to life than work, news stories and promotions.

There was also love in life, and as he slowly ran his fingers down Noah's hard chest and stomach, and loved the feeling of attraction that pulsed through him, Arthur honestly realised that love was the most important part of life after all.

And as Noah took Arthur's tablet away and started kissing him and got on top of him, Arthur just knew that they were made for each other. They both loved their work, they both loved exposing corrupt companies and most importantly they both seriously loved each other.

Those were the three most important things to Arthur and he was seriously looking forward to spending a lot of time with Noah and definitely growing old with him.

Because this really was true love.

AUTHOR OF BETTIE ENGLISH PRIVATE EYE MYSTERIES

CONNOR WHITELEY

MATED AT THE MORGUE

A MYSTERY CRIME SHORT STORY

MATED AT THE MORGUE

This was bad! This was so so bad!

In all my life I have never been in such a bad situation, because I am currently paralysed and laying on a fucking morgue table.

Now I do not blame you in the slightest for not exactly knowing what it feels like, but for starters, I'm not dead. I'm just very, very paralysed which is horrific in itself. And to make matters even worse, the massive metal slab of a morgue table I'm currently on is freezing cold.

I mean it must have been put in a freezer overnight, because I am freezing here, and I'm deadly certain (probably not the best idea to use *deadly* in a place like this) that if I could move I would be shivering.

But sadly I am completely paralysed and the strangest thing about all of this is whenever the morgue attendees come in they talk about me like I'm dead and I'm about to be sliced into.

Personally I really don't like the idea of that, I don't know about you, but I don't like being thought of as dead when I'm very much alive. And to make matters worse, the entire morgue smells so horrible of extremely strong orange, cloves and clementine scented chemicals.

I don't want to have to breathe in all that until one of two things happens. Even a very smart person realises I'm alive and they help me. Or the admittedly (and far more) terrifying option is someone cuts me open and then I die.

Truly.

So as I laid here and stare up at the massive white ceiling with a massive white light shining overhead, which I took as a massive cruel joke, I was seriously starting to doubt I would ever survive.

In all honesty I'm not even too sure how I ended up in such a situation. I'm an office worker you see by day and I work in a massive investment bank doing computers, accounts and admin things. It is actually a lot more interesting than it sounds, and because I helped the CEO get a few million pounds of investment yesterday. I went out for drinks with my friends.

We went out for dinner first, of course, because I learn during university that dinner was critical if you want to spend all night drinking. And that's a very pro tip.

But I suppose things started to become a problem when I was on my tenth cocktail (and the real key there is not to mix drinks!) and my mouth started to burn and I could taste my golden chicken goujons and crispy juicy deep fried chicken.

Then I woke up here.

The only thing I can possibly think of was I can vomited, become paralysed and now I was here in this morgue on a wonderfully cold slab on a Saturday morning instead of in my bed, hopefully with a gay guy that I picked up the night before.

The sound of some kind of door opening made me want to look around, blink and do something else. But that was impossible and I really wanted to scream when an elderly man with a face covered in ache looked at me and licked his lips.

I wanted to really fucking scream then!

"Don't worry," the elderly man said, "the good Doctor will find out what happened to you,"

I wanted to shout at him and tell him I didn't need anything because I was alive, fit and very well. I didn't need him doing anything to me.

"Doctor," the elderly man said dipping his head slightly.

If I could move I would have breathed a sigh of relief when I saw this man was only a volunteer helper. But I wasn't exactly sure if that was very comforting, because who the hell volunteers to help out at a morgue in their retirement!

"Thank you Wilfred," presumably the doctor said.

I just wanted to roll my eyes. *Wilfred.* I'm sorry but that was such a stupid name and so old fashioned, and when I saw *Wilfred* walk away I was seriously happy.

"That will be all today, Wil. I'll deal with this body and if anyone more come in over the weekend I'll deal with them on Monday. Go home and enjoy the weekend," presumably the doctor said.

"You sure doc?"

I didn't know what the doctor did, but I really hoped he only nodded as I heard the door shut behind Wilfred.

Then it locked.

Now I am no expert in doors, how they work and how they lock. But I am extremely sure morgues and their doctors and their dead patients wouldn't have a reason to be locked in the same room together.

I seriously didn't want to be here anymore!

A few moments later the massive white light moved away from my face and focused on my chest, and... wow?

I was staring at a seriously hot sexy man with an angular face, model-like looks and the most stunning emerald green eyes I had ever seen. This man was hot!

Yet I was a little unsure of him because he looked so young (about my age to be honest), so I couldn't understand how he was a doctor and was conducting autopsies all by himself.

But god this man was hot.

The Doctor smiled at me as he looked into my unmoving, paralysed eyes. Then he checked my patient information, presumably from the police and paramedics.

"Mr Luke Ashley," the doctor said, "you're quite the looker, and I locked the door so we can have some privacy,"

Shit!

This was just my fucking luck wasn't it. I wasn't actually dead, I was alive and I was going to be "touched up" by a doctor that liked dead bodies. What the fuck!

I really, really tried to lift a finger, blink and kick. But nothing was moving, I was perfectly alive and there was no way to prove it.

The Doctor gently ran a finger down my slightly muscular chest and my slightly six-pack abs, and then I felt his finger hit something. Then I realise was I extremely grateful for the towel covering my lower section.

"You know Luke," the Doctor said, "you actually remind me a little of my ex-boyfriend. He left me a few weeks ago when I graduated medical school,"

Now I felt so stupid for really wanting to shiver with excitement at the way he said my name. He sounded so sexy, charming- and utterly creepy as I saw him trying to decide which scalpel to use to cut me open.

I had to do something!

"And I'm sorry. I'm Doctor Calum Limestone and I'm covering the current doctor whilst he's on holiday for the weekend," he said.

I had to admit Calum was a good name, and he did look great.

Calum pressed the cold scalpel against my chest and I really wanted to scream, lash out or just do something to stop him.

"If you were alive, I would never do this to you. You're beautiful and I'm sure you have an interesting life. It's wrong that great looking guys like you die,"

I'm not fucking dead genius!

The scalpel sliced into my flesh and I felt my bright red blood drip down my sides onto the freezing cold morgue slab I was resting on.

"Wait," Calum said gently. Then he started to inspect the blood.

He might be starting to understand.

Calum sliced a bit more.

Fucking idiot!

More blood dripped out of the wound. I just wanted to scream.

"This isn't right. That's a lot of blood and it's too bright for this to be normal," Calum said.

No shit Sherlock!

Calum just shook his head like he was overreacting and sliced a bit more. I felt more blood drip down my sides and even pool slightly on my chest.

"Shit!" Calum said.

Then he instantly started to apply pressure to *his* slices and his stunning emerald eyes just stared into mine.

Calum weakly smiled. "I'm sorry. I'll fix this. I won't let you die,"

***

I didn't know how long I had been out (well, not in the gay sense at least), but when I opened my eyes slowly. Bright natural sunlight shone through a massive floor-to-ceiling window and I was thankfully in a very comfortable hospital bed with fine sheets, a comfortable pillow and various pieces of equipment all around me.

The entire place smelt great with hints of lavender, roses and tulips filling the air and I was really glad to be out in the land of the living.

And I could move!

I raised my hand in front of my face and just focused on how great it felt to be able to move my fingers, toes and arms. It was such a great feeling.

The sound of the equipment humming, buzzing and beeping was actually a good reminder of what normal life sounded like instead of the cold silence of the morgue.

Then I looked at the massive window and saw a very hot man looking back at me. I wasn't sure why Doctor Calum was here, but I was rather glad he was, even after he kept cutting into me.

There was just something about his amazing smile, emerald eyes and his angular face that I just loved. And I seriously just wanted to ask him out and see where the future might take us.

Calum slowly walked towards me and sat down on a wooden chair that I hadn't noticed before was sitting there by my bed.

"I am sorry," he said.

"Sorry about the privacy and locking the door," I said, smiling.

Calum looked so scared for a few moments, but then he smiled too.

"You were awake then? How long?" he asked.

"All of it. But that elderly man's creepy," I said.

Calum laughed. "Yea. That's why they rejected him at the hospital. But I'm really glad you're okay,"

"What happened to me? How long was I out for?" I asked.

Calum gestured if he could take my hand and I didn't even hesitate.

"This might be hard for you to hear," Calum said, slowly rubbing my hand. I loved the feeling of his hands against mine. "You were poisoned on your night out by your CEO,"

It was amazing to feel my eyebrows rise as he said that.

"Turns out your CEO felt embarrassed by your success, and he was a bit psychotic anyway. So he poisoned you and planned to watch your paralysed face as he killed you later on,"

I held his hand tighter.

"Thankfully the poison acted too quickly and your friends got the cops involved. So you were declared dead, the police investigated and your boss was arrested,"

I just nodded. At least I would never have to worry about him again.

"Thanks for waiting for me," I said, I managed to surprise myself at that.

When I first met this amazingly hot man, I had been terrified of being "touched up" and more as he believed I was dead. Then I believed I was going to be killed by him. And now... and now I really wanted to him.

This definitely has to be the weirdest meet-cue in history.

Calum lent closer. "I know you... you might not be into men. But I was wondering-"

I couldn't help but laugh as Calum turned all nervous, shaky and like he was a little schoolboy again.

"Yes," I said. "I'll go on a second date with you,"

"Second?" he asked.

I just smiled. "You saw me naked in the morgue. That's a date to me,"

Calum laughed and he really had the cutest laugh ever, and I loved it.

As we kept talking, laughing and smiling at each other like two teenage boys, I never thought I would meet my soulmate like this. But I was so glad I had, Calum was an amazing guy and I was really, really looking forward to the future.

And spending the rest of my life with this man who always made me feel utterly amazing.

AUTHOR OF THE BETTIE ENGLISH PRIVATE EYE MYSTERIES

CONNOR WHITELEY

UNWANTED
RETURN

A GAY ROMANTIC SUSPENSE SHORT STORY

UNWANTED RETURN

Adam Penn had always loved the wonderful warm feeling of love, respect and Christmassy goodness that he felt in Canterbury's breathtaking Christmas markets. He normally walked through the historical cobblestone high street at the weekdays when he lectured at the university on psychology, and then at the weekend when he went to volunteer at the soup kitchen, heart attack charity shop and occasionally helped out coaching an under-10s football team.

Adam really did love helping people all through the entire year and really try to amplify the Christmas spirit.

But he never ever wanted to see his abuser return.

Of course some people might have said Adam had only seen the merest of glimpses of Jamie Button through the immense crowds of people with their thick winter coats, their laughter and joy echoing in the high street and fathers carrying little kids on their shoulders.

But Adam knew what he saw.

Adam just stood to one side against the icy coldness of a white wall of a local bank as he assessed the situation. He tried to focus on the immense sea of people in front of him, people walking up and down the high street singing, dancing and spreading Christmas cheer.

It was too much and all the people there were just checking the little wooden Christmas stalls. Like the doughnut stall in front of Adam with all its rows upon rows of festively decorated doughnuts.

The loud sound of Christmas music, people laughing and even the sound of arcade games echoed off the walls of the high street.

There was no chance whatsoever Adam could possibly hear his attacker coming.

It wasn't even like Adam could call the police or anything because they would only turn around and say that James was in prison for stalking, psychological abuse and trying to kill Adam in the end. They wouldn't believe what Adam saw.

But James was here.

Adam had spent five long years being attacked, mocked and bullied by that monster.

Adam had carved every single youthful, stunning pore on his ex-boyfriend's face into his mind so it was flat out impossible for him to forget what he looked like.

The police hadn't even been too interested the last time when Adam had first reported the abuse. Apparently gay people didn't abuse their boyfriends that only happened to straight women.

Well that was a fucking joke if there ever was one.

There was one cop that tried to help and support Adam and eventually got James arrested and charged. But that strikingly beautiful cop AJ had fled soon after the trial.

There wasn't a single explanation, goodbye or anything. And it was then that Adam realised that he could only ever depend on himself.

And that most men were simply awful.

"I can see you," James said.

Adam looked around but he couldn't see him.

Adam could recognise that voice anywhere. James was here and he sounded just as deranged, insane and scary as he always did.

James had been caring and loving once but after his plan to isolate Adam from everyone who ever loved him had worked he had revealed his true self.

And even after the abuse and attempted murder, his family and friends still wanted nothing to do with him. apparently he deserved it.

Adam looked around trying to see where James might be in the sea of happy joyous visitors to the Christmas market. He couldn't see anyone strange or anyone looking at him.

Adam was completely invisible to everyone else and that was actually what James had said about the reason why he had chosen Adam to target.

All Adam had to do was just leave, get home and try to call the police. There was still that restraining order in place so hopefully the police could do something.

Yes. That was exactly what Adam had to do.

He pushed himself off the white wall of the bank and started to carefully go back up the high street. He didn't dare go into the crowd of people because that would make it too easy for James to sneak up on him with a knife.

And kill him.

Adam kept walking pulling the black hood of his coat over his head in some lame attempt to make himself even more invisible.

Adam realised his heart pounded in his chest. Sweat was pouring down his back despite the icy coldness of the night. And all Adam could think was that he was going to die tonight.

He tried to focus on the lumpy, bumpy texture of the cobblestone high street he was walking on but it was useless. He just couldn't stop thinking about dying.

Adam even tried to see if anyone was following him in all the different glass windows of the stunning shops in the high street.

He looked at the glass windows of a little coffee shop that Adam loved because of their milkshakes. But he couldn't see anyone.

Someone grabbed Adam.

Pinning him against the wall.

Adam tried to scream. Someone slammed their hand over his mouth.

Adam struggled. Kicked. Tried to fight. He couldn't.

"It's me," a very familiar voice said.

Adam's body recognised the voice before his brain could and all the tension was released, his heart calmed down and the sweat stopped pouring down his back.

Adam just looked at the strikingly beautiful man that was pinning him to the wall. His AJ had returned to him after so many years, so many years of not knowing what happened, wondering if their brief fling during the trial had been real and so many years of not trusting men anymore.

AJ got off Adam, grabbed his hand and started walking him up the high street.

"James was released from prison two days ago. It was down to a clerical error instead and train tickets show he arrived in Canterbury an hour ago," AJ said.

Adam loved how manly, husky and serious his voice was but Adam just wanted answers.

"What happened to you? I waited for you after the verdict. I wanted to thank you, love you, care about you,"

AJ frowned and looked around.

"Answer me," Adam said a little louder than he wanted to.

AJ shrugged. "It's personal and I just want to keep you safe and alive. I can't lose you,"

Adam wanted to bite back about how AJ had lost him for years without AJ even daring to call but now wasn't the time.

If James was here and released from Prison then he was a dead man walking. Adam had had a few self-defence classes over the years but clearly Adam didn't know how to use them when it actually mattered most.

"Backup is on the way but they won't be here for another twenty minutes at most," AJ said.

"Fuck you police," Adam said. "First you don't believe when I'm being abused. Second you AJ the one cop that I trust runs away. Third you release my abuser by accident without telling me,"

AJ looked around again and stopped and grabbed Adam's hands. He grabbed them so hard Adam hissed in pain.

"Oh sorry," AJ said as he released them. "I am sorry what happened but I don't want to lose you. I love you for God sake,"

The words slammed into Adam like hammer blows and AJ had

never even hinted that was how he felt those years ago during the trial.

Adam wanted to believe he was lying or just trying to manipulate him, but AJ wasn't. His eyes were too wet and emotional for him to be lying.

Someone tackled AJ to the ground.

AJ screamed.

There was a loud thud.

Someone jumped off AJ.

Adam rushed over to AJ. He was lying on the cobblestone ground. Still breathing but out cold.

"Ha. You were always a fairy boy," James said.

The icy coldness and twisted edge to the words sliced through the cold air and Adam felt his stomach twist into a painful knot.

Adam slowly stood up and just stared with utter horror as James was only a few metres from him.

James was still beautiful to some extent with his broad shoulders, amazing body and gorgeous sapphire eyes but Adam now knew those eyes were only windows into the darkest soul he had ever seen.

"I'm glad you kept your hair long. At least I can rip it all out again," James said grinning.

Adam felt a lump form in his throat as he realised that he was still the stupid little boy with no muscles, long brown hair and a handsome face that James had met all those years ago.

James rushed over to him.

Adam spun around. He ran.

James gripped his hair.

Adam screamed as James wrapped it around his fist.

He started dragging Adam up the high street.

"What are you doing!" Adam shouted but no one seemed to care.

"I'm taking you back to my car. I'll have fun with you and then I will kill you this time. Nice and slowly,"

Adam kicked, punched, struggled against James but he was still too strong.

James threw him against the cold marble of another bank. Adam slammed into it with a thud.

James slammed his fists into Adam's face.

"That is enough fairy boy," James said.

"That is enough for you too!" AJ shouted.

Adam kicked James in-between the legs as hard as he could.

James hissed. Adam tried to run past.

James gripped him. Putting Adam in a headlock.

"You didn't find your dead leso of a sister Detective?" James asked.

Adam gasped. That explained so much and AJ had spoken a lot about the fact he knew his sister was dead but they had never found the body.

"You killed her," Adam said.

"Of course. All fairies must die. That is what the bible has said for thousands of years and so it shall be until the end of time," James said.

Adam stomped on his foot. James hissed.

Adam elbowed him in the ribs.

James released him. Adam spun around.

Whacking him round the face.

Adam ran towards AJ.

James whipped out a gun.

He aimed it at AJ.

He fired.

Adam tackled AJ to the ground.

People screamed around them. James kept firing.

Adam jumped up. Charging at James.

James looked scared. His hand was shaking.

Adam leapt into the air.

Extending his leg to kick James.

James grabbed his leg.

Throwing Adam against the marble wall of the bank.

Adam landed with a crack. His chest ached.

James stormed over to him. Placing the gun in Adam's mouth.

James's head exploded. Blood, brain matter and bone shards splashed over Adam's face and all Adam could see was a sniper on the roof opposite him and as the entire situation became all too much for him, Adam simply collapsed into unconsciousness.

***

After a rather wonderful hospital visit, finding out Adam had some fractured ribs and the doctors had tried out a brand-new experimental treatment on him to make his ribs heal faster, it was thankfully only two days later after James's death that Adam was out of hospital.

Beautiful AJ had offered to pick him up and Adam just sort of knew that it would be healthy for him to let AJ do that. He still didn't really know what happened that night, why AJ loved him and Adam wasn't sure if he was ready for another relationship.

He had never really been too good at them and all the guys he had picked up were foul in the end. Maybe Adam was just meant to be and die alone.

Adam sat in the very warm and comfortable passenger seat in AJ's large black SUV as they drove down a narrow country road with thick oak trees lining the road and their branches gently blowing in the delightful crisp and warm afternoon wind.

The scents of vanilla, lavender and oranges filled the air inside the car and Adam just looked at beautiful AJ. And he actually looked at him properly now his life wasn't in danger.

AJ was just as striking now as he was a few years ago, but he seemed to have gotten even more beautiful, Adam still loved AJ's blond hair that was so soft and Adam loved spending hours running his fingers through it and playing with all that softness.

AJ was still as fit and sexy with his stunning body as he was a few years ago. His body was sort of James in a way, and clearly Adam had a type. He wanted to be with "real" men that weren't weak and pathetic like him.

But most of all, Adam still loved AJ because *he* was beautiful.

"I am sorry for everything," Adam said. "I should have been stronger, tougher and more ready for this. It's my fault that-"

"No!" AJ shouted as he turned the SUV into a little gap in the trees and just stared at Adam.

"I'm sorry," Adam said looking at the floor like he had always done with James whenever he had shouted at Adam.

It was amazing how the reflexes were still there after all this time.

"Damn," AJ said softly. "I didn't know your reflexes were still... you know,"

Adam didn't dare look up. He knew that AJ loved him and was trying to be nice but Adam just knew that not looking at AJ was safer. It was always safer never to look at men when they were angry.

"No," AJ said as carefully as he could. "I am sorry for shouting. It's just none of this is your fault. Not James. Not your abuse. Nothing is your fault,"

Adam looked up and loved seeing how innocent, cute and real AJ was being with him. And that he actually meant what he was saying.

"Listen to me," AJ said. "You, Adam Penn, are beautiful, perfect and the sweetest guy I have ever met. When that nob sent me away looking for my sister's body I thought every single day about you,"

Adam's throat went dry.

"I thought about how cute you were, about how much I wanted to plait your hair after we have sex, I wanted your body and I wanted you most of all," AJ said. "I never stopped thinking about you,"

As much as Adam just knew that AJ was telling the truth without a shadow of a doubt, he couldn't understand why AJ he had never called, texted or tried to contact him whatsoever. So he asked him.

AJ looked to the floor like he was the abuse victim then Adam realised what had happened.

"James had friends you know," AJ said, not daring to look at Adam. "Two friends really so I went to where, James had told me my sister would be, and yea, the two men found me, beat me and, yea life happened,"

Adam leant closer and unclipped his seatbelt and he hugged AJ but he was surprised when AJ hissed.

Adam gently ran his hand down AJ's amazing body but AJ was biting his lip more and more and Adam just knew that he wasn't okay.

"That's why I had to come back to you when I heard James had been released by mistake," AJ said, looking at Adam.

Adam just stared into his beautiful AJ's stunning eyes and really focused on the warmth, emotion and utter love they held.

"I couldn't, I just couldn't face the idea of losing you," AJ said. "I need you. I need to love you. I want you,"

Adam slowly nodded a little and realised that this was all he had ever wanted a man to say to him but it also felt strange. Like he almost wasn't alone anymore and sure he knew the road to recovery and living a happy life was very possible, his therapist had been teaching him that constantly over the past year.

But it would be difficult.

AJ kissed Adam's hand and he realised that no journey in life that was worth it was easy, and this time round Adam and AJ would be helping each other overcome the past, helping to love each other and finally getting the life that they both deserved.

Because Adam definitely deserved to know what true love felt like. Not the sort of "love" that James and so many men before that had "gifted" him, but the type of love where AJ would kiss him gently with passion, make love with him because AJ loved him but didn't need to channel some aggression, and most importantly AJ would never ever hit Adam or abuse him.

And right now, right in this little moment in time, that was all that Adam wanted. A relationship that loved him back and didn't abuse him.

Sure in the future that might change and Adam might want a house with AJ, maybe kids and maybe even marriage, but that was in the future.

And as Adam kissed AJ again and again, that was okay and the future was looking very exciting and Adam couldn't wait for it to come.

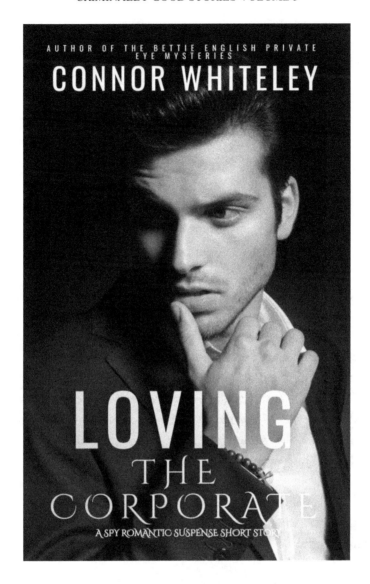

AUTHOR OF THE BETTIE ENGLISH PRIVATE EYE MYSTERIES

CONNOR WHITELEY

LOVING THE CORPORATE

A SPY ROMANTIC SUSPENSE SHORT STORY

LOVING THE CORPORATE
20th July 2022
Southern England, United Kingdom

Professional Corporate Spy Anna Smith sat on a very uncomfortable bus seat surrounded by her follow beauty product factory workers in all their outfits, height and sizes as they all talked and laughed with each other about their busy workday ahead.

Anna simply looked out the window and watched the rich beautiful English countryside roll past them as the little bus drove onwards to the factory in the middle of nowhere. She wasn't exactly keen on her fellow workers after the past six months, but a job was certainly that. Just a job.

Normally in July Anna tended to focus more on spying on ice cream, holiday agencies and sun cream makers because it was about summer time when the rivals pay extremely good money for information. But even Anna loved a good sob story from time to time.

So when a client contacted her through her extremely encrypted email address and told her the story about a local factory that was brainwashing their workers into mindless drones and poisoning the soil, leading to crop failure for the local villages. Anna was a little more interested in this potential job.

Granted she was hardly impressed by the sheer stink of some of the workers with their constant and immensely strong body odour, smell of alcohol and cheap whiskey on their breath. But they all seemed to be good people, and the management seemed to be even better.

She couldn't completely understand why her employer, who had already paid her a hundred thousand pounds, believed the workers were being brainwashed. Yet her employer was right about one thing, the upper-upper management was mysterious and mystical and definitely hiding something.

The bus shook a little as it turned onto a dirt road and Anna rolled her eyes as she knew that they would soon all be at the factory.

It had taken Anna six months just to get into the main production area of the factory instead of being in the office section. Yet even the office was rather fascinating because all the documents, invoices and other essential paperwork seemed perfect to the untrained eye. But Anna knew a lot better.

Someone in upper-upper management was forging the paperwork that was later sent to investors (who invested up to a million pounds a year) and government agencies.

This was fraud on a massive scale.

Anna just smiled to herself as she got more and more excited about her day ahead. After she had managed to… prevent the normal worker from taking the upper management their afternoon tea, Anna had spiked the tea, cakes and scones with eyedrops so needlessly to say the management would be very ill today.

That was why Anna always made a point to carry round a green fanny pack that looked like a first aid kit. It always contained official first aid supplies and underneath were a bunch of spy equipment. Like knock-out drops, a USB drive with password unlocking software and a little EMP device that her ex-husband made her one Christmas in case she ever needed to knock out a building's power supplies.

He really was amazing back in the day.

Anna was more than excited about finally getting a chance to go into the management's office, look around and finally get some proof on what was going on. And ideally she would be able to find out who was behind this fraud and corporation.

Her fellow factory workers started to get more and more excited as the bus started to drive up a gravel road, and the workers could see the very top of the factory that was situated in the valley below.

As much as Anna smiled every morning to look like the rest of her fellow workers, every morning she felt her stomach twist in both excitement and fear. She had been doing spying too long to get easily caught so that was hardly a problem. Her real concern was getting caught and never being able to deliver the justice that her employers hired her for.

That was her only fear.

And if she got caught then it meant she would never be able to see her beautiful little daughter again who she visited once a month when her ex-husband allowed her to. It wasn't that they didn't get on, it was just he wasn't exactly a fan of her work.

She couldn't exactly disagree with his reasons, that was why Anna just wanted to live in a world where these corporations weren't so corrupt and dangerous and polluting. And all that one day might affect her precious little girl.

Anna wished more than anything else in the world that she could have enough money one day to buy a little ranch for her and her daughter. Her daughter was obsessed with horses and it was definitely beyond a phase, Anna just wanted to be a good mother.

The bus slowed to a stop and Anna smiled. It was time to get to work and Anna was really looking forward to stopping this factory once and for all and definitely helping to make the world a better place for her daughter.

She just hoped no idiot was going to get in her way.

***

20th July 2022

Southern England, United Kingdom

Amateur Corporate Spy Joshua McDonald was waiting at the god-awful gates of the immense beauty product factory that looked like a large cuboid building as he waited for the bus of workers to arrive.

He leant against the hot metal of the factory and liked the almost burning sensations of the metal heating up his skin through his blue worker's uniform. He hated the entire factory, people and management.

But he was here for a purpose.

The stupid factory had popped up nine months ago and immediately cleared all government checks within days (a process that was meant to take a year) and then within a week the factory started pumping out toxic chemicals into the local river that went straight into the farms.

The local farms and surrounding areas used to smell amazing and Joshua loved hiking the footpaths as a teenager with the refreshing hints of apples, pine and ferns that filled the air. Yet now the entire area just smelt of horrible chemicals, rotting fish and rotting plants from where the water was killing the local environment.

The local villages and wildlife couldn't last much longer.

Joshua hated everything about this situation. He hated how he had seen so many of his friends in the local village lose their farms, crops and livelihoods all because of a corrupt factory. Then the teenagers started to get sick, then the women and now the men. Everyone in the village was slowly starting to get sicker and sicker and all the governmental officials denied it was to do with the factory.

Joshua wanted nothing more than to burn the entire place to the ground. He wanted to kill the entire management, but as his mother had said before she died two months after the factory opened *violence was never the way*. It was such a motherly thing to say, but she was right.

Damn her.

Joshua had slowly worked his way into the factory, becoming a good worker and gaining the trust of the management. There was a rumour going round that Joshua was meant to be promoted any moment now and that would give him access to exactly what he needed.

He had an ex-girlfriend at a national newspaper that had promised to leak the story to the public if he got her some proof.

Even as he waited for the bus to turn up Joshua felt so nervous. His knees were shaking, his heart was pounding and his breathing was rapid.

He needed today to go perfectly so he could get the promotion and get access to the files he needed so he could prove to the world (or local authorities at least) that this factory was a monstrous place.

The sound of something hitting the gravel road in the distance made Joshua weakly smile, because soon the workers would be here.

He knew it was a silly fear but every single day he feared that someone new was going to get on that bus who was a spy hunter or something, and that same person could catch him and damn him and his family and local villages to death.

Joshua's phone buzzed and he took it out and rolled his eyes when he saw it was a text message from his manager.

He read the message and smiled when it told him the security codes to the main office because they were mysteriously ill today, so he was temporarily manager. He was a one man band running everything that five people normally ran.

Joshua didn't really care too much because after today he would have his proof and then he would be in the wind.

Then his phone buzzed again and Joshua cursed under his breath. He was still in charge but the head of the factory and corporation was heading there to keep a close eye on everything.

Joshua had never met the big boss but from subtle whispers and murmurs from other workers, the big boss was not a good man, not kind and definitely not the type of person you wanted to screw over.

Joshua was tempted to cancel his plans for today but this was the best shot he had had in the past five months of working here. He didn't know if he was going to get this chance again. He needed to try.

The large bus filled with workers drove into the factory

compound and Joshua smiled at all of them as they popped off the bus and looked so excited about starting the day.

Joshua was about to call them all over to him when someone caught his eye.

A tall elegant woman popped off the bus and Joshua's mouth just stopped working. She was the most beautiful woman he had ever seen and there was just something about her.

Joshua flat out loved her long slender legs, long brown hair that perfectly framed her circular head and strong jawline. She easily could have been a model in another life and she certainly could have had any man she wanted.

And Joshua seriously loved how she carried herself with such pride, confidence and like she was in complete control. She was like some sort of god walking amongst little human ants that she could easily deal with if she wanted. Not in an arrogant way, but in a way that made Joshua drawn to her.

He had seen the woman about a few times but there was something different about her today. She wasn't normally this confident or maybe she was and she was just hiding it better.

Whoever this woman was, she definitely didn't belong here. All the other workers seemed really happy and drawn to be here, but none of them were confident or felt in control. No one in the local area did as they were all waiting for their own damnation because of this factory.

This woman was different.

And as hot and sexy as she was. She terrified Joshua.

He couldn't let her get in his way. And that was a promise.

***

20th July 2022

Southern England, United Kingdom

A few hours later, Anna was extremely impressed by her amazing, if not a little out-there, plan with the eyedrops had actually worked so perfectly. All five managers were out sick with extreme bowel problems and that was just flat out perfect.

As it was approaching lunchtime and everyone who the time the normal managers went to lunch (so she couldn't see why this new temporary manager who she hadn't met yet would be any different), Anna had slipped away from the production line and had made it into a long grey corridor on the top floor of the factory.

Anna wasn't a fan of the god awful grey paint job that covered the smooth walls of the corridor and even the bright blue fire-doors that were the entrances into the main offices weren't attractive. Anna could still hear the factory below her and she was hardly impressed that the noise of the factory machines were so loud it would be difficult to hear if someone was returning or walking about up here.

From her position on the production line from earlier, Anna had managed to get a clear view of the staircase up to the top floor, and by her count everyone was meant to be up here wasn't at the moment.

That was another advantage of paying off the chef yesterday to cook something very special for the workers, managers and even the big boss if he decided to show up. Anna wasn't exactly sure how the hell you were meant to pronounce it, but what she understood was that the chef knew the management liked some special French dish.

So he was cooking it, and it had drawn a crowd.

Anna carefully went along the long corridor and subtly checked to see if any of the doors were open, and surprisingly enough most of them were. She wouldn't have minded going into some of them just in case they were useful.

But the only office of interest up here was the main office used by the management themselves. The rest of the offices were all Human Resources, Accounts Payable and Bookkeeping. Not exactly what Anna wanted at the moment.

The sound of someone walking up the stairs made Anna roll her eyes and she quickly dipped into one of the other offices with the open doors. Keeping it just open enough to hide her but make sure she could still see the person.

Anna wasn't impressed with the smell of cheesy feet that filled the little box office that was used by an accountant judging by the finance books on the desk.

A few moments later a very fit man walked past wearing a blue worker's uniform. Anna had sort of seen him before but never really looked at him. He was so beautiful and handsome with his tight ass, tight uniform that highlighted how skinny he was with some muscles around his biceps and calves, and there was just something rather stunning about him.

Anna supposed he was the new temporary manager and with those looks she definitely would have minded following him. Yet it was strange how he was up here in the middle of lunchtime, as a manager (even if only temporary) it was expected of him not to be up here.

He could have forgotten something important that he needed, but that wasn't how any manager worked in all the corporations Anna had spied on.

He was up to something.

The hot man went up to the very end of the corridor, took out a key and opened the door to the main office.

Anna wouldn't have had a problem opening the door because of the tools in her fanny pack, but this stunning man was troubling her now. Why was he going into the main office during lunchtime?

Heavy footsteps pounded up the staircase and Anna felt her stomach twist. Something was wrong here.

Anna went into her fanny pack and got out a little device that looked like a smartphone. It was technically a smartphone but she had added a lot of software to it recently. Including an app that scanned for radio signals.

Anna was seriously not impressed when radio signals were being sent from the main office to someone from inside the factory. Chances are that the handsome man triggered some kind of alarm when he entered the office.

That's why Anna always scanned important offices before she went inside because now someone knew that handsome man was up to something. That meant security would get tighter and her mission would be even harder.

Not good.

A few moments later an extremely overweight man stomped down the corridor and Anna wanted to be sick as she smelt his immense body odour. The man was wearing a large, unflattering suit that only highlighted how overweight he was.

"Ouch!" the handsome man shouted.

Anna carefully watched as the overweight man grabbed the handsome man by the collar of his uniform, grabbed the key from him and spat at his face.

"I'm calling the police you little shit!" he shouted. "You try stealing from and I'll gut you if the cops don't get here soon enough. I gutted peeps before. You'll be no different,"

Anna almost wanted to laugh at all the trouble the handsome amateur was getting himself into but then the overweight man dragged the handsome amateur over to the office she was hiding in.

Anna ducked behind the door as it opened and the overweight man through the hot amateur inside.

He locked the door behind him.

Anna simply smiled at the hot amateur as he looked dumbfounded at her. This was going to be amazing fun.

***

20th July 2022

Southern England, United Kingdom

Joshua was absolutely steaming about getting caught by the big boss idiot himself. He didn't know how he had been so stupid but now everything was completely at risk.

And to make matters even worse, he was completely trapped in a little account office with an extremely hot beautiful woman who just smiled at him.

Joshua recognised her as the beautiful woman from the bus and even now she looked so relaxed, confident and like she was in complete control. Joshua didn't know who she was exactly but she was amazing. And even with the office heating up more and more and Joshua's palms were sweaty, she still looked as cool as a cucumber.

"Anna Smith, Corporate spy at ya service," she said extending out her hand.

Joshua was so confused. She was clearly just stupid or something because if she was really a spy then why the hell did she just admit it so easily? Surely that was against the spy code or something.

The hot woman gestured him to shake her hand. He did.

"A little weak of a handshake but acceptable," the woman said, her smile only growing.

It was only then that Joshua realised she didn't let go of his hand. Her hand was so silky smooth and beautiful and Joshua even felt like sexual energy was flowing between them. He really, really liked her. Joshua even wanted to hold a little more of her.

Then he forced himself to let go, the woman looked slightly disappointed.

"Corporate spy?" Joshua asked. "Why are you here?"

"Judging by your accent you're very local. I surveyed the local area before I started my mission. I presume you want the same evidence as me but our reasons are different," Anna said leaning against the wall by the door.

Joshua felt his stomach fill with butterflies. Anna was clearly as smart as they come but they needed to get out of here and get the proof.

Joshua went for the door and Anna gently placed her hand on his and shook her head.

He didn't want to back away from the door but for some reason he just trusted this woman.

"I'm Joshua," he said.

Beautiful Anna smiled and nodded her thanks for sharing that with her. Then Anna took a few steps back.

"I'm getting paid a lot of money to do this job," Anna said. "I don't need an amateur screwing it up,"

Joshua frowned. "This isn't about a job or money! This is about my friends, family and community that is dying!"

Anna nodded slowly like she was mulling something over in her mind. Joshua hated it when people did that normally but on her it looked so cute.

"I understand that. I saw it for myself. I just… have my own reasons for why this job cannot fail," Anna said looking at the floor.

Joshua had seen that look too many times on his mother's face before she died. It was the sort of look you give someone when the truth was too painful to reveal.

Joshua gently went over to her and lifted up her chin so the two of them looked into each other's eyes. And Anna certainly had some great lifeful eyes that Joshua didn't mind looking into.

"What's wrong? And how can I help?" Joshua asked.

Anna looked almost shocked and confused by his offer, Joshua didn't know her very well but he could tell she was in pain, and very beautiful. She was the last person he ever wanted to be in pain.

Anna gently pushed him away and started studying the door frame.

"My daughter. She's ten right now and loves horses," Anna said. "My ex-husband loves me and her but he doesn't agree with my work so our relationship could never work out. I just want to get enough money to give her the life she deserves,"

Joshua could only nod. He definitely knew the feeling from a child's viewpoint. His own parents had fought a lot, argued and barely agreed on anything so his father was hardly about. And it definitely made childhood a little less fun, interesting and solid.

Joshua had always felt like he had been missing half of himself until he became an adult.

He was definitely going to help her. Not only because she was beautiful but because it was the right thing to do.

Joshua placed a loving hand on her shoulder. "What can I do to help?"

Anna gave him a seductive smile. "Let me to do my job and

don't fuck it up again,"

Joshua wanted to be offended but there was just something so seductive and fun about her words. He could only smile.

Anna took out something from her bright green fanny pack that looked like a key and she pressed it into the door. The key-like device hummed a little then the door unlocked itself.

Joshua didn't know where in the hell she got it from or whether it was legal or not. But he was very excited to see what other incredible things she could do.

Anna went into the corridor and he followed without hesitation.

***

20th July 2022

Southern England, United Kingdom

Knowing the utterly silly mistake that beautiful Joshua had made, Anna was never ever going to make the same mistake as him. She was professional and now she had a stunning sidekick, the pressure was even more on to complete the mission.

The moment Anna reached the large blue fire-door at the end of the grey corridor she took out her smartphone again and scanned for radio signals. Just as she suspected the big boss had increased security.

There were currently scanners monitoring every inch of the main office, storage areas and every other millimetre of the factory where people were not meant to be.

Just in case the corridor they were standing in would soon be scanned, Anna activated a special feature of her smartphone that sent out radio signals that caused the scanners to report that everything was okay no matter what.

Anna smiled when her phone reported it was working. Her spy gadgets were amazing and she seriously loved her job.

A very quiet gasp behind her made her smile even more as beautiful Joshua was also clearly impressed.

Anna took out her little key device that moulded itself to any lock and the main office door opened with a simple click.

They went inside.

The main office was a lot larger and emptier than she had first imagined. She had pictured the office containing endless rows of computers, files and other office-y things. But this office only had a single desk and computer.

Anna stopped Joshua when he was about to rush over to the computer and she carefully scanned the ground with her eyes and smartphone to make sure there were no more surprises.

Thankfully there were none so Anna and Joshua went over to the large computer and Joshua cursed that it was locked.

She was really starting to lose hope with him because he was such an amateur. He was hot as hell but not a very good corporate spy.

Yet she supposed she might as well ask just in case he knew something she didn't.

"What's wrong?" Anna asked.

"The security codes I got texted earlier mentioned how you can only put it each code once before a full system wipe starts. It's a protocol to stop people like us,"

Anna wasn't exactly impressed with the term *us* but that didn't matter right now. This was just another problem they faced because even her password decoder would technically enter the password more than once and that could trigger the wiping programme.

Joshua thankfully got out his phone and huffed.

"The password for the main computer isn't included," Joshua said. "The management only gave me the passwords to the computers in the bookkeeping, accountants and human resources,"

Anna rolled her eyes. This wasn't what they needed. Any moment that big boss idiot was going to return and find them, and Anna didn't like violence in the slightest.

"Text your boss and get the password. Make up some excuse or something," Anna said.

Joshua nodded and texted his boss. Something about needing to access records because a government official turned up for a surprise inspection.

"For God sake," Joshua said.

Anna smiled. The boss had texted him saying that get the big boss idiot to sort it out.

"Use your decoder," Joshua said looking defeated.

Anna wanted to but she could see how much it was paining Joshua. He wanted to succeed but he also needed to make sure that the evidence was intact. This was a massive risk for both of them.

But Anna did what he said.

The computer unlocked straight away.

Joshua gently moved her away and thankfully he knew exactly where the secret files were located.

"Wow," Joshua said.

Anna agreed as Joshua pulled up the real environment reports, confidential emails and even health reports about the certainty of destroying the local environment.

This was exactly the proof they needed.

Anna took out the last USB she had in her fanny pack that contained an automatic transmitter that used satellites to send the information to her personal computers back at home. That if she didn't send a special password within six hours would send the information to every single news outlet in the country.

Joshua started transferring some of the documents to an email address and Anna rolled her eyes. Emailing these documents would take too long and would lead to too much of a paper trail.

Heavy footsteps pounded up the stairs.

Anna pointed Joshua to hide under the desk.

"Fucking bastards!" the big boss idiot shouted.

Anna put her transmitting USB into the computer and hid under the desk with Joshua.

She just hoped the big boss idiot didn't find them before the files were transferred.

***

20th July 2022

Southern England, United Kingdom

As much as Joshua loved being this close to sexy beautiful Anna, he was not impressed in the slightest that the big boss idiot was coming for them and he was going to find them.

He didn't even think that Anna could find a way out for them this time. She was extremely smart and just amazing in how she handled herself but this was beyond his skills and surely hers.

The heavy footsteps of the boss pounded into the main office.

Joshua felt his heart rate shoot up. His breathing turned rapid. Sweat poured off him.

Anna gently grabbed his hand and smiled at him. Joshua flat out loved how this amazing person was so confident under pressure and he was really starting to believe that nothing phased her.

"I gonna gun. And I'm gonna use it," the big boss idiot said.

Joshua took large deep breaths and Anna's smile simply grew.

Joshua could see the big boss idiot's large feet under the desk. He was standing centimetres from them.

He walked round the desk.

Joshua couldn't let him hurt Anna. She was too smart, important and clever to die. He had to save her.

Joshua put his feet under him so he could jump out if needed. Anna shook her head.

The big boss idiot stood within striking distance.

Joshua leapt out.

Tackling the idiot to the ground.

Joshua climbed on top of him. Knocking the gun out of his hand.

The idiot whacked Joshua across the room. Pain flooded his jaw. The idiot was strong.

The idiot got up. Charging over to Joshua.

Anna climbed on his back. Slashing his face with her nails.

Joshua ran over to the idiot. Kicking him in the stomach. He didn't react.

The idiot grabbed Anna. Throwing her against the wall.

The idiot rushed over to Joshua. Punching him.

Joshua collapsed to the ground.

Police sirens echoed outside. The idiot cursed.

Grabbing the gun. Aiming it at Joshua.

Joshua tried to move. He was too battered. Anna tried to stop him. She couldn't move either.

The idiot pressed the barrel against Joshua's head. His fingers tightened around the trigger.

The cops swarmed in. Tackling the idiot to the ground.

Joshua forced himself up and helped Anna up. She kept holding her hips like they were hurting but at least this beautiful woman was alive.

As Joshua left the office, he purposefully tripped near the computer and Anna subtly grabbed the USB transmitter so the police would never find out what they were doing.

And Joshua had a feeling that was exactly how Anna liked it. And Joshua definitely liked her.

***

20th July 2022

Southern England, United Kingdom

A few hours later, Anna sat under a wonderfully cool oak tree with stunning Joshua as they both watched police, environmental agency and other government cars drive into the factory compound.

Anna had made sure to plaster the evidence all over the internet, and now it was a major news story all over the country as everyone was asking how the hell this sort of thing had happened in the first place. Anna knew it was all down to money and that was what made this pathetic country go round at times.

But at least people were now aware of the corruption and there was even local politicians promising each affected family half a million pounds in compensation, so things were getting done.

And as strange as it sounded to Anna, she honestly believed that the environment was already getting better with the factory getting shut down, and no more toxic chemicals were getting pumped into the river. Amazing hints of pine, fern and crisp fresh air were slowly returning to the local area.

Anna was so happy to see the locals and workers celebrating as the police descended to investigate everything. But most importantly she was just happy to have Joshua by her side, he was so smart, cute and amazing in his own special way.

Anna might have been a professional corporate spy with all the gadgets, knowledge and confidence that the job needed, but it was Joshua that had the balls, boldness and fighting spirit that the job also required.

In all honesty Joshua probably wouldn't have made a bad spy if he was trained correctly and learnt a few things. Anna just smiled at the idea because it was a great idea.

After a good decade of spying alone, unloved and secretly yearning for some kind of human connection. Anna was excited to finally have it in Joshua and with the money alone from this mission she could live out her days on her horse ranch with her daughter.

She didn't need to keep doing this spy lark, she could just be a mother and Joshua becoming part of their amazing little family if he wanted.

Anna knew she was getting ahead of herself but it was such an amazing dream. But Anna also knew that she loved her job too much. Spying wasn't about the money, it was truly about the justice, adventure and the rush of the job.

She was never going to give it up, or at least not just yet. She would save the money for the horse ranch and still give her daughter the best life she possibly could with the thousands she sent her ex-husband every so often.

But she was a spy first and foremost, and with beautiful Joshua by her side, she could be a great lover.

"What will you do now?" Anna asked as she seductively rested her chin on Joshua's amazingly beautiful shoulders.

He smiled at her and kissed her on the forehead. She loved the sheer power and affection from the kiss.

"I don't know. I've saved my community. My family is basically gone. The future is whatever I make it," he said, giving her an evil smile.

"I could train you if you wanted. I would like you as a partner and if you really wanted, we could explore whatever *this* is between us," Anna said.

Anna almost felt embarrassed for sounding like such a schoolgirl but it was the truth.

Joshua smiled but bit his lip. "Thought you had a ranch to buy and a daughter to raise,"

"I will in time. My ex-husband treasures our daughter and gives her a normal life. And I love this job too much to give it up yet. So, what do you say? Want to join me and explore whatever relationship we have?"

Joshua kissed her again and again, and Anna seriously loved the passion, love and affection in every single kiss that made her feel like a teenager again.

Within moments Anna had been lovingly pushed onto her back and Anna just knew they were going to go on a lot of missions together, have a lot of fun and definitely explore what their relationship actually was.

But that was all after an afternoon rolling around on the grass together. And Anna couldn't think of a better way to spend a very victorious and wonderful afternoon.

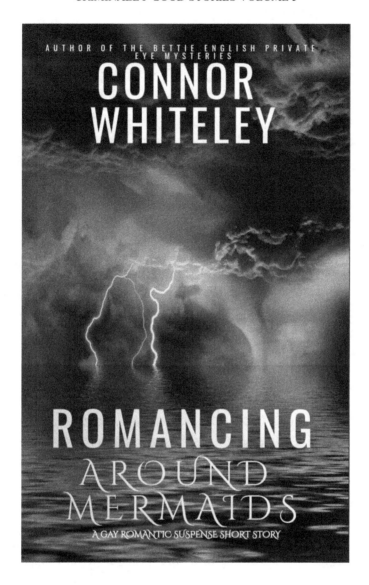

AUTHOR OF THE BETTIE ENGLISH PRIVATE
EYE MYSTERIES
CONNOR WHITELEY

ROMANCING
AROUND
MERMAIDS
A GAY ROMANTIC SUSPENSE SHORT STORY

ROMANCING AROUND MERMAIDS
20th September 2022
Dover, England

Noah had never really liked the sea, water or even sailing because he was very much a land lover, and as his ex-boyfriend had said plenty of times Noah was next to useless out in the open water, and for some silly reason that ex-boyfriend actually still wondered why he was an ex.

Noah stood on the bow (front to normal people) of a large white fishing boat with strong bright white metal sides, or a hull to fishing people, two large engines on the back and a small white metal hut-like shelter near the front of the boat that was what Noah called the bridge, were he controlled the boat from.

He had absolutely no idea if it was actually called a bridge, the only reason why he was out here twenty miles off the coast of Dover in the middle of the wide open ocean with the famous white cliffs being a mere line across the horizon, with deep blue water swirling, twirling and whirling around him was because he was trying to help out a great friend of his. Since Brooklyn had received a cancer diagnosis in July, and whilst she was thankfully in remission because of a crippling dose of chemo that she was slowly recovering from, she still sadly couldn't go fishing and exploring like she normally did.

And that was what earned her a lot of money after all, so to make sure Brooklyn didn't lose too much money Noah had volunteered to take her ship out and try his hand at fishing for her.

He was never ever going to do it again.

There was a bunch of so-called special clothing that Brooklyn normally wore and when Noah told her he was taking out her boat to help her, she had insisted on Noah wearing the special clothes but he didn't like them.

Noah had no intention of wearing an ugly drysuit, some weird shoes and a black cap. Especially as he wanted to wear something that would keep him warm and dry very quickly, he wasn't a complete idiot out on the water.

But Noah had to admit there was something so peaceful about being out in the wide open water with the massive aroma of the salty crisp water everywhere that left the amazing taste of fish and chips on his tongue, and only the sounds of gently rolling waves crashing into the hull of the boat for company.

Noah already felt great and comfortable and like he was going to be amazing at this, and for Brooklyn's sake he really hoped he was. Noah definitely didn't know how to fish, and Brooklyn had only given him a few instructions on how to work everything, including releasing the massive nets below the main deck.

Granted it was a little strange that Noah had to release the nets from the bottom of the boat, instead of throwing them over the back but at the end of the day Noah wasn't a fisherman and he was more than sure that Brooklyn's equipment was all normal.

But as the bright fiery sun started to set on the horizon, Noah felt the air start to turn colder ever so slightly, the water turned darker and Noah just couldn't help but feel like he wasn't alone anymore, almost like he was being watched by something or someone.

After a few moments of having that strange feeling, Noah forced himself to shake it off because having weird feelings wouldn't help him. Granted he was a little curious as to why Brooklyn only ever went fishing in the evening or at night time, he had always imagined fishermen and women to want to go out first thing in the morning and be back as soon as it got dark but clearly that wasn't how Brooklyn operated.

Which was strange considering how much of a rule follower she was in everyday life.

As a gentle howl of icy cold air rushed past Noah's cheeks, he seriously started to wonder if he was going to be okay out here, and that sense of unease only grew as the water turned pitch black and massive fish-like things started to swim about under the boat.

Noah wasn't sure what was going on but he really, really didn't want to do this anymore but he just had to.

He absolutely had to do some fishing for Brooklyn and get her some money to help with her recovery no matter how much it scared him.

***

20th September 2022

Dover, England

Peter Franks had always absolutely loved fishing at night, and even more so when he was recruited by the UK Government to fish for Mermaids. Apparently, and Peter seriously doubted this in normal situations, he was the perfect man for the job considering he was gay and mermaids did nothing for him unlike all the other agents and government assets they had sent after the Mermaids.

And the pretty cool thing about hunting mermaids were the clothes that the government gave him. Peter really loved his dark blue drysuit that made it impossible for water to get his clothes wet, anti-mermaid black wetshoes that were made from a certain cloth that mermaids hated and Peter really liked the black baseball cap.

It didn't serve a single purpose, it just looked cool.

As Peter stood with a wonderfully warm mug of strong bitter coffee spiced with cloves like the tribes of Africa that Peter had visited did with their own drinks, Peter just leant against the large metal steering wheel of his blade-like fishing boat, and looked out intensely into the darkness of the sea and sky beyond his little cabin through the large glass windows.

Peter really loved his cabin, it was a small metal structure in the middle of his fishing boat filled with his maps, anti-Mermaid weapons and the beautiful steering wheel that allowed him to control the boat even if Mermaids were attacking it at full force.

The last time the evil mermaids had done that it had just been a nightmare, there had been a lot of shouting, swearing and mermaids were just evil. It was exactly how Peter had lost his last two boyfriends and Peter had lost an entire crew of ten to the mermaids as they ripped Peter's nearest and dearest limb from limb.

Peter seriously hoped that no one was stupid enough to be out tonight, and as much as it would have been great to see Brooklyn hunting the mermaids tonight, Peter just wanted her to stay away and focus on recovering.

Peter felt his boat rock, jerk and shutter as the pitch black water around him began to swirl and react, and Peter just smiled because it meant the mermaids were starting to hunt tonight.

Peter looked at a little piece of paper that he had stuck on the window to his left that detailed out the timings of the most recent beginnings of the mermaids' stirrings and he was right the mermaids were definitely starting to hunt sooner and sooner.

It wouldn't have surprised Peter in the slightest that come the spring, the mermaids would start hunting in broad daylight when all the fishermen, families and tourists were out on the water.

Something that would cost a lot of lives if they weren't stopped or at least deterred before then.

A quiet bleeping sound made Peter look behind him where he kept a lot of his anti-mermaid equipment including a very small black scanner and to Peter's utter surprise the scanner was detecting the Lady of Mortem on the water. Peter had no clue why Brooklyn was out sailing and doing things considering her chemo and if the mermaids did attack then she would be so weak she might not be able to survive the attack.

Peter immediately grabbed the steering wheel of his own boat, *The Gay Revenge*, and started driving off in the direction of the Lady of Mortem. And when Peter found the boat he was definitely going to tell Brooklyn off because she should not have been out here tonight.

But right now Peter just needed to save his friend.

***

20th September 2022

Dover, England

Noah flat out couldn't believe how choppy the pitch black water was getting as the water swirled, twirled and whirled around him, and it was even weirder that the water only seemed to do it around the boat not anywhere else.

Noah was firmly hiding in the little metal hut-like structure now and fighting to hold the silver steering wheel straight to stop the boat from spinning out of control.

Besides from that the little hut-like bridge was rather great with its little heater, strange weapons on the back wall that Noah had only discovered by accident and a little bleeping scanner that Noah didn't understand in the slightest.

Noah had always known that Brooklyn was a little weird but it was confusing that she would have all of these things on her boat when she had never revealed them being here before when Noah and their other friends had come aboard.

He was definitely going to have to ask her about it later.

"Hello," a woman shouted outside.

Noah had no clue whatsoever who would be outside at this time of night in this sort of storm but Noah put on his large black coat that he had hung on a strange jade dagger, pulled it tight and went outside onto the deck through a small metal door.

The bright white colour of the deck was a great contrast to the pitch blackness of the sky, sea and the lashing rain but Noah couldn't see anyone.

"Hello," the woman shouted again.

Noah traced the sound of the voice over the lashing thundering rain to the very edge of the deck and when Noah looked over the metal side of the boat he was stunned to see a woman down there.

Noah supposed to straight men and lesbians she would have been beautiful with her long blond hair that covered her female assets so perfectly, she was clearly fit and had slight muscles on her arms and body, and she really did have the most sensational smile he had ever seen.

But she wasn't beautiful to him or attractive in the slightest.

The woman started singing a rather pretty song and seductively looked at Noah in a suggestive way but he just looked at her.

He was a lot more concerned about if she was okay. The water had to be freezing cold and rather deadly to be in so Noah just wanted this woman to be okay.

"Are you okay in there?" Noah asked. "Do you need help?"

The woman gave him another seductive smile and looked like she was really trying to make him do something but Noah felt nothing.

"You're a very attractive man. You're so brave, clever and heroic for being out this late. Not many men could do what you're doing," the woman said.

Noah shrugged. He was hardly doing anything special, he was only trying to help out a friend.

"Can I get you a coat or a line to pull you out with?" Noah asked.

The woman frowned slightly. "Do you think I'm beautiful? Do you want a little kiss?"

Noah shook his head. "Na sorry you aren't my type and I'm a lot more concerned about your safety in the water,"

"Abomination!" the woman shouted.

Noah screamed as the woman's mouth twisted and changed to show immense fang-like daggers shoot out of her teeth and fingers.

The woman started climbing onto the boat.

Noah didn't know what was happening.

There was a light in the distance. Another boat. Noah didn't know how to reach them.

The woman climbed over the edge of the hull. She grinned at Noah. Gesturing she was going to slaughter him.

Noah rushed into the bridge. He went to lock the little metal door but it didn't. There wasn't a lock.

Noah went to hold the door shut but it opened outwards.

All the woman needed to do was pull it open and she would get to him.

Noah watched the woman slash her claws around the boat. Trying to scare him. It was working.

Noah went backwards. Pressing against the strange daggers and weapons. They were glowing a light blue.

Noah grabbed the jade dagger.

The woman ripped open the little metal door. She flew at Noah.

Noah screamed. Waving the dagger wildly.

The woman slashed Noah's chest.

Someone smashed into the boat.

The woman flew into the steering wheel. Smashing her head.

Noah pointed the dagger at her.

The woman screamed. She launched herself at Noah.

Noah shot forward.

Thrusting the jade dagger into her chest.

And as soon as he did that Noah felt terrible as he watched the woman turn to ash and her cold deadly eyes just stared at him until they turned to water and Noah felt a shockwave rip through the boat and down into the deepest darkest depths of the ocean.

A few moments later Noah heard someone step aboard and he pointed the jade dagger at the now ripped-open little metal doorway his hands becoming blurs as they shook.

Then the most beautiful man Noah had ever seen stepped through the door frowning and looking completely shocked to see Noah there.

Noah seriously loved the man's amazing strong jawline, stunning deep blue eyes and even though he was wearing a very unflattering drysuit, strange wetshoes and a black baseball cap that looked to be hiding some beautiful locks of black hair, Noah just had to admit he was so beautiful.

Noah didn't know what had just attacked him but if this

beautiful sexy man had been the woman instead, then Noah was certain that he would have been dead already.

"And who the hell are you?" the beautiful man asked with a smile.

A smile that Noah was sure could melt his heart and the polar ice caps if the beautiful sexy man really tried.

Noah just had a feeling he was going to love getting to know this beautiful man even if the circumstances were a little too deadly for his liking.

***

20th September 2022

Dover, England

Peter was absolutely stunned as he stared at an extremely gorgeous sexy man standing in the bridge of the Lady of Mortem. He really wanted to know where the hell was Brooklyn but this man was just so beautiful and perfect.

Peter really loved the man's smooth youthful baby face, even though Peter could sort of guess they were both the same age in their mid-twenties, and the man had the most gorgeous green eyes, longish brown hair that was starting to curl at the ends and the man's fit skinny body was also pretty great to look at.

His hands turned sweaty, his stomach filled with butterflies and even Peter's head felt light something that hadn't happened for years and a feeling that made Peter very unsure about himself. Yet this beautiful man in front of him was simply stunning.

But what really surprised Peter was that the beautiful man clearly didn't know a single thing about mermaids or what the hell he was holding in his cute little hands, but he wasn't completely clueless about the open water. He was wearing thick clothes that wouldn't only keep his body warm but would dry quickly too.

A very smart choice.

"I'm Noah," the beautiful man said.

Peter extended his hand. "Peter, and where's my friend Brooklyn?"

Peter loved it when beautiful Noah took his hand and shook it and the purest of chemistry, attraction and electricity flowed uncontrollably between them. Noah was seriously hot.

Noah cocked his head. "I'm her friend and I said I would take her boat out for some fishing. Get her some money whilst she recovers from chemo,"

Peter just smiled and shook his head. As much as he loved Brooklyn and called her almost daily after he had been out hunting for mermaids. She clearly hadn't been focused when Noah had asked her permission because she had at least should have told him about the mermaids.

"And she never mentioned the mermaids did she?" Peter asked.

Noah laughed like he was joking then Peter just pointed to the pile of ash under the steering wheel.

Noah's beautiful eyes widened and all Peter wanted to do in that moment was hug the sweet, cute beautiful man in front of him.

"No she didn't," Noah said, "and I presume that's why she only goes fishing at night and she has nets that launch from the bottom of the boat,"

Peter nodded at least this beautiful man was a quick study and clearly intelligent.

Something smashed into the boat.

Peter dashed outside. The rain was lashing down and his boat was sinking.

The Gay Revenge was filling up with water.

Mermaids were climbing and slashing and killing it all over.

Noah gasped behind him. Peter spun around and pushed Noah back into the bridge.

Peter had no idea how the mermaids had just slaughtered his boat considering it was one of the strongest mermaid hunters in existence.

Peter had to call for backup and get some serious help now so he went over to Brooklyn's little black scanner and immediately tapped the little scanning screen.

A moment later the screen went black then changed to reveal a number pad so Peter entered a distress code that would summon the royal navy in Dover and hopefully they would come to their rescue.

Peter quickly told Noah what was happening.

"What?" Noah asked. "What are we meant to do until then? The women or whatever they are are out there,"

Peter smiled and was about to answer when the sweet melody of their singing echoed all around them and Peter just knew that the mermaids were circling the boat.

It was only a matter of time until they attacked.

Peter just looked at the insanely hot and beautiful man in front of him and he just had to protect Noah no matter what. He seriously couldn't afford to let any more hot men die because of his failures.

He had to beat the mermaids no matter what.

But just in case he died saving Noah. Peter quickly kissed the insanely hot Noah and Peter really loved the feeling and taste of his soft lips against his.

The mermaids roared in rage. The fight was about to begin.

***

20th September 2022
Dover, England

Noah was so amazed, delighted and shocked by beautiful Peter's soft and loving kiss that he almost froze but that was quickly sliced through by the constant roaring of the evil mermaids that he still didn't know too much about.

But Noah just knew that if and when he survived this the topic of mermaids was definitely going to be great first date material for Noah and Peter.

Something flew through the air.

Noah watched Peter gasp as human hacked up corpses splattered the deck. Rich dark blood poured out of them.

Painting the bright white metal deck a vivid red.

Noah gripped the jade dagger in his hand tighter. Peter grabbed another dagger from the collection behind him.

Claws slashed metal. The thundering sound echoed around the boat.

Noah watched Peter step outside. He was scared. He didn't want Peter to go.

Noah followed him. They both stepped out onto the deck. Rain lashing at them.

The thick layer of blood slippery under their feet Noah kept close to Peter making sure neither of them were attacked.

A mermaid leapt out the water.

Flying towards them.

Noah swung his dagger. The mermaid turned to ash.

Mermaids screamed around them. They climbed on board.

Climbing onto the deck.

Noah and Peter ran to the bow. Mermaids were everywhere.

They attacked. They swung their claws. Slashing at Noah and Peter.

Noah swung his dagger.

The mermaids sliced his arm.

He hissed.

Peter shot forward. Killed a few mermaids. He shot back.

Noah got back-to-back with Peter. The mermaids were gaining ground.

They formed a circle around them.

Noah kept swinging his dagger.

The mermaids lunched forward.

Slashing Noah's arms with their claws.

Blood squirted out of Noah's arm.

He screamed.

A mermaid dived on his leg.

Noah stomped on her.

Shattering her skull.

More mermaids dived for Noah.

Chomping into his leg.

Noah fell to the ground.

Peter tried to grab him. Mermaids dived on Peter. Peter fought them off.

Noah fought the mermaids on his knees. More of his blood poured out.

The mermaids got excited. They laughed. They hissed. They sung.

They grabbed Noah's sliced arm.

They pulled him towards the side of the boat.

Noah tried to kick them. Fight them. Kill them.

He couldn't. He was too weak.

Mermaids dragged him closer towards the side. Closer to the water.

Peter screamed.

Noah slashed the mermaids. They released him.

Noah spun around.

Peter had mermaids all over him.

They chomped onto his legs. His arms. His back.

Peter was dying.

Noah surged forward.

The mermaids latched onto Noah. Sinking their fangs into his feet.

Noah screamed in agony. Crippling pain filled him.

The mermaids dragged him closer to the side of the boat. Noah almost wanted to go into the water and end it all.

But he couldn't. He had to protect Brooklyn. He had to protect Peter.

They both had to live so they could go on a first date and hopefully more.

Noah kicked mermaids in the head. Smashing their skulls. They released him.

Noah shot forward.

Running into the bridge.

He grabbed as many daggers as he could.

Noah rushed over.

Randomly throwing dagger after dagger.

The daggers had a life of their own. They flew towards the mermaids.

Stabbing into the mermaids' chest. Turning them to ash.

The mermaid screamed in fear.

Noah kept throwing the daggers.

Mermaids were slaughtered.

Mermaids screamed.

Mermaids died.

Noah rushed over to Peter. Kicking the mermaids off him.

Mermaids screamed as one.

Shooting back into the water.

Swimming down as much as they could.

Noah quickly looked around to see if there were any more foul mermaids on the boat but there wasn't so Noah grabbed Peter in his arms.

Noah's own arms ached and pain flooded his senses from his feet, legs and arms but Noah just made sure to hold Peter's beautiful bleeding body in his arms.

If they were both going to die on this boat then Noah just wanted, needed to die close to this beautiful sexy man that he really wished he could have learnt more about and gotten to know a lot better.

As Noah's vision turned hazy and black around the edges Noah could have sworn he heard very human voices close by and the massive roaring horn of a Royal Navy warship but Noah wasn't sure if he was ever going to know as he collapsed with beautiful Peter in his arms and he drifted off into the darkness.

A darkness he wasn't sure he was going to wake up from.

***

22nd September 2022

Dover, England

Peter was completely shocked as two days later that he had survived it all as he sat on a cold wooden chair in a bright yellow round room in a government private hospital that looked more like a care home than a hospital to be honest.

Peter rather liked the little rows of wooden tables and wooden chairs with board games and refreshments and more for the residents to enjoy whilst they were recovering. And despite the smell of lemon, grapefruit and lime from the harsh and nasty cleaning chemicals the cleaners used in the room that left the strange taste of key lime pie on his tongue, this actually was a great place to recover.

And as much as Peter wanted to see Noah again because they had both apparently been bought here by the Navy after the attack, Peter didn't actually mind the few moments of peace before he hopefully saw that hot sexy man once more.

Peter's body still ached from all the injuries and blood loss and they were definitely going to scar but Peter was more than happy to be alive. And he was really happy that beautiful Noah had been there too.

Peter had never seen the mermaids so angry before but everyone knew that this day was coming. Everyone knew at some point the mermaids would try their luck in launching an all-out attack on humanity and the outcome of that fight would determine the rest of humanity's fate.

Thankfully because of Noah's amazingly brave actions the mermaids were scared and they would hopefully never ever attack again, and that was all because of beautiful Noah.

Peter almost laughed at himself because he had lost so much to the mermaids over the years, including friends, best friends and boyfriends, and if he was being really honest with himself then he also knew that he had almost closed himself off to love, but just the idea of seeing sexy Noah again made him feel light, happy and like such a schoolboy all over again.

Sure he barely knew Noah but Peter didn't care, because they had both experienced and fought and lived through something extraordinary and Noah had been amazing through it.

And that was exactly the sort of man that Peter wanted to be with.

"Excuse me, is this seat taken?" Noah said smiling as he gestured to the chair opposite Peter.

Peter just smiled and nodded and as his stomach filled with butterflies, his hands turned sweaty and his head went light. He really knew that he was going to love getting to know this hot beautiful man that had ultimately saved his life.

***

22nd December 2022
Dover, England

Noah had absolutely loved the past four amazing months with beautiful Peter, they had laughed a lot, hunted mermaids a lot and gotten to know each other in ways that Noah had thought was impossible, but Noah was far from ashamed to admit that he felt so connected to Peter that whenever they were apart he felt sad, lonely and like he was missing a part of himself.

As Noah and Peter laid together on their dark blue sofa in their large living room with cardboard boxes scattered around the room from where Noah had moved in with the love of his life, with Peter's amazing nautical-themed art, sculptures and books hanging on the bright white walls and just looking amazing, Noah seriously loved beginning the new chapter of his life.

They might have fought evil mermaids together, saved humanity and stopped the mermaids from hunting and feeding on human corpses (that's what Peter had told him the mermaids did all over the world) but their love didn't actually come from that. Sure it was the weirdest meet-cute in history, but Noah had little doubt he wouldn't have loved Peter if they had met a different way.

Noah really loved the great feeling of Peter's arm across him holding him tight and caringly and lovingly as the two of them just laid there in silence, not because there was nothing to talk about, but just because their relationship was strong enough for them to know they didn't always need to be talking to be intimate.

They just needed to be with each other.

And sure the mermaid hunting, fishing and sailing (something Noah couldn't believe he actually found fun with Peter), but their relationship had always been about something deeper. They both loved the same things, the same music and they had a lot in common so it was hardly difficult to bond over.

Peter kissed Noah's forehead briefly and gestured the two of them should continue unpacking Noah's things, and normally and if it was with any other man Noah would have hesitated and wanted to lay there a little longer, but this wasn't just any other guy.

This was the love of his life so as Noah got up and him and Peter started to talk about where to put things, laugh and have fun doing something as simple as moving in together. Noah just knew that their love was real, their relationship was amazing and this was going to last a long, long time.

And Noah didn't have a single problem with that in the slightest. All because Peter made him feel amazing and light and gave him butterflies like only true love could.

SPYING AND ROMANCING THE NIGHT AWAY

MI6 Officer Alexander Davies, Alex for short, had always loved the more glamourous side of spying and espionage and doing whatever it took to get the information the UK Government needed to do its business, so when he was given the opportunity to go to a black tie gallery opening filled with extremists, but admittedly hot men, he didn't have an issue in going.

Alex stood in his dark blue bedroom with the cold lonely double bed perfectly made behind him, chests of drawers filled with false passports, money and more lined the edges of the room, and Alex's favourite piece of furniture in the entire world rested right next to the large floor-to-ceiling window to his left. Alex really did love his dark brown wooden wardrobe filled with fine suits, clothes and shirts that might have been expensive but he really loved the cool, luxurious feeling of the expensive fabrics against his skin.

And on the top shelf of the wardrobe, Alex loved it that he had such a great range of aftershaves, some were poisonous to certain people and some weren't, but for tonight Alex was just going to wear his favourite. A little brand he had picked up in Paris a few years ago and even though he couldn't pronounce the name at all, he had always loved its sweet aroma of oranges, grapefruits and a subtle undertone of lemon running under it all.

That had definitely attracted a boy or two.

Alex stood in front of a large square mirror that an ex-boyfriend bought him before catching Alex in too many lies, and when the person that Alex had thought was the love of his life had found out what he did for a living, he flipped and stormed out and Alex thankfully never ever saw him again.

As Alex finished tying up his bowtie and straightening out the minor creases in his black suit made from silk that completed his outfit of a black blazer, trousers and a crisp white shirt with a little black bowtie as an added bonus, he supposed that he would have preferred to be spying on Iran, North Korea or any of the normal targets that he looked at on his computer, but it was always great to get out from time to time.

Besides from the fact that he only ever seemed to meet truly hot men on missions, but they were never the sort of men that Alex wanted to date.

They were monsters after all.

Alex had even had an offer to go clubbing tonight with some work friends, but Alex just had to go to this party, identify the leader of the extremist group that was hosting the party and leave.

To normal people that probably sounded so easy, but when the entire guest list were extremists that wanted to burn out the UK for being too soft on foreigners (but this group was talking about the Welsh, Scottish and Northern Irish who were all legal citizens of the UK) that only complicated matters.

It was even worst that Alex couldn't bring a gun or any weapons whatsoever because the party's security was so tight so Alex was hardly impressed about that.

Alex finally managed to get his bowtie perfectly straight and he had to admit that he looked great in his black suit, and it was just a shame that no one attractive or into Alex in the slightest would ever see him in it.

That was definitely one of the worst things about being a spy. Alex truly adored MI6 for having enough faith in him to let him travel the world, spying on the UK's enemies and protecting the innocent people of the UK. But the only real problem was that it was so lonely at times.

MI6 hardly hired that many gay people, unlike MI5, so it was next to impossible to date and it was even harder to find gay friends that actually understood him. Sure there were some posh snobs from the English nobility that had been casted out of their rich families for being gay, but that was far from the same.

Especially as Alex had been born to a poor family, no mother and only raised by his father who had celebrated Alex when he finally came out.

So Alex hardly fitted in with the rich posh snobs of MI6 and the English "nobility".

Alex dashed out the door of his London apartment and really looked forward to travelling across London to this extremist party.

The idea of spying on a group of extremists with certain death being the consequence if he got caught excited him way more than it should have.

***

French DGSE agent Hugo Petain had never ever understood why the English were obsessed with three things, like they were the only things that mattered in the entire world, judging by the past hour of conversations Hugo had had with these extremists, it seemed the English were only concerned with burning down the three other nations of the UK because of these dirty foreigners, killing off socialism for good and most importantly, making sure the disease-ridden French stopped invading the UK.

Hugo had no idea where some of these extremists got those ideas from, but when the President of France asked Hugo specifically to come to this awful party filled with the very worst kind of English people, he supposed he had no choice.

And it was a great benefit that Hugo could control his French accent perfectly, and it did make him very popular at French parties because Hugo could do any accent perfectly that his friends asked of him.

It was also remarkably helpful in spy work too.

After an hour of talking with so many extremists in their tight black suits, horrible oxford-laced (or whatever they were called) black shoes and black trousers, Hugo just stood at the back of the very large function room the party was in and just studied it like he had another three times tonight.

The function room itself was horrible and terribly English with its dark brown oak walls that seemed to suck out all the light of the room, there were bookcases filled with first editions built into the four walls (but Hugo seriously doubted any of these extremists could read) and there was a very large chandelier hanging from the white textured ceiling.

The chandelier itself was certainly French made judging by the craftsmanship, so Hugo was a little surprised these people wanted something so disease ridden at their party, but it just proved how stupid all these people were.

But even Hugo had to admit that he really did love the stunning skyline of London with all its skyscrapers, ancient landmarks and little lights that lit up the horizon through the massive floor-to-ceiling windows that were dotted about on the wall to Hugo's right.

Hugo had rather enjoyed tonight so far because for the most part the English were just troublemakers, or at least their politicians were, but he had to admit the English did produce some very fine-looking men. Of course mainland European men were always more beautiful than the English, but Hugo wouldn't mind bedding some of these extremists for information purposes, of course.

Hugo leant against an icy cold oak wall nursing his small glass of whiskey from almighty Scotland, now there was a country that Hugo could fully support and move to, and it was just another sign that these extremists were hypocrites.

Hugo was really looking forward to leaving the party so he could crack on with some missions whilst he was in the UK. He did need to hack into the UK Government and see what post-Brexit rubbish they were planning so at least France could prepare defence measures, a small top-secret MI6 boat patrol had already invaded French waters and killed ten soldiers.

Including Hugo's boyfriend of five years, so he was hardly impressed with the British Secret Service and he was more than happy that the Director of DGSE had given him permission to hack into MI6 too if he wanted it.

And Hugo really did want it.

"Mr Petain," a very elderly and fragile man said in an expensive suit as he walked up to Hugo.

Hugo bowed his head slightly, because that was what apparently the English did when they met a "superior" even though surely everyone should have been equal at this party.

"We are grateful for your donation to our cause, please thank your wife for us," the man said.

Hugo raised his glass. "I will thank you dear sir. It is only because of the brave men like you and your friends that there is a chance for us to be free of the smelly French and extremist Scots, Welsh and Irish,"

"Hey, hey," the man said cheering with Hugo.

As soon as the man wandered off Hugo felt like he was going to be sick. At least the money that Hugo had transferred to this extremist group's bank account had been revealed the name all their accounts were under, and with most of them being based in the EU, the DGSE was leading the charge in freezing the accounts now.

Hugo just wanted to see who was in charge though, everyone at the party had said that the boss was turning up later to reveal the new plans for an "event" that would help them to get rid of the French once and for all, so Hugo sadly had to stay a little longer.

Hugo was about to finish his drink when he noticed a new person walk in, and Hugo straightened his back just in case this guy was the boss or something.

Wow.

Hugo just stared wide-eyed and like a deer in headlights as he watched the absolutely gorgeous sexy man walk into the party, looking a little lost.

Hugo simply loved the man's tight expensive black silk blazer, trousers and white shirt that highlighted how sensationally fit he was under all those clothes. The man was so beautiful and perfect that Hugo just didn't know what to do.

His hands turned sweaty, his heart started to beat faster and he was just so beautiful that Hugo really, really wanted to run his hands through the gorgeous man's longish well-styled brown hair.

He was beyond hot, and he was far more beautiful than any English man deserved to be.

And even though he was probably a foul awful extremist that would be serving life sentences in a few years' time Hugo just had to talk to this gorgeous man.

Just in case he wasn't.

***

Alex was immediately hit with the aromas of strong whiskey, French cheese and another strange but awful smell that he just couldn't detect yet.

Alex wasn't even a fan of the function room itself, it was very upper-class English with so much poshness and snobbiness built into the room that Alex just wanted to leave. He really didn't like the dark brown oak walls, the first-editions in the built bookcases that were rather vaguer in his opinion, but he had to admit he did like the French chandelier.

Alex could instantly tell that it was French because it was so classy, sparkling and rather dazzling in a way that English made goods were very rarely done. It really did help to bring the room together but at least Alex knew that he was dealing with hypocrites, he hated fighting hard-line true-believer extremists.

But hypocrites were a lot more manageable.

Alex started looking at all the very tall and fit extremist men in their tight black suits and horrible oxford laced shoes and their pompous attitudes that Alex didn't agree with in the slightest. And whilst Alex completely believed that the UK and Britain could become "great" again, it most certainly wasn't going to become great through extremism and killing.

Yet these people probably disagreed entirely.

"Hello," a man said. "I'm Hugo Petain,"

Alex looked around to see who was talking to him and... holy fuck.

Alex's mouth actually dropped when he saw a very cute tall guy standing next to him, offering out his hand. Alex seriously loved the man's strong jawline, short but extremely cute looking blond hair and bright sapphire eyes.

He was just so cute.

And Alex seriously loved the man in his tight black suit that left very little to the imagination, at least Alex knew that he was well-endorsed below, that was always a bonus.

Alex felt his stomach fill with butterflies and blood rushed to wayward parts as he shook the cute guy's hand, and Alex thought he was going to faint as the sheer rush of attraction, chemistry and affection flowed between them.

Then Alex wondered if the man was going to kiss his hand, like they occasionally did in France at times, but the cute guy seemed to stop himself.

When Alex's face started to hurt from smiling so much, he realised that he hadn't intended to smile at this cute guy, but he was so beautiful.

But Alex couldn't understand what a French man was doing here. Sure the man didn't look French or say it in the slightest, but if the man was a spy then it meant nothing. And Petain was definitely a French surname dating back to at least to the 40s with the head of the Vichy Government in World War two.

Alex simply smiled as the cute guy as they sadly broke their handshaking and the cute guy passed him a drink of strong Scottish whiskey, but inside Alex was a bit concerned, he had only heard last night that MI6 had illegally killed a bunch of French soldiers for no reason on the orders of the Prime Minister.

Alex and basically every single MI6 agent had been outraged but if the DGSE was running operations on British soil, then he was starting to get a little concerned about what the hell this meant for his own safety.

Alex made sure no one else was within earshot and then leant very close to the cute guy, and Alex seriously loved the amazing earth smell of the guy.

"What is the DGSE up to?" Alex asked quietly.

The cute guy laughed a little like Alex had told him a joke, he was very good.

"I presume you are MI6 then, a little odd for British murderers to be operating on UK soil," Hugo said.

Alex felt his stomach flip, clearly this Frenchman was annoyed about the murders.

"I had nothing to do with that and I *flat out* hated my government for doing it," Alex said with a lot more conviction than he intended.

Hugo raised the glass to his lips and Alex just smiled because he wasn't drinking, it only looked like he was drinking. So Alex did the same, they were at a party after all.

A very elderly man walked past and Alex pulled Hugo slightly closer to him. "Believe me if I can help the DGSE I will, I am nothing like those agents from the other night,"

Again Alex was rather surprised at his conviction and it was only now that he was realising how much he utterly hated those MI6 agents, he didn't even know why they went to France in the first place and came across those soldiers.

Hugo slowly nodded, taking another fake sip of his whiskey. "I appreciate that,"

It wasn't exactly the glowing endorsement Alex had wanted but at least Hugo sounded a lot less annoyed with him than before, and that only made him seem cuter.

"What does MI6 have on the leader of the party?" Hugo asked as he led Alex through the crowd and nodded at several extremists like they had been friends for years.

"Nothing. The same as DGSE?" Alex asked.

Hugo smiled and manly hugged a very fragile man who started muttering some slogan about how the foul Scots needed to die and then only in their ashes could England rise to true greatness.

Alex took Hugo's light laughter as a yes that the DCSE had nothing.

"Gentleman!" a young man shouted near the front of the function room and all eyes fixed on him. "Our Lord and Saviour is here to enlighten us all on the Final Order,"

Alex had no clue what the Final Order was but it hardly sounded good and as Alex's stomach flipped he had a very sudden urge to protect hot sexy Hugo no matter what.

Because no one that hot and cute and wonderful deserved to suffer.

***

Hugo had to admit that Alex was really hot and beautiful, and he had actually loved spending time with him. It was such a relief to know that he wasn't like other MI6 agents, and at least he wasn't a murderer. He was just a cute little Englishman that had the power to melt Hugo's heart and his wayward parts flare to live.

"Here is our Saviour," the young man said, who was wearing the same tight black suits as all the other men in the function rooms with its French chandelier, bookcases built into the dark brown oak walls and plenty of little pieces of food now going around on little palates. Again a French invention.

A few moments later a very tall middle-aged man stepped into the room with messy blond hair, a massive stomach and the sort of grin that Hugo just had from slimy politicians that he had or may have not assassinated in his long career.

"Saviour," the young man said bowing.

Everyone else bowed so Hugo forced himself to and gorgeous Alex followed.

"Rise," the Saviour said.

Hugo focused on the man and tried to place him in all the photos he had studied of English politicians, known extremists and nobility he had studied before the mission, but he couldn't place him. He had no clue who he was.

And judging by Alex's beautiful face, he didn't have a clue either. This was a brand new player, and that never ended well.

"We have been infiltrated by the disease-Ridden, the Corrupt MI6 and even the Conspiracy Theorist Americans that broke away from our divine Empire hundreds of years ago," the Saviour said.

Hugo looked around like everyone else did in utter horror at such an outrageous and disgusting thing, Hugo really like these parts of missions when his acting skills got put to the test.

Yet he was a bit surprised that someone from the CIA was here.

"Two nights ago," the Saviour said, "I sent a group of Divine Heroes from MI6 into the disease-ridden land of mainland Europe,"

Everyone gasped like that was the most heroic and most unbearable thing they had ever heard. Hugo just wanted to laugh at these pathetic people who had probably never seen the beautiful landscapes of Paris, Budapest and the other wonders of ancient Europe.

It really was beautiful.

And Hugo really wanted to share some of those beautiful views with Alex. He even wondered if the beauty of those views would be amplified or diminished by Alex's own stunning beauty.

"I ordered them to attack a small DGSE outpost to stop them from developing a nuclear weapon to attack us with and when my agents were there from MI6 they hacked into their databases and learnt the identity all French agents tainting our most holy island," the Saviour said.

Hugo was just amazed that these idiots were buying it. France didn't have much of a nuclear programme these days and they most certainly didn't plan to use it against the British.

The opposite was quite the case.

Beautiful Alex took a step closer to him. "You should leave now. I don't want you to get hurt,"

Hugo was about to say a witty comeback to the insult of his

honour, but then he heard the amount of emotion and interest and actual caring in his voice.

Hugo had no clue if Alex wanted to protect him so he, as a Frenchman, wouldn't die or if Alex actually cared about him romantically, but Hugo wasn't leaving.

This was his fight and he had to stay and protect Alex.

Then Hugo felt the cold metal barrel of a gun press into his back and Hugo noticed two guys were standing behind him and Alex.

"And I didn't mention Swig," the Saviour said to Hugo, "but the foul traitorous Americans have earned their redemption and a single CIA asset has joined us,"

Hugo turned around slowly and just frowned at the grey bushy beard, slim body and brown eyes filled with rage of the American holding the gun on Alex.

The two men with the guns gestured Hugo and Alex to go forward.

Hugo turned back around and slowly went forward, he almost wanted to laugh at the disgusted looks of the extremists as they realised they had actually hugged a Frenchman, and a gay one at that.

When Hugo and Alex got to the front of the function room next to a bright red row of red first-edition hardbacks, Hugo just glared at the Saviour and changed his accent back to normal.

"You know half of these idiots hugged me tonight?" Hugo said.

Saviour shrugged and looked at his audience. "The real problem with the French is that their disease corrupts their voices so you cannot understand these monsters, but I think my translation of the Creature's tongue is correct,"

Bullets screamed through the air.

Twenty extremists dropped dead as men lining the outside of the function room shot all the people had that hugged and been tainted by Hugo's so-called disease ridden touch tonight.

At least that was twenty more people they didn't need to fight.

The Saviour whipped out a gun.

Alex shot forward.

Protectively placing himself between the gun and Hugo.

That was sweet and Hugo really appreciated it but now wasn't the time for romance. Especially as Hugo just needed to touch the Saviour and his friends might turn on him.

Especially if Hugo shouted French that the extremist might take as a diseasing curse.

The CIA agent punched Alex. He fell against the first editions.

"Damn it," the Saviour said. "Add burning those hardbacks to the list. We can't have fag-contaminated stuff in our party room. We can't have the mental disorder spreading to our members,"

Hugo just laughed.

Alex smiled at him and he was so cute.

"Shall we cause some trouble?" Hugo asked gesturing towards the Saviour.

The atmosphere changed in intensity. It was so tense and all the extremists looked like they were almost too shocked that something so disgusting was in front of them that they were all too stunned to do anything about it.

Exactly how Hugo wanted them.

Alex nodded. He flew at the CIA Agent.

Hugo surged forward.

Charging at the Saviour.

He screamed in pain.

A man tackled Hugo.

Throwing him against the bookcases.

Whacking Hugo across the face.

Hugo blocked the punches.

Hugo kicked him in the balls.

The man fell to the ground.

Hugo kicked him in the head.

The Saviour was running away.

Hugo jumped through the air.

Tackling the Saviour to the ground.

The Saviour screamed.

The entire room stopped. Hugo kissed the Saviour on the lips.

It was so disgusting that Hugo just wanted to vomit so badly that when two black suited men pulled Hugo off him, and placed him in a headlock.

Hugo actually did vomit all over the carpet.

Everyone gasped as the Saviour stood up and Hugo and Alex just laughed, because the Saviour's wayward parts were very excited about the kiss to Hugo's utter dismay.

The two men released Hugo and Hugo immediately made sure that Alex was okay and he was just standing on three corpses with broken necks like it was just another day at the office, because in a way it really was.

"Cover me," Alex said, as he carefully got his phone.

Hugo nodded.

"You are a fag traitor," all the extremists said as one.

"No I am pure. I am straight. I am divine," the Saviour pleaded.

All the extremists took out small pocket knives and the CIA agent punched the Saviour in the face before putting him in a headlock.

"Let's show this fag what we do to them," the CIA agent said.

Hugo watched all the foul extremists as they lined up and sliced the Saviour's flesh through his expensive suit.

Hugo quickly realised that they were going to kill by death by a thousand cuts, an extremely painful way to go but the Saviour deserved it.

"A strike team will be here in minutes," Alex said as he took Hugo's hands. "You have to go now,"

Hugo just looked at gorgeous the Englishman in front of him. A man that was so beautiful that Hugo really didn't want to leave him, because for the first time in ages, he actually felt great, alive and like there was fun in his work once more.

Three feelings he hadn't realised he had missed in spy work for a long, long time.

But he knew that Alex was right, if the strike team caught him then he would be turned over to MI6 and then the politicians would get involved with news of such a priced French asset in their custody.

Hugo would just be used by the English in their constant pointless fighting with mainland Europe, and chances are Hugo would never be freed because the English would keep changing their demands like they always did.

"Please," Alex said.

Bullets screamed through the air.

Hugo threw Alex to one side.

Bullets slammed into the bookcase behind them.

The men charged at Hugo.

Hugo punched a man.

Three men grabbed Alex.

Alex couldn't fight them off.

Hugo kicked the men in the heads.

Snapping a neck.

A knife zoomed past Hugo's head.

He caught the arm connected to it.

Slamming the arm over his knees.

Shattering bone.

Doors downstairs exploded open.

People stormed in.

Automatic rifles fired.

Corpses tumbled downstairs. The Strike team was here.

The CIA man kicked Hugo in-between the legs.

He collapsed to the ground.

The CIA man stuck a gun in Hugo's mouth.

Hugo jumped forward.

Surprising the man.

Hugo broke the man's arm.

He dropped the gun.

Hugo grabbed the gun.

Shooting the CIA man in the head.

His brain matter exploded out.

The strike team breached the room.

Hugo had to go. He had to leave beautiful Alex.

Hugo ran towards a floor-to-ceiling window.

Shot at it.

The window shattered.

Hugo grabbed a long curtain next to it.

And jumped out the window.

***

Alex was amazed as sexy cute Hugo leapt out the window, snapping the curtain rail off the wall but because the curtain rail was so long it didn't fall out the window, effectively breaking Hugo's fall.

Alex carefully went over to the window and stared down at the little balcony below that was only a few metres above the street level, an easy jump for a spy to make, and Hugo simply waved at Alex and blew him a kiss before he disappeared into the night.

And it was exactly then Alex felt absolutely awful, because it had been so much fun working and spying alongside Hugo. Alex had felt alive, young and it was the most fun he had had in ages.

As Alex watched the shadow of Hugo disappear into the night and darkness of London, he just felt so alone again. Because Alex was only realising now how much it had meant to him that he had actually got the chance to meet another gay spy, and a really, really cute one at that.

"Agent Davis," a man said behind Alex.

Alex turned around and smiled as he saw his boss Mr Blake Evans, well the person in charge of his department anyway not the head of MI6, a middle-aged man with a bald head wearing jeans, a t-shirt and some black shoes that made Alex instantly know that his boss had come here to make sure *he* was okay, and not on some official MI6 business.

As the extremists cursed and swore their revenge on the disease-ridden French and the fag English that were burning this country to the ground, Alex just laughed and when the strike and everyone had left, leaving just Alex and his boss in the function room until MI6's crime scene techs came, he just noticed that Blake was grinning at him.

"I heard Hugo Petain was in the country," his boss said. "A very cute and attractive *gay* French DGSE agent,"

Alex shook his head. "Sounds like a great guy, a real ally to this country. I hope I get to meet him one day,"

Blake laughed. "Come on Alex, you know I have power with the Head of the Agency,"

Alex shrugged again pretending to act cool, but he was surprised when Blake took a step closer.

"And in confidence, I can tell you both the UK and French Governments want more collaboration so they want two agents working together constantly, if you catch my drift,"

Alex smiled, not because the UK government actually wanted collaboration with the French, but because that might mean him and cute Hugo could be spending a lot more time together. Of course he just couldn't admit that Hugo was here tonight just because in case some idiot wanted to moan at the French for running ops on UK soil without permission.

Like the UK or any country was any better.

Alex smiled and shrugged as he walked out the function room. "If you did recommend me for it I wouldn't object it too, I have never met this cute Frenchman you're talking about but I would like to,"

Blake just laughed, and Alex was really, really excited about getting the amazing chance to work alongside with such a cute, beautiful Frenchman like Hugo.

He actually couldn't wait because he just had a feeling that he was deadly sure about would only be confirmed with a couple of dates and then even more all over the world, that the feelings of attraction, affection and chemistry was never going to fade between him and Hugo.

And what they had both personally and professionally felt was going to be amazing, fun and definitely last until death til them part.

***

Two years later Hugo leant against the wonderfully warm marble railing of their hotel balcony overlooking the stunning, magical and beautiful city of Paris with his brand new husband Alex leaning against him. Hugo had always known it was going to be magical working alongside with such a gorgeous man but it had been so much more than he ever could have imagined.

Together Hugo and Alex had taken down terror groups in the middle east, stopped the assassination of the French President (many times) and saved more European leaders than either one of them cared to think about, and whilst Hugo and Alex were heroes throughout France and European in the intelligence community, back in the UK Alex barely got mentioned in any praise. Not that either of them really cared anymore.

With the fiery bright red, orange and yellow sun starting to set behind the stunning Eiffel Tower and casting long shadows on the little narrow streets of Paris filled with bakeries, pastries and so many more wonders that Hugo just looked forward to exploring with his beautiful husband, Hugo really did feel at peace.

The air was so crisp and warm and filled with delightful aromas of pastries that Hugo never wanted to leave this stunning city again, but as he looked at the beautiful man that was his stunning husband, Hugo realised that he didn't need a place to feel at moment or at home.

He only needed Alex.

So as the sun continued to set and Hugo just held Alex in his arms, really enjoying the feel of Alex's fine expensive suit against his firm body, Hugo was of course really looking forward to their honeymoon in his home-city of Paris, but he was more than looking forward to getting back out into the world and seeing what spy missions they had to do.

There were a lot of threats in the world to stop, and before he met Alex, that concerned, scared and even worried Hugo but now he had such a great, fun-loving and skilful partner, it was simply something to look forward to.

Because they were together, and that's exactly what made them unstoppable.

Alex turned around in Hugo's arms and pulled Hugo closer, kissed him and smiled.

"Have you ever had sex with a married Englishman?" Alex asked seductively.

"I've had sex with lots of married people as a spy. Men and women, but never an English one, why?" Hugo asked, his smile only growing more and more.

Alex moved his hands slowly down Hugo's body and came so close to his ear that Hugo could feel his wonderful warm breath on his ear.

"Because when English people get married we get a lot hungrier for romance," Alex said kissing Hugo on the neck.

"You clearly haven't met French people before when they get married," Hugo said, grabbing both of Alex's hands and pulling him back into their hotel room for a very romantic night of international love that would certainly last the whole night.

But Hugo just knew that their love would last, a very, very long time indeed.

AUTHOR OF THE BETTIE ENGLISH PRIVATE EYE MYSTERIES

CONNOR WHITELEY

RETURNIG
STRENGTH

A GAY ROMANTIC SUSPENSE SHORT STORY

RETURNING STRENGTH
20th July 2022
London, England

Of all the phone calls I, Thomas Riley, had expected to receive on a boiling hot summer day in the heart of London, it hadn't been a phone call from my angry former boyfriend threatening that he was going to try to kill me yet again.

I was currently sitting just outside one of my favourite coffee shops in all of London, because the amazing thing about London was that there were so many delightfully weird little places that were hidden from the rest of the world. Like Joey's Gay Delights.

The little coffee shop was wonderful because it was a weird shape with plenty of little corners and booths for hot men to hide in, and thankfully the worst thing I had ever seen was two very fit men making out, and yes I just happened to join them for a quick one.

The rest of the coffee shop was so charming and modern and cosy with its bright light with copper hoods, black walls and golden semi-circular coffee bar in the middle of the shop that made the shop look really, really modern.

I loved the place.

I sat at my favourite spot in the coffee shop which was at the very back with my back pressed against the warm black wall because this spot gave me the best vantage point so I could see any threats walking into the bar, and I could also see what hot men were currently walking in.

Occasionally there was someone who stirred my interest enough to make me move, otherwise I tended to just read the news on my phone, do some work and think about which local charity I should support on my next charity run.

I understand this attitude might be a little carefree for someone who had gotten a death threat over the phone only a few seconds before, but there was an excellent reason why I was calm, or well as calm as I could possibly be at this moment.

I had summoned some help.

Now of course, I started originally coming to this place because I loved the name and I thought that it was a great place to meet hot sexy men because I had just moved to London, needed a new place to get coffee and if I could find hot men at the same time, well then, I was hardly going to avoid the place.

That's how I met my exboyfriend and former abuser, Callum, he was sweet and hot and sexy. He had a slim fit body that was so hard that I loved touching it at night, and his face was kind and caring, and he was just perfect.

Until he wasn't.

The only major problem was that because he had mainly used psychological abuse against me, the police couldn't prove it and the Crown Prosecution Service as much as I honestly loved them because they did the work of Gods at times, they couldn't take the case to trial and so my boyfriend went free but he's stayed away from me until now.

Calum was always an aggressive man and I had heard when we were dating that he had been arrested for assault three times, but of course I loved him so I didn't exactly pay much attention to that. And he always had a great excuse to why he had been arrested.

Apparently the men deserved it. Again, it didn't twig in my little horny mind that he had beaten up gay men that were his boyfriends each time.

"You called," a male voice said as he sat down at my small wooden table.

I just smiled, my head went light and my entire body relaxed (I hadn't even realised it had been so tensed until now) as I looked at the hottest man alive. Detective Inspector Jack Yates.

Jack was a truly gorgeous man with a very slim body, long lustrous blond hair and a face that made him look like a God amongst men. I had originally met him four years ago when Callum had abused me so much that I had decided to put a stop to it.

Personally I would have now preferred to kill him but I had naturally decided to take the legal route first of all and then Calum had left me alone. Thank goodness.

Jack was wearing a short-sleeved white t-shirt that highlighted his slight muscular biceps, four-pack and he was just so kind.

"You never called me before," Jack said smiling. "It's good to hear from you,"

I was surprised that even now Jack was being so amazing towards me considering he had actually wanted to start dating after the whole Calum incident because we had laughed a lot, cried a lot more and just bonded over the whole trauma of crime because Jack had been a victim of assault before too.

"What's the problem?" Jack asked leaning closer to me and he really looked like he wanted to kiss me.

Something smashed through the windows.

An explosion ripped through the air.

Flames engulfed the coffee shop.

People screamed. Staff shouted at people to get out.

The flames engulfed tables. Walls. Everything.

Someone screamed in agony. A man was in flames. He was running around.

I shot up. Charged over to him and knocked him to the ground.

The man rolled around. The flames went out and I pointed towards the exit.

He ran away.

Jack grabbed me. Pulling me towards the exit.

The temperature rose. Toxic smoke filled the air.

Flames shot ahead of us.

Glass bottles exploded.

Slicing my arm.

More things smashed through windows. Giving the fire more oxygen.

The fire roared to life.

Flames engulfed the exit. We were trapped. We were the only ones inside.

Jack screamed as he picked up a wet cloth.

The cloth caught alight. It wasn't wet with water. But alcohol.

I picked up Jack. Throwing him over my shoulder.

I charged towards the exit.

Flames licked my flesh.

I kept running.

I jumped into the air on instinct.

We smashed through a weak window.

Flames caught our clothes.

But me and Jack quickly dropped to the ground and started rolling about and thankfully the flames went out. Our clothes were well-damaged but I was just glad to be alive.

Three gunshots went off.

People screamed around us.

I jumped up and all I saw were men and women in posh business suits and dresses running away down the concrete road with little shops and houses lining the street.

Three more shots went off but I saw they were aimed upwards as I saw Calum was standing in the middle of the street with a massive gun.

The deafening roar and crackling and popping of the fire burning away the coffee shop filled the air, and even now I could still feel the extreme heat of fire.

"I told you I would kill both my exes," Calum said grinning.

I gasped as I finally understood what he had meant by that on the phone call and I had completely forgotten about it until now. He had always wanted to kill me but I had never realised he knew that I liked Jack and also that Jack was one of the three men Calum had abused.

Jack stood next to me and I noticed that lines of soot and ash covered his beautiful face. And I was so mad that Calum had dared to do this to beautiful Jack.

Jack was one of the kindest, bestest and most amazing people I had ever met so how dare Calum hurt him.

"I was hoping you would die in the fire," Calum said. "I had a lot of time to think about killing you and Jack together when I was cooking my poison pies, painting my landscapes and hurting little insects,"

I had actually forgotten how bat-crap crazy Calum was now. He had had so many weird little hobbies that I suppose I should have taken them as warning signs but he was just so hot.

"The police will be here soon," Jack said.

"That is a lie Inspector. We both know Tommy didn't call the police about my death threat. We both know you wouldn't have called your bosses about the death threat and well, this is a bad part of London so a few gunshots will not scare the cops enough to come running,"

I had no clue why Calum thought this was a bad part of London but I just hoped that someone would call the Police.

Calum shot at me.

The bullet screamed through the air.

I tackled Jack to the ground out of instinct.

The bullet slammed into my left shoulder. Crippling pain filled my body and eyes turned wet.

I could barely move my shoulder and my left hand was shaking so badly that I couldn't get it to work properly.

Jack wrapped his arms around me and tried to shield me from Calum but that only made my dick of an abuser laugh.

The coffee shop exploded. Thankfully we weren't right in front of it.

Flames shot out.

The shockwave threw us a few metres.

Jack screamed as flames licked against him.

Calum slowly came over to us and kicked me in the stomach and slapped Jack across the face.

Jack leapt up.

Grabbing the gun. Calum punched him. kicked him in-between the legs and stomped on his ankle as Jack fell to the ground.

A loud crack and Jack's scream echoed down the little narrow street.

My heart pounded. Sweat poured off me. My breathing turned rapid.

This abuse couldn't be happening again. I had stopped Calum before. I had to stop him again.

And then I took a deep breath of the smoke-scented air and I just looked at my pathetic excuse of an exboyfriend. He really was the scum of the earth and I just stared at him as I stood up.

"You always were a weak boy," I said to Calum. "You were always a nobody and even now you need a gun to be strong. Pathetic,"

Calum frowned at me.

"You see Calum," I said, "I don't need a gun to be strong. I don't need a weapon to be strong. I have what you will never have because I am a strong person inside. And I don't fear you anymore,"

Calum laughed, came over to me and pressed the gun against my head. "I still have two bullets left so I think I have all the power here,"

Now I laughed at this idiot. "Sure you can have all the power that the gun provides. But you will always be a weakling little boy that has to punch others to feel strong. Maybe your mother and father were right to cut you off after the first time you punched them,"

Calum spat at my feet.

"Nice knowing you," I said as I turned around and went over to beautiful Jack and helped him up.

"Look at me!" Calum shouted. "I will kill you. I will end you. I will paint this street with your blood!"

I simply kissed beautiful sexy Jack on the head and we both started to slowly walk down the street to find the nearest A&E department so our wounds could get seen to.

"I will fucking murder you both. Fear me. Pay attention to me!" Calum shouted.

I only hugged beautiful Jack tighter as we listened to Calum shout and scream for attention and then he slowly started to break down and cry like the idiot he was.

Then a gunshot went off and a body fell against the floor.

And thankfully it wasn't me or Jack's.

***

"Why did you stand up to him?" Jack asked.

A few hours later and after a very nice visit to a local hospital where me and Jack were treated for only minor injuries thankfully, minus the bullet wound in my left shoulder, I had bought Jack home and we were both in my bedroom.

I hadn't exactly planned to have a hot man over tonight so there were small piles of dirty underwear, socks and sportswear on the floor, but judging by the hard rod pressing against my side as Jack carried me into my bedroom, that was hardly a bad thing.

We both went over to my large double bed with black silk sheets and hard supportive pillows, and me and Jack sat down on it. There was a little light coming from the street lamps outside but besides from that we were sitting in the darkness and I was getting hornier and hornier by the moment.

"Because, "I said grinning at the detective inspector that I had to admit I had liked for years, "something made me realise that he was a nobody. He didn't hold any power over me, didn't control my life and he… was pathetic and when he realised he was nothing and I wasn't scared of him anymore. He killed himself,"

Jack smiled and he sat so close to me that I could feel his amazing body warmth against me. "I wish I had the courage you did,"

I shrugged. "You were still amazing today and thank you for coming to see me. You probably had better things to do. More important people to help,"

Jack laughed so hard he kissed me on the shoulder. "No one is more important than you. You might have rejected me four years ago but I never stopped thinking about you. Your kindness, your little cute smile and your amazing ass,"

Well he was hardly wrong about my ass. Apparently it was one of my best assets according to many men across the UK and the world.

"So I know today's been difficult," Jack said, "but I was wondering if now our abuser is gone. If you wanted to… go on a date,"

"What was today then?" I asked. "I took you to a hospital and you got treated wonderfully. We laughed and joked and kissed a little. That's a great date to me,"

We both laughed.

"No," Jack said. "A real date without abusers, hospitals or injuries,"

I hissed a little as I stood up right in front of him and pressed my legs against his. "Well I cannot promise anymore about the no injuries because I do like to be active with my dates. But a date does sound very nice,"

Jack bit his lip and smiled, and that really was the same sensational smile that I had seen and fallen for all those years ago.

Jack gently grabbed my ass and pulled me closer. "I also can't promise no injuries too,"

As we both started making out, we both laughed, kissed and our stomachs filled with butterflies. And it was only now that I was realising how desperate I was for Jack's touch, body and most importantly love.

We had both been wanting this for ages and now we were finally going to give a relationship a try, we were certainly going to savour it and take our love as far as it would possibly go, and that certainly wasn't a short distance in the slightest.

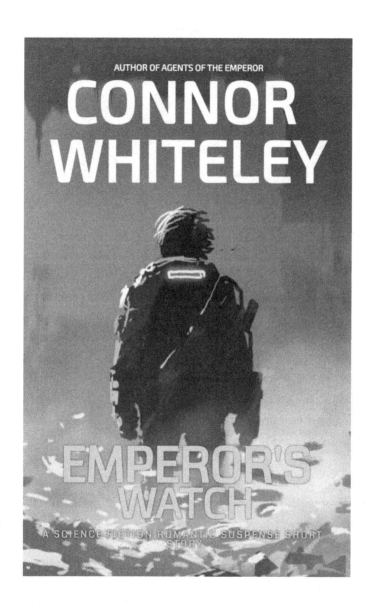

EMPEROR'S WATCH

He woke up to find a hand reaching down covering his face, mouth and nose. He couldn't breathe but a normal person might have overreacted and lashed out in tiring uncontrolled moves. But he knew better from his training, he didn't know what training he had had but he knew that he had some.

John Doe focused on his attacker as the skinny stupid idiot tried to kill him faster and faster. But it was useless.

Most people would probably try to attack the idiot's eyes and face. It was foolish. John noticed how the attacker's elbows were exposed and they were perfect weak points.

John hit them. Hard.

The attacker screamed and John knew at least one of the elbows were broken. Good. John threw the attacker off him and got up.

His body was already weak from staying at the hospital that was perfectly based on the hospitals from London from Old Earth. John hopped over to the little metal door and opened it.

He went out into a long cold corridor that seemed to stretch on forever and he quickly locked the door behind him.

"John?" a woman asked in a very posh elegant voice that John just loved.

John was beginning to get used to that name. Of course John wasn't his real name, it was the name that the hospital workers had given him. Including the Lady Matron here, the wonderful woman who had made it her mission to look after every one on this floor like they were her own family.

John loved the Lady Matron's sterile white lab coat, small black bag of instruments and the square glasses that only seemed to amplify the natural beauty of her bright blue eyes. John had little doubt he could use those eyes as a nightlight if he was scared of the dark. Which he wasn't.

"What's wrong John? You should be in bed," the Lady Matron asked.

John just rolled his eyes. He was so done with lying in bed. Sure he might have been beaten within a millimetre of his life a few months ago in the planet's desert region, but he had done nothing but healing just right.

He needed something to do and he needed to stop that attacker.

"There's an attacker in my room. He tried to kill me," John said.

He had no idea that it was a man until now. He had been far too focused on surviving and attacking to notice something so silly as who the attacker was, could that be more training?

The lady Matron just laughed. "Come on John. I'm sure it was just a bad dream-"

Someone smashed their fists into the metal door.

The Lady Matron recoiled but John didn't. There was nothing to fear here, these hospitals were made from some of the toughest steel in the entire system. Nothing was getting through that door.

The smashing stopped.

"Call the Arbiters. We need detectives here now," John said calmly.

The Lady Matron nodded and quickly walked off. John was rather impressed with himself actually, he would have imagined himself to be an emotional wreck at being attacked. But this was all just… training?

He really wished he could remember what he actually was before the attack a few months ago.

The sound of a building collapsing ripped through the corridor.

John instantly knew what it was. These doors might have been made from steel, but the thin white walls that separated these hospital rooms were made from prehistoric material known as plaster.

It was useless.

John dashed over to the two hospital room doors next to his room. He locked them both.

He heard the attacker shout in frustration and pound his fists into the door.

John knew that all he needed to do now was wait for the Arbiters to arrive and they could investigate. The attacker was clearly some crazy criminal but why did he want to attack John?

"The Arbiters will be arriving within minutes John," the Lady Matron said.

"Excellent," John said.

An intense wave of apple, cloves and coffee-scented cleaning products filled the corridor, and then John realised that this was the first time in ages he actually focused on the environment.

Then what was even stranger was how he already felt like he knew a lot about the hospital. It had been built over a decade ago by a wealthy mysterious investor born on Earth and wanted everyone to have access to great medical care, even in the harsher systems of The Great Human Empire that wanted people to pay for their medical care.

"Will the room contain him?" the Lady Matron asked.

John shrugged. "The other side of these walls is a three kilometre drop to the ground so I doubt he'll be climbing out any windows. Isn't it?"

The Lady Matron nodded.

Something smashed.

John unlocked the hospital door to the room where the noise came from and John laughed as he saw that the window had been smashed.

He didn't know why the attacker had decided to risk falling to his death but John was interested now. It was just a shame he was going to have to wait for the Arbiters to investigate.

***

Arbiter Elena O'Leary absolutely hated strange calls like this. As she stood on the awfully large circular landing platform over the immense Capital City with all its flying ships, spires and bright lights, Elena hated waiting for a so-called Lady Matron to allow her access into the hospital.

Elena had never liked Hospitals too much for that matter, or at least these stupid pretend hospitals based on the barbaric practices of Old Earth technology. There was a reason the Emperor united humanity and threw them into the future. So stupid places like these just pissed Elena off big time.

Elena would have much preferred to be joining her Arbiter friends down in the Capital City below hunting down a newly discovered traitor cult, The Emperor's Watch, and killing them.

Elena had spent ages learning about the cult, their deluded ideals about how the traitor superhumans and their allies were there to liberate the Empire from the corruption of the Emperor (complete bullshit) and how the cult was working to overthrow the planetary governor.

The Emperor's Watch needed to die.

She would have expected some kind of purified pine-scented air to help give the hospital landing platform a nice relaxing atmosphere, but nope. All Elena could smell was the horrible smell of burnt ozone from all the flying vehicles below.

Elena had wanted to bring a full investigative team, another Arbiter and more support to investigate this stupid attack, but as her Lord Arbiter kept banging on about. It was the job of an Arbiter to be a law unto themselves with them only ever answering to their Lord, the Inquisition and the Emperor.

Elena just laughed at him, which certainly didn't help improve the chances of her request going through, she would have no problem answering to her Lord Arbiter or even the glorious Emperor himself.

But by fuck was she going to answer to some Inquisitor prick who was a part of a secret organisation policing the Empire from the backgrounds like spies and puppet masters do.

The sound of massive metal doors opening made Elena gently smile at the three people walking towards her. The tall elegant woman in the middle dressed in all white like some kind of Matron from ancient Earth just looked awful and terribly ugly. And the two shorter men dressed in white armour hardly looked any better.

Elena definitely preferred her thick black Arbiter armour with her two sidearms at her side and her communicator in her backside. She looked like the Emperor's law and Will incarnate and that was what she wanted to look like. Yet the Lady Matron oddly enough barely looked scared.

"Arbiter. I am the Lady Matron of this facility. Follow me,"

The Lady Matron woman didn't even wait for a response. If it was anyone else then Elena would have happily shot her but this was outrageous. She was an Arbiter of the Emperor, everyone showed her respect, fear and admiration.

This Lady Matron woman was clearly going to be a problem.

Elena followed the Lady Matron and her two idiot men for over an hour through a network of tight corridors, purification chambers to get rid of the bacteria she bought in from the Capital City below and the Lady Matron seemed to be obsessed with taking wrong turns.

Elena knew that she was doing it on purpose and asking ever so pointed questions about who she was, why was Elena here and Elena just wanted to throw her against a wall and force her to reveal why she was asking so much.

But she behaved.

A few moments later, the Lady Matron led Elena into an endlessly cold metal corridor and Elena saw a man in the distance sitting on a chair with a cup of something on his lap.

"That is your witness, my lord," the Lady Matron said.

Elena didn't care for the change in tune at all, but she thanked her and went over to the man.

Elena was rather impressed that the man looked so... amazingly hot considering he had just been violently attacked. But he looked amazing with his strong muscular jawline, fit but muscular body that made him look like a Greek god and his longish brown hair looked like sheer perfection.

He was gorgeous.

Elena wanted nothing more than to just run her fingers through his amazing hair, kiss his big soft lips and really, really get to know him. He was amazing.

"Arbiter," the man said without getting up.

Elena was a little irked at him not standing up. For so many humans even if they didn't learn it at school, it was basic instinct to stand up and at least salute an Agent of the Emperor, something that the Arbiters were definitely classed as.

"Thank you for calling it in," Elena said.

"I trust you have your units and Junior Arbiters tracing the aerial traffic around the hospital at the moment he jumped out the window," the man said.

Elena was just flat out shocked that the man knew that was what they did. It was actually Elena's Lord Arbiter that had given that duty away but it still stunned her how this wonderfully sexy man just knew something no one should.

"Former Arbiter?" Elena asked.

The man laughed like that was the funniest joke ever.

"Emperor no my dear. I would never be an Arbiter," the man said.

Then Elena noticed that he was equally confused by his answer. It was almost like he was giving answers that he had no clue he knew.

Clearly there was so much more to this amazingly hot man than meets the eye, and Elena so badly wanted to talk to him more but Elena felt her pocket vibrate.

Elena took out her small square communicator and answered it. She was getting a call from a Junior Arbiter.

"Me Lord Elena, I traced the traffic report as requested. I am standing outside an old petroleum station in the Deserts. My teleporter homer is activated if you care to join me,"

"Confirmed," Elena said.

"The Emperor Protects," the man said.

Elena just loved that little saying of the Empire that could mean anything from goodbye to hello to good luck. Elena just loved this sexy man.

As Elena activated her teleporter, she locked onto the Junior Arbiter's location and she just looked at that amazingly hot sexy man one last time.

"The Emperor Protects," she said as she teleported away.

**

John was so confused at himself. That insanely hot woman had been asking him questions and he just knew the answers. It was so strange and it made no sense whatsoever.

John just knew that he had never been an Arbiter. He actually didn't like that because on planets they pretended to be judge, jurors and executioners. But when it came down to it they were honestly so pathetic compared to other people in the Empire that actually made it a safer place.

Again John had no clue how he knew that or what made that opinion, but he just knew it is was true.

Another intense wave of apple, coffee and cloves hit him and finally having ask the Lady Matron about it all. He had found out that every thirty minutes an energy wave washed over the hospital. It killed all the viruses, bacteria and fungi in the hospital, without hurting any humans and it had the side effect of creating the smell of apples, coffee and cloves.

John just loved technology.

John kept sitting on the cold chair staring down the large endlessly cold metal corridor that had been his home for so long, but it never actually was his home. He knew he lived somewhere he just didn't know where or who with.

"Mug of tea John?" the Lady Matron asked.

John shook his head. He couldn't have cared less about drinking.

"Did you send my medical records to the Arbiters?" John asked.

It was a very sad fact that because the Arbiters were all-powerful and in the age of traitors, superhumans and civil war, privacy laws were a joke. John just wanted her to confirm that little detail for him.

"Of course John it is the law," the Lady Matron said.

John shivered as she said that. *The Law.* John was shocked at how disgusted he felt about it like the law was about to be broken and it was a hindrance to his work. But what work?

John was starting to get so annoyed at not being able to remember who he was, what he did and anything else. He just needed to know why he didn't like the Law and was shocked to be following it for a change.

"Lady Matron?" John asked.

"Yes dear,"

John carefully looked around to make sure no one else on this floor was awake or up.

"I need you to get me all my medical records please. It seems some kind of training is returning to me and I want to see if this training could help me understand what I was before all this. Could you help me?" John asked.

The Lady Matron smiled. "Of course John. It would be my pleasure,"

John knew it was a long shot but he couldn't help but feel like there was something so important to him, his job and his past that was so critical to the future of the Empire.

He just didn't know what that was or why.

***

Fucking hell that was a bumpy teleportation if there ever was one, Arbiter Elena flat out hated Junior Arbiters and their teleporter homers. They were always given the cheap versions that made it a pain in the ass (literally) to teleport to them.

Elena was hardly impressed as she stood in a massive open desert field that stretched on for miles beyond miles. There was meant to be an old station here but Elena couldn't see it, smell it or

117

even hear it. All she could see was an endless stretch of desert that looked horrific.

"Arbiter!"

Elena rolled her eyes and firmly placed her hands on her sidearms as a Junior Arbiter walked over in much thinner black armour.

Elena nodded her respect to her junior who was nothing more than a short little man barely out of the academy.

"My sorrys for the constant movement my Lord Elena. The suspected cultist was moving away from the station and I had to track him,"

Elena nodded. That was okay in this single instant and it was good that the young man had at least some good instincts.

The low sound of humming got louder and louder as a small hover bike drove towards them.

"Is this the cultist?" Elena said as the hover bike got closer and closer.

The Junior nodded. Elena wondered if he was actually going to do something but that clearly wasn't going to appear.

So Elena whipped out her sidearm. Shot the hover bike's engines. Throwing the cultist forward.

The Cultist was hardly an attractive example of the human gene pool that was a certainty that no jury (not that he was ever going to get a jury or trial for that matter) would disagree with. The Cultist was a young man with awful cuts, bruises and slices in his face and body.

Elena wanted to shoot him right there and then for being such a disgusting human (some Arbiters had actually killed for a lot less) but this idiot had threatened the sexy human she was seriously missing so she had some questions for him.

The Junior Arbiter kicked the cultist in the head and forced him to stand in a headlock.

"I am Arbiter Elena, Agent of The Emperor and you will answer me," Elena said firmly.

The cultist cackled. "I do not recognise your or His Authority,"

Elena was so going to enjoy snapping his neck. He was definitely a member of the Emperor's Watch, which was actually a stupid name considering how badly this cult hated the Emperor. But that was the thing about cults, the traitors and their allies. They were all beyond stupid.

"You attacked an innocent man tonight. A man from the Old Earth Hospital, why?" Elena asked.

"He isn't an innocent. He is an enemy of the Traitors and the Watch brotherhood. He is a servant of Dark Powers and had to die,"

It took a moment for Elena to understand what the cultist meant by the whole Dark Powers thing, and from what she had read about the cult. They believed anyone siding with the Emperor to be corrupted by the Emperor's dark magical powers (even though the Emperor had none).

"He's a servant of the Emperor?" Elena asked.

The cultist spat at her. "I donno. I just know he betrayed the brotherhood and stole from us,"

The sound of more and more hover bikes echoed around them as Elena knew that the Brotherhood must have discovered they were there. They had to leave now but Elena couldn't leave him alive.

Elena whipped out her sidearm and shot the cultist in the head.

His corpse collapsed and both Elena and the Junior Arbiter activated their teleporters.

Elena had to get back to the hospital now.

***

John was a little surprised to see beautifully sexy Elena and another young man in thinner black Arbiter armour rematerialize in front of him as he kept sitting on the hospital chair in the long cold metal corridor.

"What you doing?" Elena asked.

John noticed she was looking down at the large black dataslate he was holding in his hands with his medical records.

"Lord Elena I will notify the Arbitration of our findings," the young man said as he walked away.

John and Elena grimaced. John hated how they had probably found all the cultists there that wanted to kill him. He had been doing the job for decades and he had been still shocked when he had discovered their base of operations.

John just huffed. At least certain parts of his memory was returning but all he could focus on right now was this beautiful woman standing in front of him.

"You knew about the cultists, didn't you?" Elena asked.

John shrugged. "I didn't really. I just remembered the desert was their base of operations. There were thousands there, all ready to attack the Planetary Governor and take over the system for the traitors,"

Elena laughed. "I didn't know quite that much but I did interrogate a cultist before I killed him. He mentioned you were an Agent of the Emperor, do you know what division you were?"

John just laughed. Now she mentioned it with her perfectly seductive lips, it made perfect sense, but he just wished he could remember which division and why the hell he was on the planet in the first place.

Elena came over to him, knelt on the ground and took his hand. John loved the amazing warmth of her rough hands that showed she seriously liked serving the Emperor and John even smiled at the little sparks that flew between them.

"Who are you?" Elena asked.

John didn't know if he was ever going to know the answer but he had a strange feeling of not, actually never, wanting to tell her even if he did know.

"If you told me would you have to kill me?" Elena asked.

John didn't react. It just felt like training. The training of not reacting, never revealing anything to the enemy but this woman was hardly an enemy. She was so beautiful, so perfect and so dedicated to the Emperor that John just wanted to kiss her.

"I think you're an Inquisitor," Elena said.

John recoiled at the idea. "No. Why?"

Elena smiled. "Because it explains your training. It explains why you were here investigating the Emperor's Watch and why you stole something from them,"

Again training kicked in and he scanned the cold metal corridor. There were no enemy hostiles and plenty of escape rooms if needed, and damn, she was right.

John wasn't his name in the slightest and he remembered everything.

John stood up firmly. "I am Lord Inquisitor Ezra Grayson of the Emperor's Holy Inquisition. I came here 6.2 months ago with my team to investigate the Emperor's Watch. I declared them a heretical organisation and was about to order their extermination by the superhuman Angels of Death and Hope when I was attacked,"

John… Ezra felt amazingly powerful again now he knew exactly who he was. He was a Lord Inquisitor, one of the most powerful members of the most secret organisation in the entire Empire, and he had a job to do. He had to stop the cult, save the planet and then travel on to the next mission.

But first… but first Ezra just looked down at the beautiful woman that he towered over. She might have been an Arbiter, a silly little police officer fighting in an Empire she honestly couldn't even begin to understand, but she was so beautiful.

Ezra just loved her stunningly beautiful face, soft lips and her mind. She definitely wasn't stupid and she had some balls confronting him as an inquisitor, no normal human would have dared do that.

He couldn't leave her.

"Good to see you again my Lord," the Lady Matron said with an evil grin.

Ezra went over and hugged her. She was no Lady Matron, she was a member of his team, an assassin in fact by the name of Clarice.

"Trust you to stick close to my side," Ezra said, kissing her on the head. "I trust the others got the information I stole,"

"Of course, my Lord. The others are in high orbit waiting for your return," Clarice said, shifting her gaze to Elena. "And we do have room for more, my Lord,"

Ezra looked at Elena who was now standing up perfectly straight and looked as if she was carefully weighing up her options.

Everyone in the Empire knew that no one just happened to walk into an inquisitorial operation and survive it. Elena had seen their faces, gotten a chance to know them, it was too risky. All that needed to happen was for the traitors to grab her, interrogate her and she could crack. Risking their lives.

She had to die, be mindwiped or maybe she could serve the Emperor in a brand new way.

"Has the extermination order been given?" Ezra asked.

Clarice shook her head. "That order is one only you could give my Lord. I'll order a secure line to be established immediately,"

"Thank you," Ezra said, as Clarice walked away to do her master's will.

Then Ezra slowly walked back to the beautiful woman he seriously wanted to get to know better. Elena was definitely a woman made of the hard stuff, the right stuff and sexy stuff.

And Ezra had learnt long ago never to waste talent, even more so when it belonged to such a stunningly perfect woman.

"You got a family? Boyfriend? Friends?" Ezra asked, already knowing all the answers.

"Of course not. No one with family or relationships joins the Arbiters, and you know they don't allow us to get friendships outside the Arbitration," Elena said, frowning.

"Then how about you serve the Inquisition? You'll be a part of my team, you get to get the traitors, superhumans and all threats against Him On Earth," Ezra said. "I can't promise it's a safe life but we'll have each other, and the rest of my team to support us,"

Elena looked deep into Ezra's eyes. Ezra seriously wanted more chances to stare into hers.

"Inquisitor, are you asking me out in the weirdest fashion I've ever seen?""

"I am," Ezra said.

He was never going to change his mind but he didn't want to give Elena the impression he could for a moment. He loved her and really wanted her at his side.

"Then yes," Elena said. "I want to be with you too and hell, this might be fun after all,"

Ezra hugged her. She really had no idea what world she was walking into with all the dangers, impossible missions and gadgets she could get to experience. But Ezra would always protect her and love her and be there for her because after serving the Inquisition for decades without someone by his side.

It was finally time to let someone in and love him.

And Ezra couldn't think of a single person he would rather have than Elena. Not a single other person.

THE CRUISE

I, Jordan Russell, was very quickly starting to realise a rather horrible fact about being stuck on a cruise in the biting cold rivers of Norway. My problem was that I really didn't believe there would be enough mead in the entire world to possibly make this cruise very enjoyable for me.

You see the problem with being a PhD and technically doctor of history specialising in the Vikings was very simple, you were always the person your family turned to whenever they wanted to know something.

Or in my case, wanted to drag on a cruise with a Viking theme.

I suppose as I sat on a very comfortable golden metal chair with a large round dinner table in front of me with a white silk tablecloth, that it could have been worse. This could have been some kind of touristic event filled with historically inaccurate depictures of Vikings like the horns on their helmets. Something that still irritates me even now.

But thankfully this was a grown-up historical cruise that my grandma had invited me and the rest of her senior friends on, for free I should probably mention. And my philosophy is don't turn down freebies.

Normally that philosophy supplies to hot men only, but I did need a holiday.

The entire dining chamber on the cruise ship was immensely big, able to fit almost a hundred people inside on massive round tables with a piping hot buffet at one end of the chamber and a live band playing soft classical music at the other end. I actually didn't mind the classical music so and even some of the Norwegian band players were rather hot and I was starting to wonder if I had a thing for Scandinavian men.

The hard wooden floor of the dining chamber was perfectly polished which was a little surprising because I knew of two elderly women who had chipped the floor early during a very entertaining argument about something I couldn't understand because they were shouting in Finnish.

"Are you okay dear?" my grandma Heidi asked.

I smiled at her and nodded and my grandma really did look beautiful in her long red dress, pearl necklace and black high-heels that didn't hide her age but she really accented it. Making her long neck even more beautiful.

I returned my attention to the table where all of her university best friends (she had known most of them for fifty years or more) sat around the table eating, drinking mead and wine and brandy and just being happy.

"Are you enjoying yourself Jordan?" my grandma asked.

"Yes, thanks Grandma," I said.

My grandma smiled a little and gestured I should return to my plate that was empty, and as amazing as the buffet was with its juicy succulent chicken strips in a rich curry sauce, golden crispy goujons of prawns and amazing fluffy white chocolate mash (another historical inaccuracy I'm not complaining about) I wasn't sure if I actually wanted some more.

There was just something so nice and peaceful and calming about being with all these older people and hearing them enjoy themselves. Especially after all the chaos and pressure and utter nightmare that turned out to be my PhD, even now I was rather surprised I got it.

"Oh Roope," my grandma shouted.

My stomach instantly tensed as my grandma embarrassingly (like all overprotective women do) waved over to a very hot and sexy Finnish man with beautiful broad shoulders, a killer smile and hair to utterly die for. He was hot as hell and he was certainly gay but I didn't want my grandma to sign me up for a random blind date.

Not on this trip. Not ever.

So I quickly stood up, I didn't even take my plate and I made my way over to the buffet on the far side of the chamber.

Thankfully, there were plenty of long red silk curtains covering open windows near the buffet area. I was just glad there were places to hide, and at least I could get to smell all the amazing food whilst I hid from grandma and Roope if need be.

"I'm sure my grandson is here somewhere," my grandma said as I could hear her little feet shuffle towards the buffet.

As much as I wanted to grab some food out of the enticing silver buffet trays, I dashed behind the nearest red curtain.

I was surprised that I backed into something very soft.

I slowly started to feel the thing behind me and realised that it felt like a living person wearing a very expensive suit.

"What are you doing?" a man with a Swedish accent asked.

I had to admit that I was rather turned-on by the voice. It was husky, manly and very sexy.

"Hiding from my grandma and a man she's trying to hook me up with," I said, trying to keep my voice as quiet as possible then I realised something. "Why are you hiding here?"

"Make you a deal. Don't tell anyone I was here and I'll help you hide from your grandma," the man said.

I didn't really have a choice and the man's voice was so sexy I couldn't say no to him at this point.

"Deal," I said.

"Good," the man said. "Don't make a sound,"

I didn't know what he was talking about until he wrapped his wonderfully strong arms around me and I found myself being thrown out of a window.

Then I quickly realised the man holding me was abseiling down the side of the white cruise ship with the icy cold Norwegian water below us.

I wanted to scream but for some reason I trusted this man and I felt him touching me up, putting his hands all over my body and as much as I liked it and my wayward parts flared to life I realised he wasn't touching me up.

He was searching me.

I carefully touched his waist and felt something very hard. I wished it was his hard dick to be honest but it was a gun.

Why the hell did this man have a gun?

A few moments later the blur of the past thirty seconds stopped as I felt the hard wooden ground of the ship's swimming pool area under me.

The massive crystal clear heated swimming pool was only a few metres from me, and I looked up at the immense height we had just come down from and I'm flat out not joking when I say we probably abseiled thirty metres.

I went to look at the hot man that had dropped me down but he was gone.

And all I could think of (besides from how hot he was) was he must have been a lot of an expert to abseil that quickly and controlled in such a short amount of time.

Who the hell was he?

***

As much as I had tried to forget about that hot sexy man with the Swedish accent, which was very hard because considering I hadn't seen his face and body, his voice was very memorable, the next day at breakfast which my grandma and her friends had decided to have in a much posher area of the ship, I found myself really thinking about him.

The place where my grandma and her friends had decided to have breakfast was somewhere we had never been before.

It was a very large room with immense floor-to-windows that were perfectly clean, blue carpeted floors and only enough white square tables for about fifty people to have breakfast. It was very impressive and a lot more intimate than last night's dining chamber.

Which I seriously loved because there wasn't a single place I would have rather been than spending time with my amazing grandma and her friends.

Despite the absolutely amazing breakfast of crispy bacon, juicy sausages and the softest, tastiest eggs I had ever had (again this was another historical inaccuracy that I was prepared to live with), I still couldn't get his smooth, sexy voice out of my mind. And the question of the gun was still on my mind.

Why did he have it?

"You okay Jordan?" my grandma asked as she gently tapped my arm.

"Yea," I said, "I was saw something strange last night,"

"What?" my grandma asked leaning a little closer.

"I accidentally brushed against a man last night and I felt he had a gun on him," I said leaning closer. "Is that normal on cruise ships?"

My grandma gave a gentle laugh as she finished off a mouthful of her freshly made spinach omelette. "Of course not honey, but the Norwegian and Swedish Prime Ministers are coming aboard tomorrow. It was probably just a security guy,"

She was probably right like always.

"Oh Heidi. This must have cost you a small fortune," my grandma's oldest friend said called Rose.

"Na not really," my grandma said. "My old insurance company wanted to reward me for so-called decades of service and you all know I don't pass up a freebie,"

"Like that time in Spain in the 70s," Rose said, and everyone laughed. "You didn't pass on those four Spanish men,"

If there was ever a time I didn't want to hear about my grandma's sex life, it was right now. And if the sea could have taken me I wish it would right this second.

My grandma laughed for a few moments and hugged me. "Rose my grandson doesn't want to hear about my sex life. And what trip are you doing later? We'll be arriving in Oslo shortly,"

I instantly smiled at that. I had been so looking forward to exploring the beautiful capital of Norway for so long, and it would be simply brilliant to see the sites, explore the city and speak the language as I had been studying hard for ages.

"Me, Pickett and Robin are going to explore the museums," Rose said.

"Brilliant," I said trying to sound excited but being careful not to get myself roped into a day of babysitting my grandma's (and to be honest my) friends.

"Are you coming with us?" Rose asked.

And there I was in the trap.

I had basically just confirmed that I was happy about them going to the museum and that excitement sort of implied I was going there too and glad for the company.

"It will be like having our own historical expert there too!" a short woman with silver hair called Pickett shouted.

I subtly looked at my grandma but she just grinned, she wasn't going to help me out of this.

"I'll join you a bit later," I said holding my thin stomach like it was hurting. "I don't think my sausages were cooked very well,"

Then I pretended to cough and my grandma subtly shook her head at me.

"Hello everyone," Roope said as he came over to the table.

I instantly swore under my breath. He was so hot and sexy and he was probably the best looking Norwegian man I had seen on the trip so far but I just felt weird about him and not in the good way.

I pretended to hiss in pain again and grab my stomach and I quickly walked away from the table.

Thankfully I hooked an immediate right out of the room we were having breakfast in and I found myself going down a long silver corridor deeper into the cruise ship.

A few moments later, I came out onto a very long blue metal platform that I had heard was where the scuba diving sessions took place when the ship was in warmer waters. The icy cold water was only metres away and at least I now knew that the ship was in Oslo harbour.

The harbour was so beautiful with its bright lights, ancient-looking red wooden houses and it was really nice to see all the fishing boats preparing to go out.

Someone climbed onto the deck.

I instantly jumped up as I saw a large, very fit man crawl onto the deck wearing a black drysuit. He just smiled at me as he took off the dry-suit revealing a very expensive black suit, black shoes and a killer smile.

Damn he was hot. I seriously loved his smooth facial features, dark sapphire blue eyes and dark brown hair like all Swedish men seemed to grow so naturally and make it look perfect every time.

"Hello again," the man said.

I recognised it as the man from last night and damn he was so cute and hot and sexy.

But why was he in the water diving?

"What are you doing here?" I asked.

The man shrugged. "I don't have to tell you that and... I'm more interested in why you're following me,"

As much as I wanted to tell him it was because I found him extremely attractive and I seriously hoped he was gay. I noticed a minor edge in his voice like he actually wanted to know, almost like I was a danger to him.

"I think my grandson's down here somewhere," I heard my grandma said.

"I'm sure we'll find him. It would be good to meet him at last," Roope said.

Damn it. Not bloody Roope again.

I just looked at the really hot man in front of me and just went for the only play I knew.

"I'm sorry," I said.

I grabbed the man, pulled him closer and I kissed him. I kissed him a lot.

I heard the man put his diving stuff behind me as he pushed me against the wall. And believe me, this hot man was very gay and he was an excellent kisser.

The sheer attraction, passion and power in the kiss was amazing and far better than anything else I had ever experienced.

Thankfully it only took a few more moments to hear Roope walking away so he had probably seen this very hot making out scene and ran away.

Thank God.

Then I realised that the hot Swedish man wasn't stopping. He kept kissing me.

I sadly pushed him away. "He's gone,"

The man smiled. "Thanks for that. You really saved me. What agency do you work for?"

I just looked at him. I actually had no clue what he was talking about? I didn't work for an agency?

"What?" I asked, trying to be polite but seriously wanting to just get out of there.

"You can tell me. We'll all intelligence officers here," the hot man said. "I'm Swedish Secret Service, what about you?"

"I'm not anything," I said walking very quickly away.

The problem was I actually didn't know what the hell I had just walked into.

The hot man was either was a madman with a gun pretending to be a spy or he was a real spy who had just revealed his secret identity to me.

And whatever the answer was that scared me a lot more than I ever wanted to admit.

***

After an amazing day walking round Oslo with my grandma's friends, telling them all about the history of the city like how the area modern Oslo was located in used to belong to Denmark in the Viking age and throughout the middle ages it constantly switched between the Danish and Norwegian kings until the Danish finally lost control of the city in 1241.

Then after the best dinner of historically accurate Norwegian food (with some liberties I will admit actually made it taste good), me, grandma and her friends had played some poker and finally me and Grandma were off to bed.

I was laying on my perfectly warm, toasty single bed with its very thick sheets just staring up at the ceiling in the pitch darkness, and I seriously couldn't stop thinking about that damn Swedish guy.

I was actually starting to think that I had a thing for the guy. He was so beautiful, handsome and damn sexy that I was very surprised at myself. I never normally reacted this intensely to guys but there was also a great air of mystery to him. Not the dangerous kind but the interesting kind that I really did want to explore more.

Our hotel door buzzed and clicked open.

I instantly froze.

My grandma was safely in her bed and I was doing the same. No one should have come in and even my grandma's friends wouldn't dare do anything like this.

Slivers of light poured into the room as someone slipped into the room. I didn't know who they were but I just knew that there was a light switch next to my bed.

And the criminal breaking in would have to come right past me to get to grandma.

I flew off my bedsheets.

Punching the light switch.

The lights exploded on.

A massive man dressed in black appeared next to me.

I dived forward.

Slamming him against the wall.

I punched him.

He hissed.

The man slammed his fists into me.

Kicking me in the stomach.

I went to punch him.

The man blocked me expertly.

He punched me in the throat.

Throwing me onto the bed.

Grandma jumped out of her bed.

Aiming a gun.

The man charged at her.

Grandma fired.

The man hissed.

He jumped into the air.

I jumped off my bed.

I missed him.

I slammed onto the floor.

Grandma hissed.

She punched him.

The hotel room door exploded open.

A man stormed in.

Firing something.

The attacker screamed as he slammed onto the ground.

Then I noticed the man dressed in black had a taser coming out of his back and then the very hot Swedish man holding the taser came over and handcuffed the man in black.

I went over to our attacker and ripped off his mask and I was very surprised to see it was Roope.

"Area is secure Madame," the hot man said. "The Prime Ministers are secured. The decoys are still alive and-"

"Stop," my grandma said.

"Why Madam? I thought you said MI6 didn't want any of the prisoners of this op?"

I just looked at my grandma. "I think she means stop because I'm not cleared. And really grandma, is an insurance company the best MI6 could come up with?"

She shrugged. "Budget cuts. I wanted to be the owner of a bank but that was too pricey apparently,"

I just hugged her because she was perfectly okay and that was all that mattered.

But she definitely had some explaining to do in the morning.

***

"So this was all an op?" Rose asked.

The next morning we were all back out sitting in the very large dining chamber with its wonderful live band filled with so-called attractive men, bright white walls and immense size. But my favourite feature this morning was the out-of-this-world Swedish breakfast and I didn't care how historically inaccurate it was.

It was the best breakfast ever.

And there was another change to this morning that I was seriously a fan of. The hot sexy Swedish agent was actually called Ludvig and he was sitting with us. He looked utterly beautiful with his smooth and lifeful brown hair, smooth handsome face and he looked divine in his pair of tight black jeans and white t-shirt.

He looked like a god to be honest.

"Yea," my grandma said. "This was an op between MI6, the Norwegian and Swedish Secret Services. The UK needs trade deals and Norway and Sweden wanted to get rid of a problem without paying for it,"

I laughed. "Clever. Hence the need for an English cruise ship, crew and tourists. That would spend English money in Norwegian towns and cities,"

"Exactly," my grandma said. "We had all known that Roope was an international assassin for years and this seemed like the perfect opportunity to take him out of the game and learn what he knew. So we set a trap and thankfully caught him,"

"That's why I saw you behind the curtains," I said to Ludvig, "and why I saw you in the diving area. You had just returned, from what? Seeing if the ship was sound in case Roope had placed any bombs on the outside?"

"Your grandson's smart," Ludvig said.

I was liking this hot sexy man more and more.

"Say my name," I said, very seductively and felt so embarrassed when my grandma's friends laughed at me because of how cute they found it.

Ludvig looked into my eyes and I really loved staring into his dark sapphire eyes.

"Jordan," Ludvig said, "you're very smart, clever and beautiful,"

My stomach filled with butterflies and I didn't want this moment to end.

"That's why I bought him here actually. MI6 and the British government wants to strengthen our Scandinavian relationships so they want to post a permanent agent here," my grandma said.

My smile grew so much when I heard that. "You want me to join, don't you? Get trained up and stationed here with this beautiful man,"

Out of the corner of my eye I saw my grandma shrug like this was nothing.

"I have friends in high places and a lot of dirt if they say no," she said smiling. "What do you say kiddo? Want to join the intelligence game?"

All I could do was stare into the dark sapphire eyes of the beautiful man in front of me and I kissed him. He kissed me back and all my grandma's friends smiled and laughed for a moment before they went back to their breakfast and planned the next few days of the cruise.

Not because they found the scene of me and Ludvig kissing wrong or disgusting or not appropriate, but because they all had their answer.

I was going to get trained up, posted in Scandinavia and I was going to spend a lot of amazing years (maybe, hopefully forever) with wonderful Ludvig. The amazing man I was starting to fall for, the man I found fascinating and the man I was seriously looking forward to getting to know better.

And that really was the perfect end to a crazy two days.

LOVING TO SPY

Part-time Intelligence Officer Steven Page really loved working in the secret computer labs at Kent University. He really enjoyed the labs' smooth white walls filled with anti-scanning technology, perfectly soft blue carpet and all the little computer booths that shot out from the main area he was sitting in so other officers could work.

Thankfully, it was only him working the labs today so far, and in all honesty he wasn't really sure why it was called a computer lab considering the only computers in the room were in the little booths that shot out from the main area. And even then, all the computer booths were shut behind monitored wooden doors.

But Steven didn't really mind the strange detail, he just loved the location because it was quiet, peaceful and he could actually crack on with all his university assignments, readings and Intelligence work without anyone watching him.

Steven sat at a large round wooden table that leant to one side because of a dodgy leg that no one had cared to fix just yet, and Steven wasn't too bothered either. He had dealt with a lot more trouble than a simple wobbly table leg.

The wonderful aromas of fruity blackberry tea, strawberry pastries and rich creamy hot chocolate filled the air from Steven's breakfast that he had bought in with him, but at the moment he was a little too busy looking at his black high-security laptop going through the various morning emails he had been sent.

Steven seriously loved having parents that were some of the

UK's best Intelligence Officers, and he loved that he got to work with them from time to time with other students at the university, but he had never known how many emails he would have to deal with.

Most of the emails were great. Like new assignments, new threats to the university (because it handled a lot of top-secret government research that China, Russia and Iran were very interested in) and there were even some well-done emails from heads of departments congratulating Steven and his friends on their work.

But some of the emails were a lot less interesting.

Officially, Steven was a political psychology student at the university so it didn't sound strange for him to talk to his friends with an in-depth knowledge about how the political worlds worked around the world, but some emails from the British secret service (MI6) made it sound like impossible terrorist threats were headed to the university.

Of course, it was just MI6 being overdramatic because they weren't meant to be operating on UK soil, but they still made Steven's stomach tighten each time he read them.

The sound of students laughing, talking and discussing their latest assignments outside made Steven just smile for a few moments, because he honestly couldn't imagine not knowing what he knew about the world, the university and the threats he faced.

He loved the work, it was amazing and he got to work with his amazing friends that were meant to be showing up later, but he was still a young man at the end of the day. And it had been so long since he had hooked up, spoken to or even smiled at a cute man.

Steven was in his final year at university and he had only had one hook-up with a sexy guy in those three years, that wasn't a good sex life by any definition, and now Steven was finding that he was having to lie more and more with his non-intelligence friends about his non-existent sex life.

It was even worst that Kent University had a thriving gay scene, but Steven had never actually gone to any gay events to meet people, and with the months ticking down until he left for good. He was definitely starting to doubt he was ever going to find some fun, action or maybe even a boyfriend whilst he was still a student.

Steven's laptop pinged and Steven smiled at the email from his amazing mum that was addressed to him, his best friend Natasha and another straight man in their friendship group. There were a lot of files attached but the email mentioned something about Iran preparing to do a massive cyberattack against the university at any moment.

Steven instantly knew exactly what the Iranians were after, it was so typical that as much as MI6, Counterterrorism and the entire UK intelligence community tried to hide the fact Kent University was conducting nuclear research for the government, the UK's bloody enemies always found out.

Steven had been stationed and studying at Kent University for years and he still refused to believe the government's logic for conducting nuclear research at a university. Apparently, the UK's enemies were less likely to target a university compared to a government-owned site.

Steven didn't believe that for a second.

But there was one line of his mother's email that really caught Steven's eye, *Find out how the attack will be launched.*

Steven was almost an expert in Iran, geopolitics and intelligence work. But he knew next to nothing about the inter-workings of cyberattacks.

Not a single clue.

And with a major cyberattack happening any time now Steven was growing more and more concerned by the second.

***

University Student Phill Lee leant against the wonderfully warm red brick wall of his best friend Tom's accommodation block at their university. The day was perfectly warm for an autumn day without it being too cold, too warm and there was even the subtle dampness that made him just know it was autumn.

Phill had always loved the amazing season of autumn. It was nowhere near as awful and cold as winter, nor was it was as boiling and unbearable as summer, or a weird combination of winter and summer like spring. Autumn was a perfect standalone season that was perfect for Phill.

Phill wrapped his hands round the piping hot takeaway cup of coffee that was steaming and he was holding onto the cup like his life depended on it. That was the weird thing about the cold, it was only his hands that tended to feel cold or icy.

The rest of him was fine.

Phill waited for Tom to come out of the large glass doors next to him, but in the meantime, Phill focused on the amazing calmness of the early morning outside the accommodation block.

The large miniature lake that had a few ducks bobbing along twenty metres away was a great natural feature in amongst the concrete university campus that led onto a massive green field covered in white frost sloping down towards the city centre a few miles away.

Phill had always loved Canterbury, it was still a city but it didn't have the crazy feel of London or Manchester or Leeds.

And this early in the morning, the area around Tom's accommodation block was almost perfectly empty with no one walking along the narrow concrete paths that zig-zagged in-between all the different accommodation blocks.

Phill watched a cute young gay couple that he only knew were gay because the two fit men (clearly first years) were holding their gloved hands together, as they smiled and walked towards Canterbury City Centre. That was going to be a bit of a hike for them but Phill was really happy for them.

That was exactly what he wanted.

As bad as it sounded (and Phill couldn't believe it), he had been at university for four years now studying advance computer science with a year's work experience doing research at the university, and he hadn't dated a single man.

He had always been gay, his family had been the ones pushing him to find love and get a boyfriend, but Phill had just found himself too busy to get a boyfriend at university. Phill had dated a little during 6th form and at secondary school but he was a kid back then, he didn't know anything about relationships.

All Phill wanted now though was to have a real love at a relationship, sex and maybe love.

It was just annoying that Tom was straight, then all of Phill's problems would be solved and that was the standing joke between him and Tom.

But Phill still couldn't understand why in the world Tom had wanted to meet up with him early. They were already going into the city later tonight with some of their other friends to go clubbing, drinking and dancing.

Yet apparently Tom just had to see Phill this morning, it was so important that Phill couldn't miss it.

"Hi," Tom said as he walked out of his accommodation block.

Phill always just smiled at his best friend for a few moments whenever he first saw him. Phill really liked how great Tom looked in his black jeans, denim jacket and black designer trainers that made him look so cool and hot.

It was just such a shame he was so straight, and actually had a girlfriend.

Tom gestured they should start walking down the narrow concrete path that led towards the main campus, and Phill followed.

"Why you wanna see me?" Phill asked.

Tom grinned. "I can't tell you, but you will not be sorry you met up with me,"

Phill wanted to say something a little pathetic like he was already glad he called because he got to see him this morning. Damn it, Phill seriously needed to get with a man a lot sooner rather than later. He hated being this desperate.

"Okay," Phill said. "But why all the secrecy? Why don't you just tell me where we're going?"

Tom shrugged as he led them through a little concrete tunnel that went through an accommodation block towards the main campus. It was a great shortcut but Phill would never go through it in the dark, he wasn't that brave.

Phill was a little surprised when they came out of the tunnel and Tom hooked a right. No one ever went that way because the main campus was straight ahead.

Phill didn't argue, he only kept following Tom as they went down another narrow little pathway with bright orange leaf-covered trees to their left and grey concrete to their right.

After a few moments Tom went into a dark brown wooden building that Phill knew was the computer labs used by the Social Science Division and Phill just couldn't understand why Tom was taking him in there.

Phill didn't know a single person that actually used that building. It was often the butt of a joke because the computer labs looked like a massive shed-like building from the outside because it was completely made of wood.

"Come on please," Tom said, grinning. "You will definitely love this,"

As much as Phill didn't want to go in and he sort of felt like he was making a big mistake, he knew that Tom was a great friend and he wouldn't make him do anything bad.

Phill went over to the computer labs, went through the large glass door and went into a room that he could only describe as a main area of sorts with its bright white walls, horrible blue carpet and tons of wooden doors that were presuming computer pods or something lining the walls.

"Who's that Tom?" a woman asked.

Phill looked at the group of people sitting at the end of the main area with their laptops resting on a round wooden table, but there was only one thing he could focus on.

Phill had absolutely no idea who the hell was the hot sexy man was sitting at the table. But by God he was the hottest man Phill had ever seen.

The man was wearing a very smart almost-business-like dark green jumper that made him look so stylish, hot and seriously highlighted how fit he was. Phill wouldn't have been surprised in the man had V-cut abs or something.

And the man had the most adorable face ever, he had massive innocent looking eyes, a killer smile and a strong, very manly jawline that Phill was really falling for.

Phill just looked at Tom quickly and he quickly realised that next to this man, Tom really didn't look that impressive.

"Who is he Tom?" the woman asked again.

"This is the man who's going to help us," Tom said.

And as much as a little voice in the back of his head was telling Phill to run and that he had walked into something very wrong. All he could do was focus on the sexy man with the smart dark green jumper.

He was seriously hot.

***

Steven had always known Tom was probably the smartest and most resourceful of their group of three, and Natasha had only showed up moments before Tom had turned up, but for Tom this seemed very, very strange.

For a spilt second, Steven had even thought that the new guy could be an enemy agent that had forced Tom to come here, but they had all been trained far too well for that to happen and Tom wasn't giving any of the twenty subtle signs that he was in danger.

With that possibility now thankfully dead, Steven allowed the black plastic and fabric chair he was sitting on to take his full weight, and he really focused on the new man.

It thankfully didn't take him too longer realise how amazingly hot and very cute this hottie was.

The man was seriously fit with his slim waist and the white t-shirt he was wearing definitely highlighted how fit he was, and if anything years of intelligence training definitely told Steven it was that the hottie worked out. Not a lot, but enough to keep himself fit and looking very, very nice.

Steven really loved the hottie's pointy face, slightly brown beard and his blond crewcut that looked so smooth, attractive and alluring. It was taking every single gram of Steven's willpower not to go over to the hottie and run his fingers through that soft hair right there and then.

Then he realised the hottie was actually staring and smiling at him too.

Steven's stomach tensed. It tightened into a knot. Sweat poured off his forehead.

It had been ages since a man had liked him and focused on him. It wasn't natural and Steven had no idea what to do. Should he speak? Introduce himself? Offer the hottie a seat?

Steven stood up then realised his throat was too dry to speak and now everyone was staring at him.

"I…" was all Steven could manage.

"What do you mean this man is going to help us?" Natasha asked.

Steven forced himself to sit back down and focus on Natasha in her long brown hoodie (that was bound to be hiding a knife or two, or three), jeans and winter boots.

"Help you?" the hottie asked. "Why would you need my help?"

Steven had to admit that he needed to say something to get answers but his damn throat was still too dry.

"You have an assignment to do and we need the expertise of a computer science expert and HQ has cleared him," Tom said.

Natasha threw her arms up in the air and Steven completely agreed that Tom should not have mentioned HQ.

"They also wanted to recruit him," Tom said.

Now Tom had really crossed the point of no return and Steven gave a careful eye on Natasha in case she went for the hottie.

"What the hell is this?" the Hottie asked, clearly getting more and more concerned. "What the hell do you want to recruit me for?"

The only major problem with all of this, and Steven seriously hated this problem, was that their work at the university was extremely top-secret because not even the university itself knew that MI5 and MI6 and other agencies were running operations to keep the university's research out of enemy hands. And even if their operation was hinted at and even partially exposed then this would all end very, very badly.

All of their careers in intelligence work could be over way before they had even begun.

"Why the hell are you telling hottie this?" Steven asked, a little more forcefully than he meant to.

"Because the Iranians are here. There's an attack about to happen and we need expertise," Tom said.

Steven just looked at Natasha. "Well I guess we now have to brief the hottie,"

"You think I'm a *hottie*," he said.

Steven's mouth dropped instantly as he soon as he realised how silly he had been. Damn it, he was never this silly around a boy normally.

"Sit down," Natasha said to both Tom and the hottie.

Steven just stared at the hottie as he carefully walked over to their round wooden table and Steven was really fighting the urge to run his hand under the hottie's white t-shirt and kiss those amazing lips.

Steven wanted to laugh at himself for being so head-over-heels for this guy, but he forced himself to behave.

After a moment of hesitation the hottie sat down next to Steven, and Steven had to sit on his hands to make sure he didn't accidentally do anything.

"I know your name is Phill Lee," Natasha said, "and I know Tom wouldn't lie about HQ clearing you and wanting you to join us. We are a small unit working for the UK government on protecting the university's top-secret research against the UK's enemies,"

Steven had to admit Natasha was always great at giving the

official talk about what they did and she did it with such a serious tone that Steven didn't know whether to be scared or not.

And Phill was a very hot name for a very hot man.

"Really?" Phill asked, laughing like this was all some kind of joke. Natasha folded her arms.

"You guys don't work for the government," Phill said, laughing so hard no sound was coming out.

"It's true," Tom said.

Phill kept laughing and shook his head. Steven just smiled because he had seen this reaction plenty of times and it was always fun to watch, but not when they had a deadline and an attack to stop.

Against his better judgement, Steven took out a hand from under his butt and gently grabbed one of Phill's shoulders.

Steven was instantly amazed at how wonderful Phill's shoulders were. He definitely worked out and his shoulders felt amazingly toned.

Now Steven was just wondering what else was toned so perfectly. And Steven really enjoyed the sheer chemistry that was flowing between him and Phill.

"It's true," Steven said, amazed he could even force that out.

Then Phill stopped laughing, grinning and smiling. His face just went pale and he frowned.

"And," Steven said, "unless you help us figure out how to stop a cyberattack Iran is going to get their hands on a lot of nuclear research,"

Phill's face went even paler and Steven fully understood why.

This was bad. Very bad indeed.

***

Phill flat out couldn't believe this was actually happening. He couldn't understand in the slightest why the hell the government was spying on the university? And could these people really be trusted?

Phill didn't really know how he could possibly believe them. It just seemed so crazy that they were spies or whatever they called themselves, it was so strange because they looked so normal. Phill would have imagined them to look like older men in posh suits.

They definitely weren't wearing them as they all sat around the little round wooden table.

And the fact that they wanted him to join them or help them or just do something for them was even crazier.

"Time is ticking," the woman called Natasha said.

Phill slowly nodded his head. He didn't know what to do. This was all too much information, he had truly believed that he was going on a nice meet-up with his best friend. He didn't know he was about to enter the spy game.

Then Phill just focused on the really cute beautiful man sitting next to him. He had to admit the man had been acting strange ever since he saw him, but there was something so cute about him.

"We need to know how Iran could pull a cyberattack on the university," the cutie said. Phill was surprised, it was the most the cute man had said to him all day.

"Who are you?" Phill asked.

The cutie smiled. "Steven,"

"Boys. Men. Lovebirds," Natasha said. "Focus. Focus. Focus,"

Phill and Steven laughed and it was so great to feel their attraction to each other run through Phill. He really wanted to get to know Steven a lot better.

"Well," Phill said, deciding the best way to make Steven like him was to prove his intelligence, "Iran, if what you say is true, couldn't pull off a normal cyberattack by hacking into the computer systems from the outside. The university has security too good for that,"

Phill loved it how Steven was on the edge of his seat and hanging onto Phill's every word.

"At best Iran might be able to break the first few levels of defence into student records and stuff but they wouldn't be able to get to the research," Phill said.

Natasha nodded and looked at Tom.

"How would *you* commit the attack?" Steven asked grinning.

Phill loved Steven's sense of humour. It was a very well-kept secret that most of the time computer science students wanting to focus on security had to think just as much about how to break into computer systems as how to defend them.

"This is a university with a lot of deliveries. I would infect of the new pieces of equipment being delivered," Phill said.

"Oh," Tom said. "He's good. Can we keep him?"

Phill loved how wide Steven's grin got. He looked so cute and everyone looked at Natasha who he was starting to understand must have been their leader or something.

"Maybe," she said. "Tom look into what deliveries are scheduled to be made today. Focus on new equipment being delivered to the Georgian Building,"

Phill was impressed. He had always wondered why the Georgian building was basically off-limits to students and most staff members. He never would have guessed it was a top-secret research building.

"None," Tom said looking up from his laptop.

Steven clicked his fingers. "Actually I like Phill's idea but you're thinking about it wrong,"

Phill moved his chair over to be closer to this insanely hot man. Phill got so close to beautiful Steven that he could feel his body warmth radiating off him.

"There is a lot more equipment that goes into that building than deliveries," Steven said.

"What the researchers bring in themselves," Phill said. That was seriously clever of Steven to work out.

"But all researchers are checked weekly by MI5," Natasha said.

"Yes," Phill said, "but if what your saying is true. Then that only checks if they have turned against the government, not if they accidentally picked up something by mistake,"

"Oh God," Tom said.

"What?" Natasha asked.

"My stupid university," Steven said.

It took a few moments for Phill to realise what Tom and beautiful Steven meant but they had all received tons of university emails about it.

Today was the only day staff members, postgraduate students and researchers were allowed to attend the Careers Fairs in the sports hall. There would be so many freebies and USB sticks being given away that it would only take one infected USB stick and one careless researcher for Iran's mission to be done.

Everyone stood up and packed their laptops away.

"How do we know what we're looking for?" Phill asked.

Everyone laughed.

"We won't until we get there," Steven said.

Everyone started heading out the door.

"Phill with me," Steven said as the others grabbed earpieces.

Phill's stomach filled with excitement at the idea of spending more time with wonderful Steven.

Even if they were about to hopefully stop a deadly cyberattack that would cost hundreds of thousands of lives if they failed.

***

Steven hated the massive sports hall that was the size of football pitches with hundreds of researchers, lecturers and other staff members tightly packed between rows upon rows of stalls.

It was a security nightmare and this was flat out not what Steven wanted at this moment.

But he was more than glad sexy Phill had joined him and Phill was so closely behind Steven that he could enjoy Phill's warmth against him.

Yet not quite as much as he wanted to because of the massive security threat looming over them as Steven glided through the crowd.

"What are we looking for?" Phill asked.

"Anything that isn't right," Steven said knowing exactly how vague that sounded to non-intelligence officers.

Steven seriously didn't like how many international governments and companies from the middle east were present today. Anyone of them could be an Iranian agent or none at all. Iran wouldn't be the first enemy of the UK to use its own people as agents.

This was a nightmare.

"No sign of anyone yet," Natasha said through Steven's earpiece.

This wasn't good. Steven felt completely lost in the sea of people that kept bumping and smashing into him.

Then he heard something.

Steven could have sworn he heard some Arabic but it was mutilated. Arabic normally sounded beautiful and rather lyrical in a strange fashion but the English accent in this Arabic murdered it.

Steven looked around but he couldn't see anything.

Phill carefully turned Steven around and looked into his eyes. Steven really loved looking at Phill but this wasn't the time.

"What's wrong and think it through," Phill said.

Steven just nodded. He was too caught up in all of Phill's beauty but he was right, damn him. Steven needed to focus on the problem and not get overwhelmed in all the chaos this sports hall represented.

"We need to find possible Iranian agents in here. They want to give an infected USB stick to one of the nuclear researchers," Steven said.

"We need to go to the biggest physics research company here," Phill said.

Steven just nodded and glided through the crowd a lot more forcefully. He bumped into tons of men and women as he almost charged towards the government's stand here.

The UK government had a massive stand trying to show the researchers and lecturers how great and powerful it was. Steven knew it wasn't but it was always good to see the government try.

There were five middle-aged men standing behind the row of silver tables talking to researchers. Including one of the nuclear researchers from the university that Steven recognised.

The nuclear researcher with his balding head was talking to the only white man at the station and Steven just knew that he was the Iranian agent.

Steven charged through the crowd.

He watched the man give the researcher a USB stick. They were talking in Arabic. The researcher was in on it.

"Stop!" Steven shouted.

The nuclear researcher legged it.

"We have a runner!" Steven shouted into his earpiece.

The white man whipped out a gun.

He fired.

People screamed.

Phill tackled Steven to the ground.

Steven rolled onto the ground.

Everyone ran to the exits.

He leapt up.

Charging across the sports hall.

Steven jumped into the air.

Leaping over the silver tables.

The white man fired again.

Missing Steven.

Two black men and an Asian woman tackled the gunman to the ground.

Steven landed next to the gunman.

Punching him in the face.

"You fool!" the white man shouted. "You have stopped nothing. My friends will end you and your pathetic country,"

Then the idiot started shouting and screaming in murdered Arabic and twisting the peaceful religion of Islam to their messed up ideology.

Steven just shook his head because their intel was very wrong here. This wasn't a plot sanctioned by the Iranian government this was just a group of sad pathetic men wanting to do terror for no real reason at all except the silly ideas in their heads.

Three gunshots echoed.

Steven spun around.

A gunman fired at Steven.

Steven saw the muzzle flash.

The bullets screamed towards him.

Steven started to move.

Phill kicked Steven out the way.

Blood splashed against Steven's face.

Another shot went off.

Tom killed the gunman. Presumably the white man's only friend here.

Steven's eyes just widened as he looked at Phill. Phill was bleeding. Heavily.

"Call a fucking ambulance!" Steven shouted. His training kicking in.

Steven went straight over to Phill. Pressing down all his weight on the gunshot wounds.

Steven's hands were covered in blood but he just hoped he could stop the bleeding enough until help arrived.

And he seriously hoped it would arrive soon. Steven just couldn't lose beautiful Phill.

**

The next few hours were a complete and utter blur to Phill, the only thing he could possibly remember was the shouting of doctors in the operation theatre, them demanding more blood and the massive blinding light that shone in his face every single damn time he regained consciousness.

Phill didn't even really know where he was now. He of course knew that he was in a hospital of some sort because he was in a white plastic chair with more than enough medical equipment stuck into him, down his nose and constantly monitoring him, but he wasn't sure if he was still in Canterbury or not.

Phill managed to see the bright grey walls of the hospital room out of the corner of his eye, but Phill felt like he had been parked by the nurse or whoever had gotten him here, in front of a very beautiful view of a lustrous green field with sunflowers and wheat and blackberries gentle blowing in the wind through large floor-to-ceiling windows.

Of course Phill knew that this wasn't real and it was just an extremely effective TV screen, but it was beautiful.

And thankfully, the hospital didn't stink of horrible cleaning chemicals, death or anything else that Phill normally associated with hospitals. This one smelt very pleasant with hints of lavender, jasmine and orange that reminded him of Christmas pudding as a child with his family.

"I didn't think you were going to make it," Steven said behind him.

Phill felt his stomach churn and tighten for a moment.

He was only realising now that he was so relieved that Steven was well. When Phill had heard the gunshots and seen the man aim at Steven, Phill didn't know what came over him he just ran and had to make sure Steven wasn't hit.

It had never crossed his mind that he might be putting himself in danger or risk of injury or even risk of death. It just felt like the right thing to do and Phill honestly knew he wouldn't have changed it for anything.

He would always save Steven no matter what, which was weird in a way because Steven was a cute beautiful man that Phill had only met a few hours before.

But it was still true.

Steven walked into view and laughed at the TV screen in the windows in front of them both.

"These windows have gotten better since I was here last," Steven said folding his arms and looked at Phill.

Steven looked so cute in the same clothes as earlier, and for some reason Phill didn't know whether to be disturbed or not that Steven's hands were still covered in his blood.

Phill watched Steven get on his knees so his beautiful eyes were level with Phill's.

"Why did you save me?" Steven asked.

Phill laughed because it was such a weird question that Phill didn't see the point in. As his stomach tensed and flipped and filled with butterflies, the answer was so obvious because Steven was a beautiful man that was clever, kind and Phill could see how much he loved his job and helping people. It was those sort of people that just had to survive no matter what.

But Phill wanted to tell Steven a short answer.

"Because I like you and want you to live," Phill said, only now realising how true that was.

Steven laughed. "It isn't every day I get shot at and even have cute men trying to save me,"

"Tom's cute. Doesn't he save you?" Phill asked poking his tongue out at Steven.

"I prefer you to Tom," Steven said.

Phill smiled because it was amazing to see how much Steven's eyes were lighting up the more they talked, there was such a glimmer in his eyes that was so cute and Phill really wanted to get to know Steven a lot better.

"Just ask me out already," Phill said seductively.

Steven shrugged like this was nothing. "How do you know I'm into you. I am an intelligence officer, I could be playing you,"

Phill laughed and started coughing as his medical equipment bleeped. "I don't even know how long I have left. Do you really want a dying man to die not knowing if you like him or not?"

Steven playfully hit Phill and kissed him on the lips. Phill almost jumped out of his skin at the sheer electricity and passion that flowed between them. It was the most passionate and sensual kiss Phill had ever had.

"You aren't going to die," Steven said. "I won't let that happen,"

And as Phill stared into Steven's perfect dark eyes, he just knew exactly what was going to happen now. They were going to keep talking, making each other laugh and almost certainly kiss a lot more for the rest of the day.

And beyond that, Phill had a very strong suspicion he had a boyfriend. A boyfriend that he would always protect, kiss and probably fall in love in a few weeks' time. Because Steven really was a perfect guy that was caring, clever and loving.

Exactly what he had always wanted in a man and now he was thankfully going to get it, and it had only taken him being shot to realise it.

***

After an amazing afternoon and evening with Phill, Steven just stood leaning against the perfectly warm wooden doorframe of Phill's hospital room as he watched Phill fall asleep. Phill looked so cute, peaceful and alive when he slept.

After the chaos and stress and worry of today and not knowing if wonderful Phill was ever going to make it, Steven just focused on Phill's fit sexy stomach rise and fall under the thin blue bedsheets that the hospital had provided him with. At least the little white plastic hospital bed was comfortable, but it would have been great if it had been bigger.

All Steven really wanted to do was spend the night with Phill just to make sure he was okay.

The quiet sound of nurses and doctors and porters doing their rounds echoed up and down the bright grey corridors of the private hospital just south of canterbury that the UK Government had agreed to pay for, in exchange for Steven not going public with it was one of their people that was the danger today.

"Are you ever going to wash your hands?" Natasha and Tom asked as one as they kissed Steven's cheeks.

Steven looked down at his hands. All the blood had mostly gone away for the most part but they were still streaks from where he had tried (and thankfully had) saved Phill's life.

"The government and MI5 are grateful," Natasha said. "I caught the nuclear researcher with the memory stick before he could use it and it was their plan to use the careers fair as a cover so in case the stick was traced back to the researcher. He could say someone at the fair gave it to him,"

Steven nodded and forced himself to look away from beautiful Phill. "Thanks both, but Tom, why did you bring him today?"

Tom shrugged. "Because you need a boyfriend. Like seriously, when was the last time you had dick or something?"

Steven was so not going to dignify that with a response (mainly because he didn't know himself).

"Oh," Natasha said pulling out her phone. "I got an email just now and we all have a new assignment together and we have a new trainee with us who had accepted a job offer,"

Steven just grinned. He loved it that Phill had accepted the job offer he had been emailed about an hour ago.

"The three of us with Phill," Natasha said, "are heading to Sweden to go to university there as part of a joint operation with the Swedish Secret Service. Apparently, there's some neo-Nazi group trying to recruit British students,"

Steven felt his stomach buzz with excitement, all the tension in his shoulders and body relaxed and he was seriously looking forward to the future.

Because he was with his best friends in the entire world and now he was going to be with a very cute man that he could finally call his boyfriend, and after years of being an intelligence officer, Steven had very good senses about people and things and relationships.

And he just had a feeling that him and Phill weren't going to be breaking up for ages, if ever and he was perfectly fine, happy and delighted about that.

SPYING AROUND AN AUCTION
8th November 2022
Classified Location, Southern France

To MI6 Officer Scott Brody, there were exactly three things that classed a party as "too posh", "snobby" or "silly" for his liking, and with him being British he only knew all too well how stupid some English parties could be. For a party to be too much for Scott, it had to involve miniature food, formal suits and a live classical band that played such classical music that not even operas would dare to play it.

This event had all those three things perfectly.

Scott leant against the dark brown oak railing on the upper-level of a great chamber inside a very wonderful castle in the south of France. The floor Scott was standing on was a massive circle that didn't jet off into any rooms or serve any practical function, it was just an upper floor to allow guests to look down on the guests below them.

That was another definition of poshness or even pompousness to Scott.

He really enjoyed the amazingly soft red carpet under his feet that was bouncy to walk on, the bright white walls with classical French paintings done by artists he had never heard of was pretty to look at and even French waiters walking round with champagnes flutes were very hot.

But Scott couldn't really focus on any of that, and he seriously wanted to focus on the hot French waiters because the French definitely knew how to produce gorgeous men. Instead Scott had to focus down on the floor below him.

To call it was a floor was a massive understatement because the chamber (that was probably a better word) was an immense red-carpeted dance floor where tons of hot French, Spanish and Chilian men were dancing with their wives as they both groped each other in their dresses and suits.

There was one particular Spanish man in the middle of the dance floor gently dancing with his wife wearing a particularly lovely dark blue suit that Scott really wouldn't have minded dancing with. He was so gorgeous.

Scott forced himself to look away as the classical band playing from their raised platform on the far side of the chamber got a little louder as they finished up their latest song, everyone clapped and the band immediately started into another song that Scott hadn't heard of before.

The entire castle smelt amazing with hints of freshly roasted pork, frogs (that really did taste like chicken) and freshly poured champagne. It was a symphony of pleasure for the senses and Scott just knew he was going to enjoy this mission.

When MI6 had first asked him to come to southern France, he had to admit he was a little unsure because as much as he honestly loved the French (and their men) he wasn't sure if he was comfortable running an op on French soil. He normally worked in eastern Europe working against the Russians, Polish and criminal gangs.

Working so close to home was new for him.

As Scott focused on all the men and women walking about him on the upper floor and down in the chamber below, they all screamed money, power and corruption and this really was exactly where Scott loved to be.

There was meant to be an auction tonight for a number of illegal items, like slaves, US intelligence, top-secret codes and more, but Scott was only interested in one of the items.

Someone was selling information on where MI6's Most Wanted fugitive was located. That was the information he needed, and ever since he had learnt that, Scott hadn't been at all surprised when MI6 had said to forget about the rest as they tipped off the French Directorate-General for Internal Security so no doubt there would be a raid later on.

Scott hoped to be done by then.

MI6's Most Wanted fugitive was a woman by the name of Sarah Mckinnon, a former MI6 officer turned international assassin responsible for assassinations on all 6 continents, killing entire squads of British troops in the Middle East and assassinating a Spanish Prime Minister only three months ago.

Sarah had to be found no matter what and Scott really wanted to kill her himself but that wasn't the mission just yet.

As the entire live band got even louder as they were about to finish their song, Scott was really looking forward to this event and he hoped the auction would start soon, because tonight was going to be extremely fun, exciting and with all the hot men here Scott really wanted to have some adult fun too.

***

8th November 2022

Classified Location, Southern France

Australian Secret Intelligence Service (ASIS) Officer Adamo Blackman had always found Europe a funny place filled with strange countries, strange people and extremely strange politics. And this entire castle with all the hot men and women walking around only seemed to prove his point even more.

Adamo had always grown up in Australia and that was the home he loved and treasured with all his heart, even if his slightly homophobic country didn't always care about him. But at the end of the day, he was always going to do whatever it took to protect Australia and its interests.

Adamo sat on a very old brown wooden chair that was probably from the 1800s like the rest of the ancient tables and chairs and art on the bright white walls that surrounded him as Adamo focused on the dance floor a few metres from him.

He had to admit the chamber or dance floor or whatever the pompous French owners of this castle wanted to call it, was actually very nice. There were little stylish details on the walls, ceiling and everywhere that added such texture and depth to what would be a very dull chamber without it.

That was what Adamo really liked about Europe, they definitely knew how to make things interesting and now Adamo understood why all the top artists came from here.

And an added bonus was definitely all the hot French, Spanish and even Chilian men that were walking round in their expensive posh suits. Adamo had never given European men too many looks before, but given how many of them were young, hot as hell and very fit, Adamo was so going to change that opinion.

Adamo watched a youngish gay couple, clearly French, walk around pompously with their fingers wrapped round each other and no one seemed to care. Something else that Adamo had only ever encountered in Europe.

The breath-taking smells of sexy earthy aftershave hinted with cloves, forests and another refreshing scent that Adamo couldn't identify filled the air as the live band (which wasn't bad looking either) broke out into another song, and Adamo was so glad Australia wasn't as big on classical music as these Europeans.

Classical music was awful.

That was the reason why Adamo was rather simple and he really looking forward to the auction because his bosses as ASIS has given him 50 million euros to secure the information pertaining to Sarah Mckinnon.

Adamo seriously hated the damn woman especially after killing his best friend, almost killing him and just being a massive pain in the ass.

The English were such idiots for allowing her to live so long. Considering the British MI6 was meant to be the best in the world, unstoppable and extremely resourceful they were proving to be nothing short of pathetic.

Adamo had killed tons of rogue agents in his time whenever the ASIS required him to, and it was a really fun challenge but it wasn't impossible. Clearly the British couldn't have cared less about their rogue agent traveling the world, killing people and leaving nothing but wreckage in her wake.

Damn the British.

Adamo continued to scan the dance floor and he felt his stomach churn a little bit as he looked at all the hot men hugging, loving and dancing with their wives. It must have been nice for the hotties to do that so openly and in public without anyone caring.

Adamo had been gay or sometimes bisexual depending on the woman and year for as long as he could remember, but even then growing up in rural Australia on his dad's farm wasn't exactly a paradise for a gay son, his dad's only son.

Adamo tried to force himself to smile at the memory of how disappointed, outraged and heartbroken his dad had been when Adamo had come out. His dad was so upset that he had lost his heir, he wasn't going to have any grandchildren and Adamo would be just as useless as his sister on the farm.

That was another thing that Adamo liked about Europe, it definitely had its problems but at least the sexism wasn't quite as blatant as it was in rural Australia, because Adamo's precious older sister was far from useless and Adamo still couldn't believe the entire family hadn't understood why she had fled to Italy when her boyfriend had given her the chance.

Adamo certainly understood now.

The live band turned slightly louder as they started playing some German rubbish and given how Adamo had been worried from the start about how intelligence agencies might come here to get the same information as him, Adamo looked up and started scanning the upper floor to see if anyone was doing the same as him.

Damn it.

Adamo's eyes immediately noticed an extremely cute boy the same age as him leaning on the dark brown wooden railing and staring down at the dance floor.

That might not have sounded like anything to worry about and that was exactly what Adamo would have told new recruits, but there was just something in those light brown eyes that Adamo recognised.

That cute boy was scanning the dance floor and trying to make it look like he was staring at the hot women (or hopefully men). Adamo had to admit the cute boy was good at pretending and Adamo had actually almost missed it.

Almost.

Adamo just kept staring at the cute boy and he really was cute. There was just something about how confidently the tall, fit, skinny boy stood that radiated happiness and authority and confidence from him that Adamo really respected.

The cute boy was wearing a very expensive and extremely flattening black suit, white crisp shirt and silky black trousers. The boy really did look so perfect and hot and his smooth handsome face was accented effortlessly by his brown hair in the faded style that Adamo had seen so men wear in Europe with the short hair expertly faded into longer hair on top.

He was beautiful.

But Adamo had to admit if this cute boy was a spy then he had to talk to the cutie, assess if he was a threat and then deal with him if he was.

Adamo really hoped that the cutie wasn't a threat because he was far too beautiful to be a danger.

Yet looks could be deceiving.

***

8th November 2022

Classified Location, Southern France

"Five minutes until the auction!" an elderly French man shouted in English.

Scott was so pleased to hear that the auction was finally going to happen as he leant against the warm dark brown wooden railing near a red-carpeted staircase that led down to the dance floor. Scott had spoken to a lot of French, Spanish and Chilian men and surprisingly enough he didn't even need to put on an accent, something he was extremely good at.

No one at all seemed to care that he was English and everyone had already guessed he was an intelligence officer after the information.

Scott wasn't exactly sure how comfortable he was with that fact because he was quickly learning that everyone here was current or former intelligence officers from their own countries.

Scott had fully believed this was a dodgy auction that was going to be filled with terrorists, criminals and more, but it turned out that the vast majority of people here were acting on behalf of their own governments. And Scott felt his stomach tense more and more at the idea of being trapped in a castle filled with so many professional killers, even his shoulders were tensing, something that never happened.

A whiff of strong sexy manly scent filled the air as someone leant against the railings next to Scott, and Scott could just tell that the man was pretending to focus on the dance floor below but he was really interested in him.

"You're too beautiful to be here by yourself," the man said.

Scott smiled and just looked at the man and... wow Scott couldn't believe how hot the man was.

Scott felt his stomach churn for a completely different reason now and all the tension in his shoulders, chest and body relaxed because all he could do was focus on the insanely gorgeous man standing less than a metre from him.

Scott seriously liked the cheap(ish) looking dark blue suit that told Scott instantly that the gorgeous man was an intelligence officer of some sort, but the beautiful suit really did highlight the gorgeous man's slight muscles, large arms and very fit body that Scott wouldn't have minded running his hands over to give the gorgeous man a quick pad down.

The gorgeous man's face was handsome, cute and it looked so caring in the light of the castle. He had a very slight golden blond beard that was accented by the man's blond crewcut, something that Scott hated on most men but this gorgeous man actually managed to make it work.

But what really did it for Scott was his gorgeous blue eyes that was like staring into the beautiful crystal blue ocean on the most perfect holiday imaginable.

"You really are too beautiful to be standing by yourself," the gorgeous man said. "You look cute, sweet and a little too innocent to be here too,"

Scott just smiled. This sexy man really was a smooth talker.

"I'm Adamo," he said, and Scott just nodded as he realised that it was an Australian accent he was hearing.

And Scott had to almost catch himself before falling into the classic trap of why Adamo didn't talk like a typical Australian. It was simply because in Scott's experience it was always best to train out accents and dialects. It just made intelligence work a damn slight easier.

"So tell me," Scott said, "why is the.... Australian Secret Intelligence Service in France?"

Scott loved it how when Adamo smiled, his entire handsome face lit up.

"I was only being honest with you. I do think you're cute and beautiful and I can tell you're into me too,"

Damn it. Scott was normally a master of hiding whatever he was thinking whenever he was on a mission. He was known as being one of the calmest and coldest agents when he was on the job.

Scott had to focus and hide his thoughts better, he couldn't let this hottie read him.

Adamo moved closer and Scott hated it as his wayward parts sprung to life and Scott seriously had to fight the urge to move closer and kiss the sexy man only centimetres from him.

"My question," Scott said coldly.

Adamo shook his head. "I can tell you're into me and I know you aren't all work and no play. I can just tell that about you,"

Scott was impressed. This Officer was very good at changing the conversation, playing on Scott's feelings and making him focus on different things. That had to change.

"Did you realise that after Australia pulled out of that submarine deal in 2021 with France in exchange for AUKUS the French haven't been very tolerant of the ASIS?" Scott asked.

That made the hot smile on Adamo's face melt away slightly. "I am aware of that,"

"Then you are also aware that there are at least twenty DGSE agents here that I am sure would be all too happy to kick an ASIS agent out of their country," Scott said grinning.

Adamo rolled his eyes. "Fine, what do you want to know?"

Scott was so tempted to admit how badly he wanted this gorgeous man to take him to a nearby hotel and do him, and let them explore each other's bodies but Scott forced himself not to.

Damn it. Scott hated how he couldn't stop thinking about how beautiful and downright sexy Adamo was. He had to focus.

"Why is the ASIS here?"

"We're here to make sure the British don't fuck up another Sarah McKinnon mission," Adamo said. "Australia will get the information and then we will deal with Sarah personally,"

Scott almost laughed but he could hear the anger, outrage and annoyance in Adamo's voice crystal clear, but then Adamo placed his perfectly warm and smooth hands on top of Scott's. Normally Scott would have recoiled instantly and hated the touch of someone else without him making the first move but surprisingly enough this actually felt... right, natural and really perfect.

"I'm sorry," Adamo said. "It's just that she killed my best friend, caused me a lot of problems and I just hate her,"

Scott nodded, he could understand that. He really could.

"Everyone," an elderly French man said. "The auction will now begin,"

As the man continued to explain the rules of the auction to everyone in the chamber and Adamo was focusing solely on the man. Scott just couldn't look down from Adamo.

He was so cute, gorgeous and Scott really, really wanted to get to know him better.

And he almost wished that he had met Adamo in another place in another city in another life because romances between intelligence officers never ended well.

And Scott really didn't want that to happen to him and Adamo but he wasn't sure it could be avoided.

***

8th November 2022

Classified Location, Southern France

Adamo was just flat out amazed at how weird the past two hours had been. When he had come to the auction and the castle he had of course known what was up for sale, how much people were willing to pay for these top-secret pieces of information and that some people might have even fight for it. But it had actually been rather calm.

Adamo stood right next to beautiful Scott at the very end of the lower level pressing his back against a wonderfully warm bright white wall, and right in front of him the red-carpeted dance floor had been transformed into a real auction with rows upon rows of dark brown wooden chairs with tons of posh and rich and snobby people sitting on them.

Adamo had been really impressed with Scott throughout all of it and he had actually learnt a lot about European relations and what each government was after and why it wasn't surprising who bided on what item. And Adamo had already spent 5 million of his euros on some classified Australian documents that detailed out where Australia's brand-new nuclear submarines were repaired, something that not even the British or Americans knew.

"And now the item we have all been waiting for," the elderly French man said who was standing at the front holding a thick folder.

Adamo leant forward slightly as everyone in the entire chamber fell silent as everyone just wanted confirmation that it contained the location of Sarah McKinnon, but the silence concerned Adamo a lot more than he ever wanted to admit.

He had no idea that there were so many people interested in the item and clearly this was going to get very expensive very quickly. And as beautiful, sexy and hot as Scott was he couldn't allow the British to get the information.

"I take it we're bidding against each other," Scott said with an evil grin.

But as Adamo looked into Scott's amazing light brown eyes with little flecks of whiskey thrown in to make them even more beautiful, Adamo could just tell there was sort of hurt in his voice.

And Adamo didn't want to bid against him either.

Adamo seriously liked Scott, and the past two hours had been wonderful as they had talked, laughed and made fun of each other's countries (respectfully of course) and it had even been magical. But a job was a job and sadly Adamo had to bid against Scott and stop the British from getting the information.

"You really are beautiful," Adamo said looking at the floor.

Scott hissed a little and clearly wasn't impressed, and a non-intelligence officer might have wondered why Scott didn't just avoid bidding altogether so Adamo could have it. But Adamo knew that MI6 never would have allowed that.

Both of their careers and governments had put them in an impossible position.

"Let's start the bidding at two million euros," the auctioneer said.

"Ten million," a Spanish woman said.

"Twenty million," A Chilian man said.

Adamo really wasn't liking this at all. These prices were rising way too quickly for his liking.

"Thirty million," Scott said coldly.

The bid slammed into Adamo's ears like a hammer blow and

Adamo was almost annoyed at himself for feeling like this in a way. He had been nothing but flirty, chatty and vulnerable all evening around Scott, something he never ever normally did.

"31 million," Adamo said.

Everyone laughed and Adamo instantly realised how poor he looked by only increasing it by 1 million.

"45 million," Adamo said.

Everyone went silent and Adamo looked at Scott and tried to smile. Scott weakly smiled back.

"51 million," a Russian woman said near the front.

"Damn it," Adamo said to Scott. "That's over my budget,"

Then Adamo realised if there was any way he was going to keep his job then he was going to have to use every trick in the book. He needed Scott and the British to give him some money.

"How much have you got?" Adamo asked.

Scott smiled. "I'm not telling you,"

"Please beautiful," Adamo said. "My job is at stake,"

Scott shot Adamo a warning look. "Stop trying to manipulate me. All you have done tonight is flirt with me, pull on my emotions and now you reveal your true intentions. You just want my money,"

Adamo covered his mouth with his hands. He had no idea that was how he was coming across. He hadn't meant it in the slightest.

"55 million," a Spanish man shouted.

Adamo really smiled at Scott. "Please Scott. I'm trying to not do anything to you and we need to put our governments aside or we will lose this auction,"

Adamo could see Scott was working through his options in his head. "Fine. But we don't open the folder until our bosses agree the takedown is a joint op,"

"Done," Adamo said.

"55 million," the auctioneer said. "Going once. Going Twice-"

"60 million euros!" Scott shouted.

Everyone gasped and everyone started shaking their heads.

"Sold to the British man at the back. Happy hunting and try not to fuck it up again," the auctioneer said as he handed the folder to a young woman in a black waitress' uniform.

Adamo hugged Scott and really loved how natural and right and wonderful the hug felt. Adamo seriously liked the feeling of Scott in his arms.

"Thank you," Adamo said. "How much did you have to play with?"

Scott grinned. "Fifty million euros and at least I only spent 10,"

Adamo was about to start telling Scott how beautiful he looked again because he really did look it under the golden light of the chamber but he noticed that the young woman holding the folder was staring at them and she wasn't smiling.

"Tell me," Adamo said hugging Scott again and whispering into his ear, "does that young woman look like Sarah to you?"

Adamo gently turned Scott around so he could see the young woman and he felt Scott nod.

They both broke the hug and Adamo focused on the rather short young woman wearing the black waitress uniform. She was very small with her long glossy black hair that was almost certainly a wig but it was her strong jawline, thin waist and large arms that made her look like a former intelligence officer.

Adamo and Scott started to go over to her.

Adamo quickly realised they were completely unarmed without weapons, backup and Adamo seriously doubted any intelligence officer in the entire chamber would want to help them.

The young woman whipped out a pistol ran up to the elderly French man and put the gun to his head.

"Everyone leave!" Sarah shouted. "Except the brit and the Aussie,"

Everyone shrugged and Adamo just grabbed Scott's hand tight. Not as a sign of weakness or manipulation or anything besides from love pure and simple.

Because Adamo really didn't want anything to happen to Scott in the slightest. He was too precious for that.

***

8ᵗʰ November 2022

Classified Location, Southern France

When the entire red-carpeted chamber was empty except for Adamo and Scott and the hostage that Sarah was still aiming the gun at, Adamo realised that the entire item had been a mistake and the documents had probably been entered into the auction by Sarah herself so she could kill anyone hunting her.

"Why do you want us?" Adamo asked.

Scott shook off Adamo's hand and took a few steps forward.

"I wanted you both here because I wanted to send a message to the stupid Brits and Aussies," Sarah said. "Stop hunting me. I have my jobs to do and I have my people to kill,"

"What you are doing is wrong," Scott said.

Adamo really doubted a morality lesson was going to do much good here but he wanted Scott to buy him as much time as possible.

Adamo had to figure out a way to escape this mess.

"You see Aussie," Sarah said. "The Brits always say they're the good guys, defender of democracy and more but do you want to know how many elections I have rigged,"

Adamo shook his head. "We all do things for our countries we aren't proud of. It doesn't mean killing innocent people makes you any better,"

Sarah laughed and pressed the gun harder against her hostage's skull.

Adamo and Scott took a few steps closer until they were only ten metres away from her.

"Maybe you are right," Sarah said, "but if I leave here tonight killing the former head of the DGSE, a Brit and an Aussie then my world will be a lot safer,"

Adamo had wondered where he had recognised the auctioneer from.

Scott took a few more steps towards Sarah but she aimed the gun at Scott. Adamo's stomach tensed.

Sarah fired at Scott's feet.

"No!" Adamo shouted and rushed forward.

Sarah busted out laughing. "Seriously? An Aussie officer loving a brit. Wow,"

Adamo covered his mouth with his hands as he realised what he had done. He had given Sarah the perfect weapon to use against them both and when Scott looked at him it wasn't a hateful or regretful smile it was a look of concern for him too.

Because Scott would have done the exact same thing if Adamo had been in trouble.

Sarah fired. Shooting the auctioneer in the leg. She threw him to one side.

She aimed the gun at Scott. "Don't resist,"

Adamo nodded at Scott and he allowed Sarah to put him in a headlock as he pressed the barrel of her gun against his head.

Adamo hated all of this he felt so useless, weak and unless he came up with something very quickly he was about to have the blood of an absolutely beautiful boy on his hands.

"Now this is going to be a bit more interesting," Sarah said. "I know you Scotty boy have another forty million euros. You're going to tell me the MI6 account number, password and you will authenticate my transaction when I drain the account,"

Scott laughed. "Never,"

Sarah hissed. She aimed the gun at Adamo.

"Fine then. Do it or he dies,"

"Let me die," Adamo said before he realised what he was saying. "Just let Scott live,"

Adamo was surprised at the anger in Scott's eyes like he was really pissed that Adamo was prepared to die for him.

"What's your answer?" Sarah asked Scott. "I will kill him,"

Adamo just looked at beautiful Scott just in case this was the last time he was going to see his handsome face.

"Never," Scott said with a hint of sadness and just winked at Adamo.

Adamo didn't know what Scott was planning but in all his years of experience he knew that time was an Officer's best friend.

"You know what bitch," Adamo shouted, "fuck you and your fucking government. The British are just useless pricks that pretend to know what they're doing when they're just blind idiots,"

Adamo loved how Sarah's face twisted into confusion.

Scott stamped on her foot.

She screamed.

Adamo rushed forward.

Scott elbowed her in the ribs.

Sarah released him.

Adamo tackled her to the ground.

Slamming his fists into her head.

Police sirens came from outside.

"Internal Security," Scott said.

Adamo just looked at Sarah. He saw the gun a few metres away. It was their only option.

Scott picked up the gun. Aimed it at Sarah. Adamo nodded.

The bullet screamed through the air.

And Adamo instantly realised this was a hot handsome man he could always see himself working with because he really was beautiful and clever and perfect.

***

9th November 2022

Classified Location, Southern France

Scott was completely amazed at how wonderful the Directorate-General For Internal Security agents were when they had stormed into the chamber and because they had snapped up some of their own Most Wanted because it seemed that the Chilian agents were not fans of the French whatsoever, the French really hadn't cared too much that MI6 and ASIS had killed someone in their country.

Scott was more than glad about that because the last thing he had wanted to do was had to fight the French and risk gorgeous Adamo getting hurt in the process, but Adamo really was an amazing man for what he had been willing to do to make sure he had lived.

Scott and Adamo stood in a very large field in the south of France with thick wonderful grass coming up to their ankles, a cool breeze blowing between them and messing up their hair and the pitch darkness of the field was illuminated slightly by the dazzling lights of a nearby French city.

France really was a beautiful country.

Even the air smelt perfectly refreshing with the tangy refreshing hints of autumn and Scott was slowly realising that he didn't actually want MI6 to come and pick him up from the extraction point, all Scott really wanted to do was spend just a little more time with the gorgeous boy he was starting to fall for.

The pitch darkness with the little illumination really didn't detract from Adamo's beauty. He was so fit, handsome and really had a beauty about him that Scott hadn't seen before, and it only took him a few more moments to realise that that beauty was that Adamo actually cared about him.

Something no one else had truly done before.

"Take this beautiful," Adamo said holding out a thick folder to Scott.

Scott knew exactly what it was, it was the Australian nuclear information that he had bought earlier, but he couldn't understand why Adamo wanted him to have it.

"No doubt it will come to light we fell for each other. Our governments won't like that and they'll get to kick you out," Adamo said, "because they'll be scared you're an Aussie turncoat or you're compromised,"

Scott nodded. It made sense and he could think of at least ten people back at MI6 that would try to kick him out because he was a lot better than them but he wasn't going to risk Australia's national security just to save his own skin. That wasn't right so that was exactly what he told Adamo.

"I don't want anything to happen to you because of what I did. If I wasn't so into you I wouldn't have revealed my feelings in front of a target. If it was better you could have arrested Sarah and got information from her. If I was better-"

Scott just kissed him.

Scott pressed his lips against Adamo's and was surprised how warm, smooth and lustrous they were. He had been wanting to kiss this gorgeous man for so long and now he was finally doing it, it felt so right.

"You're perfect the way you are," Scott said breaking the kiss and gently running his hands up and down Adamo's body.

Adamo's body really did feel as amazing as Scott had dreamed.

"What will you do now?" Scott asked.

Adamo smiled. "The ASIS has interests all over the globe. Europe, the Americas and Asia all have threats against Australia. Maybe we'll even meet each other again officially or not,"

As the distant sound of a helicopter got closer and closer Scott knew that his time was running out but surprisingly enough didn't feel as sad as he had earlier. Because he knew he would see gorgeous Adamo again on another mission in another country away from the eyes of their governments.

And at the end of the day, the UK and Australia were close allies and allies really did need to work *closely* together in these dark times and sometimes so close that skin and wayward parts would touch.

Scott knew it wouldn't be a hard sell to his or Adamo's bosses and Scott was seriously looking forward to a wonderful future of working with this gorgeous man who he had really fallen for in the past few hours.

The future was going to be amazing and bright and wonderful so Scott gave Adamo a final deep passionate kiss as the MI6 helicopter landed.

And Scott left Adamo. Definitely not for the last time because they would soon see each other again and Scott fully intended to pick up exactly where they left off.

LOVING THIEVES
5th July 2022
Rochester, England

International Art Thief Johnathan Blueberry absolutely loved coming home to his childhood city of Rochester with its historical castle, massive cathedral and little cobblestone high street filled with so many delightful little Victorian shops. Johnathan really did love his home city and it was always fun to return with a massive stolen painting or sculpture because then he had to hide it.

Johnathan went into a little corner shop on Rochester High Street and the wonderful aromas of spiced meats, freshly roasted pecans and roasted potatoes filled his senses as he stood next to the wooden door for a moment to really enjoy the heavenly sensations coming from the store.

The store itself wasn't anything too special because at the end of the day it was just another convenience store with five aisles of white shelves that different foods called home, like vegetables, meats and cupboard staples.

There was a long off-white counter at the back with a very short little old lady standing there on a stepping stool made from oak wood by the looks of it. Johnathan felt sorry for the lady, she deserved something more than that.

She did run a wonderful shop after all, maybe he would give her a few hundred pounds to treat herself.

It wasn't exactly like Johnathan needed all the millions he had anyway.

Johnathan was only really here for some spiced meat because it was just what he fancied tonight. He would have preferred some other manly meat but that was the problem with being an art thief, it just made dating hot men even more problematic than normal. Some men were hot and sexy and wonderful, but for some reason they just didn't like Johnathan leaving suddenly to go and steal a painting.

That was a shame.

The sound of three people walking about made Johnathan a little disappointed because he was so good at what he did because he was invisible, and there being only three people made that even harder.

Johnathan could only see two women clearly and the top of an orange hat hopping along across the top of the aisles. The two women were clearly mother and daughter and wore very nice pink jumpers, jeans and black high heels.

The two women were trying to decide what brand of chicken they wanted because apparently the daughter's boyfriend wanted to make a special recipe to treat them both, and only a very certain type of chicken would do.

Johnathan went towards the spiced meat section but he stopped just in front of the two women.

"Just get whatever chicken you can. If he's a really good cook, the type won't matter," Johnathan said.

The mother laughed and even the daughter smiled so they picked up the cheapest bag of chicken they could get and they went off to pay.

Johnathan loved helping people and that was really why he actually stole paintings because most of the time he was in Germany and other former Nazi areas recovering art from people it never belonged to in the first place.

Johnathan went down the spiced meats aisle which was nothing more than a long row of white shelves with packs of European meats on them. There were wonderful spiced meats from Germany, Poland and so many other amazing countries that Johnathan loved almost as much as his job.

"Excuse me," a man said as Johnathan felt a firm hand being placed on his ass for a moment.

Johnathan just smiled as he looked at the man who had spoken to him. Johnathan coughed out of shock more than anything else.

The man currently smiling at Johnathan was shockingly handsome with his longish brown hair, outrageously fit gym body and his smile was to die for. The man was really wonderful and Johnathan loved the smell of his earthy but spiced aftershave that definitely told Johnathan the man wasn't from around here.

And the man's hot sexy clothes only supported that idea. No one in Rochester wore designer black trousers, white shirt and a dark blue three-piece suit.

The man was seriously hot.

"Who are you?" Johnathan asked. "You're hot and I haven't seen you before,"

The man grinned. "Thank you. You aren't so bad yourself. I'm Tobias Palmer and I've been coming here for months,"

Johnathan nodded because that could have been true in all fairness. Johnathan had been in mainland Europe for months and it was possible that this Tobias fella had lived here for ages and Johnathan just hadn't been here to see him.

But the man didn't dress like a local, he didn't talk like a local and he certainly didn't know that gays in Rochester didn't do anything in public.

This man was no local.

Johnathan had to find out more about this hot man just in case he was a real threat to Johnathan's criminal activities.

"Are you free tonight?" Johnathan asked.

***

Out of everything Tobias had been hoping for tonight, it certainly hadn't been running into his target Johnathan. Tobias had moved to Rochester six months ago to try and hunt down the damn art thief that had been robbing him blind for months and it was because of damn Johnathan that no one in the criminal underworld would hire Tobias anymore.

Johnathan had somehow managed to beat Tobias to three different high-security paintings in the past year alone. That wasn't a small number and when three different very powerful and rich men hired him to steal them and Tobias turned up empty-handed, those men were very harsh.

Tobias had even had to become an office worker of all things to earn himself a living. He was a great art thief just not as great as Johnathan, so the plan was simple. All Tobias needed to do was hunt down Johnathan, get into his house and steal all the artwork back to sell on the black market.

"Wait here for a moment," Johnathan said.

Tobias had to admit as he stood in the large box room of Johnathan's living room, it was a very beautiful house. The walls were freshly painted bright white, the cream colours of the ceiling were spotless and even the light blue sofas and armchairs looked so tasteful and added just enough colour and depth to really bring the living room alive.

Tobias was a little confused as to why Johnathan didn't have any art on the walls or anything. The walls were so bare and unloved that it made no sense why an international art thief wouldn't decorate his home with any art whatsoever.

Tobias decorated his house with tens of massive pieces of fake paintings because it was what he loved, he was passionate about and it was who he was at his very core. But Tobias had to admit that right now he was really into Johnathan.

Tobias had seen Johnathan far away when they had both been on jobs but to actually see him in the flesh, now that was extremely hot.

Johnathan was a stunning man with large beautiful lips, high cheekbones and a very strong jawline. Tobias really loved staring at Johnathan's face because it really was a work of art and Tobias seriously wanted to know what Johnathan's lips tasted like. They were probably delicious.

The sound of the odd car driving past outside was the only noise on the street and Tobias was okay with that. It meant that as beautiful as Johnathan was, if he didn't give him what he wanted then there wouldn't be too many people around to save Johnathan if things got ugly.

Tobias's stomach twisted into an agonising knot at the very idea. He couldn't do that to beautiful Johnathan, so he wasn't going to do that in the slightest.

"Now then," Johnathan said walking into the living room holding a very small single-shot pistol.

"Oh damn," Tobias said.

"It is a pleasure to finally meet you face to face Tobias," Johnathan said. "I needed to flick through the photos on my phone first but I thought I recognised you from two jobs back in Budapest,"

Tobias wanted so badly to run away but he also didn't want to get shot.

"I had wondered if you would ever turn up because I've also seen you in Paris and Lyon. And wow, you really are a beautiful man," Johnathan said.

Tobias just shook his head. He had been trying to look as local as possible in those French cities, he hadn't meant to look as beautiful has he had.

"I presume you're after those three paintings I stole from your targets," Johnathan said. "Well if you want them then you need to look under my sofa,"

Tobias was half expecting that to be a youthism for something and Tobias definitely wouldn't have minded looking under Johnathan, damn it he had to focus on the mission.

Tobias knelt down and saw under the sofa was a small black photo book so Tobias grabbed it and took it out.

The picture book was filled with pictures of teenagers. Some were boys, some were girls and there were a lot of *before* and *after* sort of photos showing the boys and girls in awful living conditions only to end up in better accommodation and situations.

"Who are these people?" Tobias asked.

Johnathan put the gun away and sat on the blue sofa. "Whenever I steal a painting I of course sell it but I don't want millions upon millions of pounds so I give the money to charity and I give some money to children,"

Tobias just nodded. That was a great thing to do.

"Each of those children were in a bad foster home with foster carers that couldn't look after them properly but the carers were good people at heart. So I gave them some money to help them out," Johnathan said.

Tobias just looked at Johnathan. Damn, he was a hot sexy man and his lips were even more beautiful.

"So I am sorry that I robbed you of your targets," Johnathan said.

Tobias laughed. "Don't be silly. Your use is a lot more respectable and better than what I would have used the money for,"

The front door exploded open.

Three men exploded into the living room.

One smashed Tobias over the head.

Tobias felt Johnathan grab him and all Tobias could focus on was how badly he wanted to protect stunning Johnathan no matter what.

***

Johnathan absolutely couldn't believe what these idiots were doing as he just stared at the three really tall men in black trench coats, trousers and very crisp white shirts. Johnathan was surprised that they were all middle-aged and they just smelt of corruption, money and power but this was hardly the worst situation Johnathan had ever been in.

Johnathan subtly placed the single-shot gun into his pocket just in case he ever needed it, because right now as Tobias pressed his sexy body against him, Johnathan really wanted to protect him.

"Did you find the paintings?" the tallest of the three men asked.

Johnathan just looked at Tobias. "Did these men hire you?"

Tobias shook his head. "No. These men were my former employers. They hired me to get the paintings months ago but they must have followed me,"

"We don't need to follow you just your car," the shortest of men said.

Johnathan nodded. It made sense that the three employers had probably paid Tobias in full (a very stupid mistake) for each painting and if they could afford that then it was only reasonable to assume they could afford a little tracking device.

"I presume," Johnathan said, "that you want the money or the painting but I burnt them,"

The three men stared at Johnathan.

"He's lying," Tobias said.

Johnathan just shook his head. He had no idea how that line could have become part of a plan to save their lives but that idea was now dead in the water.

"I stole them back three months ago and that's when I started to become interested in Johnathan here," Tobias said.

"Now he's lying," Johnathan said hoping to confuse the men enough to get them angry.

Men always made mistakes when angry.

All three men took out very larger pistols that were probably big enough to take out Johnathan's foot if they really wanted to.

"Where are the paintings?" the three men asked as one.

Johnathan shrugged and told them all about the photo book that also included pictures of the receipts he had gotten when someone bought the paintings on the black market.

The shortest of the men went over to Johnathan and pressed the cold barrel of his gun against Johnathan's head.

"We needed that money," the man said.

"You should have hired better money managers," Johnathan said and Tobias shook his head to sort of say it wasn't the time for humour.

Johnathan put his hand into his pocket. Pulled out the gun. Fired.

The shortest man's corpse landed with a thud and Johnathan cursed under his breath. He had only killed two other criminals in his life but he still hated it.

Johnathan was an art thief not a murderer but at least each time was only ever self-defence. But each kill still made him feel like crap.

Tobias stood up and stared at the last two men. "Leave. The paintings are gone. The money is spent. There is nothing more here for you,"

The two men sneered at each other and Johnathan. "Fine then,"

Johnathan stood up and clicked his fingers at the two men. "Excuse me, take your friend?"

The two men spat at the body, picked up their friend and they left kindly shutting the broken front door behind them.

"Aren't you scared about the cops showing up?" Tobias asked.

Johnathan laughed as he wrapped his arms around Tobias's insanely fit body and he bit his lip. "I know I would always have to leave Rochester at some point. I don't have a family, loved one or many friends,"

Johnathan loved feeling Tobias's hands move lower.

"I also don't keep anything material in the country or house. All my property and assets are in bank accounts all over the world so I can flee at a moment's notice,"

Tobias bit his lip now and that only made him look even cuter.

"I hear Paris is beautiful at this time of year," Johnathan said. "You know, if you want to join me,"

Johnathan really hoped Tobias would say yes. Johnathan knew it was stupid that he really wanted a relationship with a man he had only just met but clearly Tobias was a hot, sexy man with a very good head because Johnathan really didn't know too many men that would have remained calm and controlled tonight.

"Let's go," Tobias said kissing Johnathan and both of the hot men moaned as they felt the sheer pleasure, attraction and building sexual tension flow between them.

"Wow," Johnathan said.

"Your lips really are delicious," Tobias said.

Johnathan just laughed and Tobias joined him and they kept kissing more and more almost like they were two old flames that were getting back together and had years of lovemaking to catch up on.

And it was exactly at that moment that Johnathan realised that they did actually have a shot at a real relationship.

Two international art thieves falling in love, having to deal with angry former employers and going on the run together. Now that really was the most perfect ending to an eventful evening that Johnathan could have asked for.

And Johnathan just knew that there were a lot more adventures to come.

AUTHOR OF THE BETTIE ENGLISH PRIVATE
EYE MYSTERIES

CONNOR WHITELEY

A ROMANTIC DROP
AT UNIVERSITY

A GAY SPY ROMANTIC SUSPENSE SHORT STORY

A ROMANTIC DROP AT UNIVERSITY
28th September 2022

Canterbury, England

Part-Time MI5 Intelligence Officer Jeremy Clarkes absolutely loved the massive sofa he lowered himself onto with its large red cushions that basically absorbed his small body, the very comfortable black fabric that was slightly cold to the touch that wrapped around his lower region and he really enjoy the peace and quiet of the wide long wooden hallway he was in.

The hallway itself probably wasn't anything too special to the university students that came here each and every day, and Jeremy supposed when he had been a student here at Kent University, this long and very wide corridor with its smooth wooden walls to the left, a few wooden doors that led into grand music halls and on the right there were massive floor-to-ceiling windows, he hadn't cared either.

Maybe the so-called grand designer of the university believed the floor-to-ceiling windows were meant to be nice, beautiful or impressive. But in reality it was a minor shame that the windows only looked out onto a narrow concrete path between this building and another grey university building that Jeremy believed was the biology building.

But Jeremy was hardly going to hold the sheer lack of view against the designer, because the wide, long wooden corridor was rather nice and Jeremy was more than happy to wait here until his contact came to meet him.

The air smelt wonderful with great thick aromas of bitter coffee, sweet creamy cakes and even the amazing smell of juicy crispy bacon came from the little university restaurant at the far end of the corridor past some stairs, groups of students and the half-broken wooden door to another lecture theatre.

The great sound of students talking, laughing and debating how unfair their coursework was this term just made Jeremy smile, because he had been out of university for a few years now after studying psychology (which wasn't profiling like every single person believed that really did annoy Jeremy) and he was working part-time on his Master degree whilst helping out MI5 at the same time.

Jeremy really loved how his dad had wanted him to work for MI5 and work for his department, but Jeremy had really wanted to get his Masters in clinical psychology (or mental health as Jeremy explained to everyone else) so instead Jeremy's dad *bullied* (more like pleaded) for Jeremy to work part time for MI5.

So Jeremy agreed.

Granted Jeremy never believed he would have to return to his old university to meet a contact that meant to be giving him a memory stick containing information. Since apparently MI5 believed one of the professors at the University was meant to be selling secrets to the Russians because Kent University had a number of top-secret government contracts.

Jeremy had to admit his old university was impressive as hell because they had managed to get government contracts on a range of issues, like cybersecurity, research new materials for body armour and even highly advanced communications systems.

It was great that Kent University was doing this sort of work but Jeremy was a little concerned that there was a possible enemy operative in the university.

Ideally Jeremy would have liked his dad to give him the mission of *deposing* of the threat to national security but apparently his dad didn't believe he was ready for that sort of responsibility.

Jeremy completely disagreed, because Jeremy had slept with

enemy agents to get classified Brazilian, French and Spanish intelligence and he had even had to kill a few of them by *accident*, so Jeremy just couldn't understand why he wasn't allowed to end this threat to national security.

The beautiful sound of two men laughing as they walked past made Jeremy smile a little, and Jeremy had to admit they really did look beautiful in their dark blue jeans, blue jumpers and smooth round faces.

Jeremy had seriously missed the university scene for young men, and university had actually been an amazing time for him. He had first learnt he was gay here, he had lost his virginity and he had really learnt the sort of person who he wanted to be.

Granted no one here would have been able to tell he was gay or even an intelligence officer, because he had really tried for the student-look today, or at least what he called the student-look. Some tight sexy blue jeans, a white t-shirt that showed how slim he was and some black trainers.

It might not have been as attractive as the sporty men walking around university with their sportswear, but Jeremy knew he looked pretty cute, and judging by the range of looks he had gotten earlier from men and women he sort of knew that he was completely right.

Jeremy checked the time on his black smartphone and it was coming up to midday, and Jeremy just really hoped that the contact he was meeting would show up soon.

He still had a lot of reading to do for his Masters degree after this meeting and after he had travelled to see his dad to hand over the memory stick.

Jeremy just really hoped that the contact wouldn't be too long because the longer MI5 didn't have that memory stick, the longer that foul rogue professor was out on the streets selling information to the Russians.

And Jeremy just knew from personal experience how deadly that really was.

***

28th September 2022

Canterbury, England

PhD Student William Conner leant against the slightly cold red brick wall of a very large and very long glass building that housed the university's libraries with tens of thousands of books and several cafes and workstations for students where William studied. He really liked the slight coldness that radiated through his white shirt, chequered blue trousers and his brown shoes.

He just felt like he needed the coldness more than anything today, and he really wasn't sure if he was doing the right thing.

William just focused on the constantly moving sea of students in all their different heights, weights and ethnic origins flow up and down the brick path ahead of him. He didn't recognise any of them at all but that was hardly surprising considering it was the first week back at university for everyone, so there were thousands of new students that had just joined.

But at least there were some cute boys that William didn't recognise. There was one very cute boy that might have been 22 or 23, just a year or two younger than himself, with longish brown hair and a perfectly round face that was walking towards the library.

The crisp, refreshing and slightly damp air surrounded William as he felt a little excited for a moment until the cute boy smiled and kissed his girlfriend, and William just laughed a little.

All the students were talking to each other, catching up on their summers, what they wanted out of this year and what they thought of their courses so far. It was so amazing to hear so many voices again and it really was like the university campus was finally back to normal after the eerie silence of the summer months.

But William just realised he must have been kidding himself if he seriously believed that dating would actually be any easier this year. He was 24 years old, bisexual and he had barely been able to do too much dating in recent years.

He seriously loved women but after dating a few last years and in his Masters and Undergraduate degrees, he just wanted to try dating a man. He had only dated one seriously hot guy in High school but that had ended awfully.

Yet the problem was always the same for all gay or bisexual people, William just had absolutely no clue how the hell he was going to meet a hot cute man to fall in love with. It was seriously the bane of his life, and he had wondered about going to the university's LGBT+ society on Friday but that just didn't seem like his sort of thing.

He tried to just forget about his dating problems as he looked at the time on his large blue smartphone and it was starting to approach midday. He still couldn't believe that he was actually meant to be meeting a spy or Intelligence Officer as they preferred to be called to hand over a memory stick.

William still felt so guilty about it all, and he really didn't want to do it, because Professor Davenport had seriously been so great to William, without Davenport William really doubted he would have gotten onto the PhD position (because of department politics for than anything else) and the professor had been a great supervisor.

It just seemed so wrong of William to hand over the memory stick and all the information that could get the professor arrested or even worse, killed.

But William had to hand over the stupid memory stick more than anything else in the world, his father had been murdered by Russia-backed insurrectionists in Afghanistan so William was not allowing the damn pathetic Russians to hurt him anymore.

And if the price to protect the UK, like his father would have wanted, was to make a "good" man go to prison then that was okay to William. It just had to be okay.

William took a deep breath of the crisp, refreshing air and took a few steps forward and merged with the endless stream of the students going in and out of the library and past it.

William just kept following the brick path ahead of him, trying not to knock into the other students as he hooked a left onto another brick path towards the university building he was meant to be meeting the Intelligence Officer in.

He didn't even know what the officer looked like, he didn't know if he was expecting James Bond, a man in a suit or street clothes or anything. William was completely in the dark, and part of him just wanted the man or woman to be hot.

That wouldn't be a problem.

But William forced himself not to get his hopes up as most intelligence officers were probably older men and women in their 30s or older. A little out of William's age range but he seriously wished the officer would be hot.

And just because he had read a few spy novels last night (something he fully admitted he should not have done because the informant always dies in them) and learnt that a lot of contacts get pickpocketed before dying, William placed his hands in his jean pockets.

Thankfully the small black memory stick was still in there so William simply wrapped his fingers around it.

After a few more moments of walking along the long brick path and got to a very modern-looking wooden university building, William went through some glass doors, hooked a right and went down a very wide and long corridor with massive sofas and smooth wooden walls to his left and horrible floor-to-ceiling windows to his right.

William really didn't like the windows because they were so awful, tasteless and the designer had to be an idiot because of the sheer lack of view and-

William stopped dead in his tracks as he looked at the most beautiful man he had ever seen sitting on one of the large black sofas in the corridor.

The man was so hot and beautiful and sexy with his white t-shirt that showed how seriously fit he was, his tight blue jeans that only amplified his raw sexual appeal even more and William really, really loved the man's cute little square face that looked so young and innocent but there was just something about his eyes.

Maybe other students here looked at the hot sexy man and presumed he was another student that was innocent in the ways of the world, but William just recognised something.

A certain type of emotional damage or experience behind the hot man's sexy emerald eyes that made William instantly know that the beautiful man was the intelligence officer he was meant to be meeting.

And William couldn't help but realise the hot man was a little young, maybe only a year younger than him, William had absolutely no problem with hopefully getting to know this sexy, hot, beautiful man a little better.

And that all came with the hopeful bonus of helping to protect the UK as well.

***

28th September 2022

Canterbury, England

As much as Jeremy loved the amazing softness of the large black sofa with its pillows and wonderful fabric, Jeremy was seriously starting to wonder if this contact would ever show up, and even worse what if the entire mission had been compromised?

That had already happened to Jeremy far more times than he actually wanted to think about. The last time in Paris with the French DGSE, the Italian Mob and a scared cute man was not Jeremy's idea of fun in the slightest, so Jeremy just really hoped that the mission was fine.

As it was lunchtime, the sound of students talking, moving and catching up on their summers got louder and louder as more students came into the university building and dived into the restaurant at the far end of the corridor, but they were all so loud that the sound carried perfectly.

Jeremy was about to move further up the wooden corridor to another large black sofa when he noticed someone coming towards him. He couldn't see who it was exactly because they were sort of merged into the endless stream of students coming into the corridor.

If this person had intelligence training then Jeremy had to admit they were excellent, because they would be far too close to Jeremy for comfort before he had properly assessed if they were a threat or not.

But then he actually saw the guy.

The second the hot sexy guy stepped into perfect view Jeremy was just shocked to the core.

He had absolutely no idea how the hot sexy guy could look so average and rather unappealing in the few photos and pieces of paper that his father had given him, but in reality the guy actually looked like a god.

Jeremy seriously loved the guy's amazing looking legs in his jeans, the crisp white shirt that made him look so intelligent, clever and sexy with the wonderful added bonus of it showing how slim the guy was underneath.

And Jeremy seriously loved how cute the guy was with his longish fluffy brown hair that he really, really wanted to run his fingers through, his slight brown beard and Jeremy just knew the guy's smooth, youthful face was simply adorable.

The guy was sheer perfection and probably one of the most beautiful guys Jeremy had actually ever seen, and that included a lot of foreign agents trying to attack the UK.

Jeremy felt his hands turn sweaty and he felt sweat slowly roll down his back and his wayward parts flare to life as he stared at the sexy hunk of a guy that was walking towards him.

Then the hot sexy guy simply came over to him and held out the little black memory stick that contained all the information to save or damn the UK.

The hot sexy guy didn't ask if Jeremy was the Officer he was meant to meet, he didn't know if Jeremy was friendly and Jeremy was just shocked at him.

If he had been anyone else in the slightest, Jeremy would have been mad, a little annoyed and so infuriated that a person with no intelligence training could have destroyed UK national security by making such a simple mistake.

Jeremy just couldn't believe this hot sexy guy had been willing to hand over the memory stick so easily. What if Jeremy had been working for the professor or the Russians?

But as much as Jeremy wanted to be annoyed with this very cute fool, he actually couldn't bring himself to be any of that. All he could do was simply stare into the beautifully soft brown eyes of this guy and really want to know more about him.

Yet he had a job to do first.

Jeremy gently smiled and shook his head as he took the memory stick of the guy, making sure their fingers grazed each other for a moment. And Jeremy seriously loved the smoothness and tenderness of the guy's warm, slightly sweaty, skin against his own.

And Jeremy could have sworn he felt the beautiful guy's fingers stretch out a little more as if they both never wanted this moment to end and they both wanted to hold each other's hands for a little longer.

Jeremy really wanted that, more than anything else in the entire world at the moment actually, but he sadly forced himself to pull away and took out his black smartphone.

One of the same benefits of working for MI5 was that Jeremy got access to a lot of great apps that he really loved, including a smartphone app that allowed him to scan memory sticks without them having to be plugged in. He had absolutely no idea how it worked but it was an amazing app for sure.

"What's that?" the guy asked.

Jeremy smiled at him and he felt his smile turn into a sexy grin as he looked at the amazing guy in front of him.

When he had met informants or contacts before, they were normally so scared, concerned or nervous, but this guy wasn't. That could have meant that the guy had no idea what he was actually involved in, but as he was doing a PhD Jeremy really doubted he was that stupid.

Or this amazing guy was clearly curious and Jeremy really liked that in a guy.

Jeremy gestured for both of them to sit down on the large black sofa and the guy slowly nodded and they both did.

Jeremy was fairly sure that if he looked at any MI5 policy or rulebook, he wasn't meant to sit back down once he had the asset (the memory stick) in case they were attacked and technically his mission now was to validate the memory stick was real and get it as soon as possible to MI5.

But around this really hot sexy guy, Jeremy just didn't want to leave yet and he even wanted to get to know this beautiful guy a little more.

"Can I know you're name?" the hot sexy guy asked.

Jeremy smiled. He said it so nervously and with such a schoolboy grin that the guy looked so cute and Jeremy was slightly willing to bend a rule or two for this cutie.

"Only my first name but I'm Jeremy," he said holding out his hand.

The guy unleashed another sexy schoolboy grin that melted Jeremy's heart but Jeremy hated it when he had to take back his hand before the guy shook it because his phone buzzed.

"I'm William," the hot guy said.

"Hot name," Jeremy said, regretting it the moment he said it. "Um, sorry I'm normally more professional than this,"

Jeremy really couldn't believe he had actually just said that to a contact, he hated being so unprofessional but this guy was just so cute.

Then it hit Jeremy that he really needed to make himself not like this guy. MI5 Officers couldn't fall for contacts or anything, it was the rules and this guy was a PhD student and he was only a Masters student.

They weren't exactly compatible.

Jeremy forced his attention back to his phone and smiled that the memory stick did actually contain all the information MI5 needed.

"Wow," Jeremy said as he scrolled through some of the data. "This is amazing. This contains email addresses, bank accounts and details every little document the professor sent,"

Jeremy just looked at sexy William and smiled. He had met some good and great contacts before during his part-time intelligence work but William might be the best. He had never seen information this detailed before, it was perfect.

Just like William so far.

"Thank you," Jeremy said. "This is amazing,"

William shrugged like it was nothing but Jeremy saw in his eyes that he was conflicted.

And as much as Jeremy just needed to leave and get the memory stick to MI5 he made himself stay a little longer.

"Can I ask your age?" William asked.

Jeremy's raised his eyebrows a little, it was nothing that he hadn't heard before.

"Sorry, sorry," William said. "I'm not normally like a teenager. I'm normally quite intelligent and know exactly what to say it's just I haven't met someone like you before,"

If anyone else had said that Jeremy might have taken it as William not meeting an intelligence officer before but he seriously hoped it was that William found him attractive.

Because Jeremy really wasn't sure what he would do if William didn't like him, because Jeremy was just wanting to get to know this amazingly hot guy more and more with each passing second.

"I do this part-time," Jeremy said wanting to be as truthful as he could with hot sexy William but being careful at the same time. "I'm a psychology Masters student by day,"

It was great to see William's eyes light up.

"Then we can all talk," someone said.

Jeremy looked up away from the black sofa for a moment and just frowned as he saw three men standing there.

Jeremy would have known the middle-aged man standing in the middle from anywhere. He had stared the professor Davenport's face too many times from surveillance footage and personnel records for Jeremy not to know what he looked like.

But Davenport seriously didn't know how to dress well. The professor was wearing a very worn and ancient grey trench coat from the 1950s, his bald head looked awful and his rough skin really didn't help the look.

Yet Jeremy was a little more concerned about the two slightly younger men with their classic Russian looks, short blond hair and strong jawlines. They were rather attractive in a way but judging how they were holding their black overcoats Jeremy sort of knew they were holding guns under them.

Not what Jeremy wanted.

If MI5 found out about this little problem then Jeremy just knew they would moan at him because he should have left already and now because of his feelings for a very hot guy he risked losing the memory stick.

But Jeremy couldn't help as his stomach twisted into a painful knot as he realised that he didn't only risk losing the memory stick but he also risked losing William.

It was so stupid to be worrying about losing a hot guy he had only just met but Jeremy really felt drawn to him and he was quickly realising he was rather desperate for a first date or something with this hottie.

As professor Davenport took a step closer Jeremy just knew without a shadow of a doubt he had a lot to do. He had to save the UK from the Russians, protect the memory stick and most importantly save the really attractive man sitting right next to him.

Jeremy just had to do all of those things or die trying.

***

28th September 2022
Canterbury, England

William just flat couldn't believe this was happening. Sure he had been nervous and concerned that Professor Davenport and his crazy Russian friends might show up and try to stop him but for it to actually happen was something else entirely.

William felt his heart pound in his chest and he was fairly certain that something very, very bad was going to happen to them all as they all stood there staring at each other in the wide, long wooden corridor.

"Let's go to my office men," Professor Davenport said as a group of female university students walked past.

William was actually about to take a step forward like Davenport and his two Russian friends were the ones in complete control but he was rather amazed that beautiful Jeremy simply sat back down.

William had to admit Jeremy was so beautiful and cute as he sat down on the large black sofa and simply allowed the massive black cushions to swallow his body whole. Jeremy was seriously cute and William really wanted to protect him.

But given how Jeremy was the professional spy, William just sort of wanted to follow his lead.

So he sat down to next to Jeremy. He was probably sitting far too close to Jeremy for comfort but given how beautiful Jeremy was William actually wanted to be even closer to him.

Davenport laughed. "Wow. William I gave you everything, I allowed you get onto the PhD programme, I supported you and I kept supporting you. And this is how you repay me?"

William looked to the floor as Davenport's words slammed into him. The sad truth was that Davenport was actually right, he really had done so much for William whenever no one else would and he was basically betraying him.

Then Jeremy handed a perfectly warm hand over William's and William's pounding heart skipped a few beats.

"You know he's only manipulating you," Davenport said. "It's what they do and you are such an easy mark,"

William glanced at Jeremy slightly and he really didn't want to believe that everything Jeremy had said in those few precious sentences between them was a lie.

He really wanted to believe that Jeremy cared about him, was attracted to him and seriously wanted to get to know him better. But what if it was all a lie and a simple spy trick?

What if Davenport was simply doing the same?

The two Russians said something loud in Russian and whipped out their guns and aimed them at William and Jeremy.

William was about to lean protectively over Jeremy but Jeremy beat him too.

Jeremy smelt amazing with his hints of his earthy aftershave but now really wasn't the time. William had to help Jeremy get them out of this situation.

The other students sitting on the other sofas screamed and shouted and ran.

William wanted to panic but Jeremy was almost projecting a very hot aura of calm that William just couldn't help but relax.

"Give me the memory stick," Davenport said. "Or believe me my friends will kill you both,"

William smiled. "Impossible. Your friends aren't your friends. They're your Masters and we all know the armed police would be coming right now,"

As William watched Davenport and the Russians tense, he found it so weird that Jeremy tensed as well.

The Russians raised their guns. They fired.

The massive floor-to-ceiling window behind William shattered.

"Give the stick," the Russians said.

Jeremy stood up. William did the same.

Jeremy took the memory stick out of his pocket. William felt his stomach twist. This couldn't be happening.

William hated it how Jeremy was about to hand over the memory stick.

Davenport took a few steps closer.

William leant forward.

Davenport's eyes widened.

The Russians surged forward.

Punching William in the stomach. Putting him into a headlock.

William hated the Russian's rough overcoat and his captor tightened the headlock.

He hated seeing Jeremy upset even more. William felt awful as Jeremy looked so disappointed, sad and like he had just failed.

"I was going to do the same to Davenport," Jeremy said.

William gave Jeremy a weak smile and even though he could sort of guess that Jeremy was a bit annoyed Jeremy still looked so cute.

The other Russian pressed the cold metal barrel of his gun against the bottom of William's jaw and looked at Jeremy.

"The memory stick now or I will paint the walls with his brains," he said.

Jeremy swallowed hard and William could only begin to imagine how hard this was for him.

Jeremy was basically going to be risking his entire country just for the sake of William. He really hated himself at that, William just wished that he was better.

But he was a PhD student as Davenport had said. Maybe he could figure out a way to save them all.

Jeremy held out the little black memory stick towards Davenport.

"You know that won't help," William said.

William hated it how the Russian headlock-ing him tightened his grip.

"Why?" Davenport said.

"Because MI5 already has the information. He scanned it earlier," William said.

"Stupid idiot," the Russian holding the gun to William said.

The same Russian took the gun away from William and shot Davenport in the back of the head.

Davenport's corpse slumped to the ground.

William really didn't like this anymore. Even Jeremy looked shocked or at least surprised.

The Russian with the gun pointed it at Jeremy's head.

"Sorry about this we need to cover up all loose ends now," he said.

William couldn't have this. He couldn't have Jeremy dying. He was too beautiful and William had to go out on a date with him.

William jumped up. His neck ached.

He slammed his feet into the Russian holding him.

The Russian hissed.

His grip weakened.

William slammed his elbow into his ribs.

The Russian with the guy looked at William.

Jeremy flew forward.

Tackling the Russian with the gun to the ground.

William headbutted the Russian holding him.

The Russian released him.

William spun around.

Punching the man in the nose.

Kicking him in-between the legs.

The Russian fell to the ground.

William jumped on him.

Some ribs broke.

William was just about to knock the man down when armed police officers in black body armour and face masks stormed in.

William spun around to make sure beautiful Jeremy was okay but he was gone.

And William honestly expected himself to be mad, sad or concerned that such a beautiful man had disappeared on him but he actually wasn't. Jeremy was a beautiful, hot man that he really, really liked but he was a part-time spy and even William knew deep down that surely a relationship between a PhD student and a spy could never ever work.

But it would have been nice to try and William seriously wondered where the hell Jeremy had gone to?

***

28th September 2022
Canterbury, England

A few hours later, William had finally finished giving his statement to the armed police officers at the university and suffered through even more interrogations with people in black suits after he stupidly mentioned the involvement of MI5, Russians and a memory stick. But now it was finally over William was so looking forward to going home at last.

William went into one of Kent University's many massive square concrete car parks that had rows upon rows of little car park spaces with large thick oak trees lining the edges. It wasn't the most attractive of car parks with the ugly grey brick university buildings slightly beyond the oak trees but it was a great car park.

And as the sky turned a fiery orange as the sun started to set, William was a little disappointed that he had spent so much of the afternoon and early evening talking to police officers, men in black suit and all whilst pining over a man he barely knew.

As William slowly walked past a lot of empty car park spaces because everyone else had already gone home, and the slight warmth from the perfectly smooth concrete gently pulsed through his shoes and into his feet, William was really surprised at the sort of impression that Jeremy had left on him.

William had been so cute, beautiful and hot so William just sort of supposed that it was normal for him to like Jeremy because he had also been searching for a hot man to date for ages, but he just felt like it was more than that.

Not only because Jeremy was a part-time spy (which was always a very attractive job) but he was clever, kind and he was a psychology student himself. William liked to believe that all he really wanted was a beautiful kind man that would love him, and he could love too and with them both being psychology students that would give him a lot to talk about.

And it would hopefully be a good foundation to build a relationship on.

As William got deeper into the massive square car park, William could see his little blue Ford Fiesta and to his utter surprise there was a very cute man leaning against it. Sure the man was wearing a baseball cap and completely different clothes to earlier but William instantly recognised it as Jeremy.

Why was he here?

William quickly walked over to him.

William had to admit Jeremy did look amazing in his slightly baggier black jeans, black shirt and boots that didn't really highlight anything about him but William wouldn't have been surprised if it helped him to blend into places where he didn't want to be seen.

But William really didn't care at that moment, not only because he had thankfully seen Jeremy in something extremely attractive earlier but because his beautiful Jeremy was here for him.

And that seriously meant everything to him.

Jeremy waved and smiled at William and Jeremy's sensational smile just melted his heart again, and there was such warmth behind it too.

William realised that Davenport had been completely wrong in his own manipulation, Jeremy didn't hold his hand to manipulate William, he had held his hand because Jeremy really wanted him.

Just like why Jeremy was here now instead of doing whatever for his own degree or MI5 job.

He wanted William and William really, really wanted him.

"I didn't expect to see you again," William said, slowly going over to Jeremy and he didn't even care that he was probably getting a little too close to Jeremy.

William only stopped when he accidentally realised that he was so close to beautiful Jeremy that he could feel Jeremy's amazing wonderful body heat against him.

Jeremy only smiled. "My bosses didn't either but it turns out, and this is all only hypothetical of course, but the Ministry of Defence is offering your university a lot more contracts and China, Russian and our other enemies are… excited about this,"

William smiled, he just hoped this was going where he seriously hoped it was.

"So I have managed to persuade my bosses and university to let me transfer here," Jeremy said.

William just grinned like a little silly schoolboy as Jeremy took another step closer to him. So close that William could feel Jeremy's wonderfully sweet-scented breath on his neck.

William so badly wanted to kiss Jeremy at that moment.

"I was wondering if you were okay with that and if you, you know, wanted to get to know each other a little bit?" Jeremy asked looking at the floor with his own very cute schoolboy smile.

William couldn't believe how cute Jeremy looked even when he looked so embarrassed and shy. William couldn't actually believe Jeremy thought he was going to reject him.

William would have loved nothing else.

But what if he wasn't the right sort of man with a spy? Even a part-time one. Would Jeremy be constantly concerned about William's safety so he would take his eye off the ball and risk his own safety.

William didn't want Jeremy to be constantly worrying about him, and William didn't want Jeremy to be constantly stressed and if the UK's enemies were really concerning the university as much as Jeremy believed then surely William shouldn't bother Jeremy with a relationship. Did he have more important things to focus on than him?

"And," Jeremy said kissing William on the cheek that made William gasp with pleasure. "My father was wondering if you would like to come into the fold. You got us the information from Davenport, I said you were great when confronted with the Russians and I... I would really like to see you more,"

William smiled a little more and his own face started to hurt as he realised what exactly Jeremy was asking him to do. And it did actually make perfect sense, who the hell would ever suspect a PhD student as a spy or *intelligence Officer* as he was probably going to have to start calling himself.

"Please?" Jeremy asked. "Will you do it?"

If it was anything else in the entire world, William was fairly sure he would have said no because he was a bisexual man that loved his sexuality, being a psychology PhD student and he loved his quiet non-spying life. But for some reason he simply kissed Jeremy on the lips.

He loved the silky smoothness of Jeremy's warm lips against his own and he simply nodded.

He actually enjoyed stealing information from Professor Davenport a lot more than he realised and as William unlocked his car and Jeremy got in with him, he really excited for the future.

Because it didn't actually matter what happened now, because William was going to become an *Intelligence Officer* and spend a lot of amazing time with beautiful Jeremy and if things didn't work out then that was okay.

Jeremy had already given him a lot of great gifts, William finally knew that he could find hot attractive men, he could finally become a spy and continue his father's work about protecting the UK and he had finally felt the start of *love* or utterly great attraction towards Jeremy.

But William and Jeremy both got in the car, and William just looked at how cute, beautiful and wonderful Jeremy looked sitting next to him, he seriously just knew that Jeremy was the one.

And he was seriously looking forward to getting to know Jeremy a lot, lot more but for now at least William just kissed him.

Again and again.

***

16th June 2023

Canterbury, England

An entire academic year later, Jeremy and William sat on Kent University's massive bright green field that looked out over the wonderful historical city of Canterbury with its ancient high street, impressive cathedral and tall spires in the distance. Jeremy really loved it how he had just finished his last exam of the year and William was resting his sexy little face on his lap as they both sat (or laid in William's case) on the grass.

It was a perfectly warm day, the sun was high in the sky and there was even an amazingly cool breeze with hints of pine, freshness and candy floss from a stall tens of metres away on the main university campus.

Jeremy gently ran his fingers through William's wonderfully fluffy hair and he was so pleased, happy and excited for what had happened over the past academic year.

Jeremy had worked a lot of MI5 cases part-time, meeting contacts and doing other work, but this was the first year that he could actually say without lying that this was a fun job. And it was only now that he realised that all the other times he had said it was *fun*, he had been lying.

He hadn't even known how great his part-time job was until he worked with William. William was still training in intelligence work and he really did bring such flare, style and sense of fun to the seriousness of a very deadly job.

Together they had found out what "students" were actually foreign agents, they had stopped top-secret military experiments being sent to hostile powers and Jeremy's favourite task was whenever the two of them had to make out to stop them from getting caught.

Because Jeremy was seriously glad that English and foreign agents and people had a massive aversion to walking into the same room as two guys making out. And it also helped that William really was an amazing kisser too.

So as the cooling breeze picked up a little, Jeremy just stared at the stunning fluffy hunk of a man who's head was on his lap, and Jeremy just bend down and kissed him.

Really passionately.

And Jeremy was expecting William to question or ask what that was for, but he didn't, and that really summed it up for Jeremy.

The problem with being an intelligence officer that had relationships were they were often needy, chaotic and hard to prioritise over the work, yet William wasn't like that at all. He was so easy to work with, love with and just be with that Jeremy really, really knew that they were perfect for each other.

Sure Jeremy was joining Kent University's PhD programme, the same one as William, next year so they could both become doctors, work in the university and still do their job for MI5, but they weren't scared about it.

All because their relationship was so strong, perfect and they loved each other so much that they were actually really looking forward to it both.

And as Jeremy kissed William again and again, he knew that they were perfect for each other and this wasn't some fling between two guys. This was real, special and something that was going to last for a very, very long time indeed.

And that was exactly how Jeremy wanted it and judging by how hard and passionately William was kissing him back, he seriously didn't mind either.

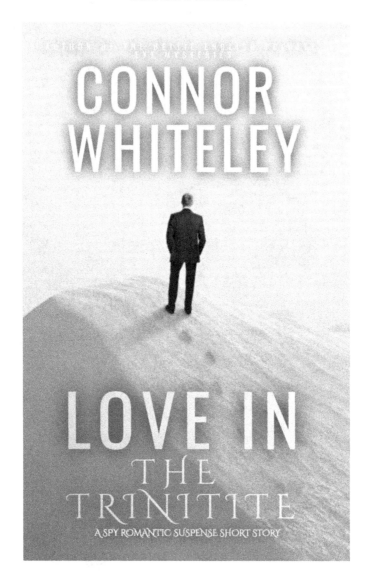

LOVE IN THE TRINITITE
Classified Date, 2022
Kavir Desert, Iran

British Intelligence Officer Adeline Zouch sat in a very uncomfortable and boiling hot seat of the top-secret military plane she was flying in over the desert in Iran. She hated being the only person in the long metal tube that the pilots called a hull and the deafening roar of the engines didn't relax her.

Adeline even hated the horrible scents of burning oil, sweat and bitter coffee that filled the air in the hull. It was such a disgusting way to travel that Adeline really wanted this Queen-forsaken mission to just be over already.

Adeline had never liked Iran or the middle east very much. Sure she knew it was a very dangerous area but she had always loved playing against the Russians and Chinese, because they had great spies. And that was what being a spy was truly about, playing games against your enemies.

The Russian and Chinese were clever, evil and fascinating people that Adeline loved to hunt down and investigate. It was only last week she had been tracking down the former head of Chinese Intelligence who had gone rogue. And Adeline was sure the Chinese Government would deny this but it was just flat out funny to see the Chinese Ambassador beg the UK government to take him out.

That was probably the only time Adeline had ever seen the Chinese play by the international rules and not actually go rogue. It was impressive, scary and just funny all at the same time.

The deafening sound of the engines roar and thunder and pop deep into the desert made Adeline's stomach tighten into a painful knot. The only reason why she was on the mission in the first place was because she hadn't been given new missions yet and the Prime Minister (also known as Mr Dickhead) apparently wanted the best person on this mission.

Adeline didn't agree in the slightest.

The mission was apparently simple, according to the exact same people who had never ever done any fieldwork or even fired a gun before, Adeline needed to go into the Kavir Desert and search for traces of a substance known as Trinitite.

Adeline had heard of the substance that was created when soil was superheated following a nuclear explosion, but this was hardly worth her time. She had investigated tons of Russian and Chinese nuclear testing facilities over the past decade, so sadly she was familiar with the substance.

Yet there were other agents who could have done this, but Adeline knew that the quicker she got this done. The sooner she could return to dealing with the Russians and Chinese agents that seemed to get more and more powerful each day, not that the UK Government was actually interested in the slightest.

Adeline held on tight as the military-transport plane banked a little and she just knew that she would be at her destination sooner or later.

All she actually knew about her mission destination was that it was a very remote stretch of desert that even the insurgents and local terrorist groups rarely went into because it was so dry and lifeless. At best Adeline would see a few animals and maybe a government patrol if this was a nuclear testing facility. At worse, the whole bloody Iranian army would be there.

Adeline had made sure she looked the part of a tourist just in case she was caught. She liked wearing her stab-proof vest, sandy shorts and hiking boots. Then Adeline picked up her small rucksack that was filled with wonderfully cool water, a gun and small satellite phone to call for an extraction when she needed it.

But her stomach still filled with butterflies as she felt the plane descend ever so slightly.

Non-spies would probably call her paranoid or something but she just knew that something was off. There was something about the extreme heat and the uncomfortableness of the air that made the entire mission feel not right.

The intelligence reports might believe that the deserts were always empty, but that was a lie. The fall of Afghanistan had proved how bad some intelligence reports could be, Adeline just really, really hoped that this wasn't one of those times.

Because if there were a lot of enemies in the desert then there would be no extraction, help or support this time. She would be well and truly alone and as much as the idea of fighting the enemies of the UK excited her, Adeline knew that these enemies wouldn't take her prisoner in the slightest.

They would kill her.

Slowly.

***

Classified Date, 2022

Kavir Desert, Iran

Former British Intelligence Officer Theo Martin really liked his brand new job working for private military contractors in the boiling, sweaty, cultural hub of Iran. He actually didn't mind this beautiful country in the slightest. Sure the country was run by crazies, extremists and corruption but the people weren't that bad. And the food was simply sensational.

Theo sat in the shadow created by a very, very tall sandstone column that seemed to rise out of the sandy desert ground just for him. Theo almost wished he was at one of the amazing little "cafes" that served him battery acid bitter coffee and sweet wonderful pastries that were specialities of Iran where he was staying. He simply loved it here.

The wonderful silence of the desert was another delightful gift away from the constant noise of the UK and MI6. And as a private military contractor he still got all his powers, gadgets and licence to kill without all the bureaucracy nonsense.

Theo loved staring out at the boiling hot desert with sand dunes that seemed to roll on for miles upon miles with sandstone columns rising up as a little scenic break to make the landscape more interesting.

The only bad thing about the desert was the awful boiling hot air that stunk of heat without a hint of moisture in it. It was simply awful to breathe and that was why he always had a humidifier on in his room, he just wanted to try and enjoy a little bit of moisture for a few minutes before the heat of the air simply made it pointless.

Theo didn't entirely know why his boss wanted him to come out here and look for Trinitite that silly little compound that was a result of nuclear explosions. Theo and everyone in the intelligence community knew exactly why the Iranians were building up their nuclear testing programme again. It was all because there was no Iran Nuclear Deal anymore so there was no incentive for them to not make nuclear weapons.

So they got excited about it and they were building a lot. Theo had once read an intelligence report proposing Iran had bought enough nuclear material from Russia to build a hundred nuclear warheads.

Theo was sure in the slightest what proving it would actually achieve. What would the international community do with the proof? Simply slap Iran on the wrist and tell it was a bad country?

Granted Theo had read a report before he left his room today about the United Nations calling a meeting to attempt to create a new nuclear disarmament bill. And even the US, Russia and China were meant to sign it meaning they would have to get rid of about a quarter of their nuclear stock piles, so maybe that new Bill had been a possible cause for the need for this proof.

Theo didn't know. He just followed orders.

Theo just laughed because of how true it was. And that was one of the reasons why he had left MI6 because the entire lack of international justice and all that stuff just seemed so pointless after a while. But at least now he got a little more freedom.

A low humming sound got louder and louder from behind Theo and his stomach tensed. There weren't meant to be any patrols this early in the morning. There weren't meant to be any patrols at all today according to his contacts in the Iranian Government.

This was bad.

Theo slowly got up and peeked around the sandstone column he was sitting behind and frowned when he saw a very large black military transport plane hover for a split second before taking off again.

Theo saw a very short woman was standing where the plane had been and she looked like a tourist perfectly. Theo was hardly impressed to have another spy in the mix, that would only complicate matters and considering she was playing the part of the tourist a little too well by wearing shorts (she would burn easily) she was definitely going to be a liability.

Granted the woman did look amazing as she started to walk over to the sandstone column, and she thankfully hadn't seen Theo yet. Theo seriously loved her fit sexy legs, amazingly toned body and her sexy smile that seemed to be lighting up the desert.

She looked amazing and her eyes were like sapphires in the desert sun, and Theo definitely liked her sensational blond hair (that was definitely dyed to match the hair of local women) that flapped about the wind so elegantly.

She was sheer perfection.

Theo almost felt embarrassed to be wearing a tanned loose-fitting shirt, trousers and hiking boots that probably highlighted how fit and muscular he was, but did nothing to make him look so attractive compared to this goddess walking in the desert.

They locked eyes.

As much as Theo wanted to stare into those stunning sapphire eyes. Theo's training kicked in.

He grabbed his gun from his back and aimed at her.

She did the same.

***

Classified Date, 2022

Kavir Desert, Iran

Adeline absolutely hated this awful desert and she was in no mood not to shoot this man.

He might have been extremely hot sexy and looked like the cover model of a GQ magazine. But this was her mission and even though he had the most kissable lips she had ever seen he was not going to stop her.

The insanely hot man slowly started to walk towards her and Adeline firmly held her finger on the trigger. She was definitely going to kill him if he tried to stop her.

Clearly the typical intelligence reports had been completely wrong and now it might cost Adeline her life. She was flat out not impressed.

"I got a little lost," Adeline said in perfect Arabic. "Do you know the way back to town?"

The insanely hot man laughed and spoke in English. "You don't speak a lot of Arabic, do you? Your accent is still too strong to form some of the sounds correctly,"

Adeline hated this man even more now. She was a highly trained operative of the UK Government, she had split the throats of greater men with just her bare fingernails. How dare he question her.

Adeline spoke in Chinese. "Sorry but who made you expert in everything Englishman?"

The hot man seemed to smile. Adeline had read a lot of faces in her time and she was surprised that the man was really smiling at her. He either liked her for some reason or he was an extremely good spy.

She had to be very careful around him.

"MI6?" the hot man asked.

"You first?" Adeline asked, pointing her gun firmly at his head.

"Private Military Contractor working for the UK Government. Authority Code: Alpha Lemur-666," he said.

That was not exactly what she wanted to hear. She didn't mind private contractors and she had worked with them before, just not in this ridiculous stupid heat. Sweat was already pouring off her forehead and rolling down her back.

All she wanted to do was get on with her mission and leave this Queen-forsaken place.

"Trinitite?" the man asked. "You know where it is,"

Adeline forced herself not to react. The mission was too important not to focus on, and this insanely hot sexy man could have easily tortured another private contractor to get the code. He could be an Iranian spy.

She couldn't trust him.

The man lowered his gun and put it into his back.

Adeline didn't do the same. "How do I know I can trust you?"

The man laughed. "We don't trust people in this spy game. But I wouldn't kill a fellow Brit for love or money,"

Adeline liked the idea of working with him for a little while and even the idea of that made her stomach fill with damn butterflies, and her hands turned sweaty unlike before.

Damn it. She could not fall for this insanely stunning man under any circumstances. Love and emotions on the field get people killed. It was as simple as that.

"Theo," the man said walking over to Adeline.

Adeline gestured with her gun to stay a few metres away from her. Then she put her gun away.

"Code name is Sarah," Adeline said.

Theo smiled. Adeline had to admit *Theo* was a hot name and now he was so close, she was amazed at how sexy and toned his body was under his slightly opened loose shirt.

Adeline started to walk off into the desert and headed towards a very tall sand dune that would give her the best possible vantage point over the area. She needed to see where would be the best location to detonate a nuclear bomb and create trinitite.

***

Classified Date, 2022

Kavir Desert, Iran

Theo was really impressed with the composure and strength and beauty of this woman. Of course this beautiful angel was not called Sarah, he doubted she actually knew a woman called Sarah in the slightest. But she was a strong spy who had good instincts.

Theo and Sarah stood on top of a very large sand dune that somehow beautiful Sarah had just managed to storm up like it was nothing. Theo had slipped over twice because the damn sand had moved so much.

Sarah was carefully scanning the horizon and local area like she was some kind of building expert who knew exactly what each and every dip and ridge in the desert landscape meant. Theo didn't have that much of a clue about geography but clearly that was why he needed this woman called Sarah.

The air was still boiling hot but now Theo was sweating for a different reason entirely. He was sweating because being this close to this stunning beauty was just too much to bear.

"You born in Southern England?" Theo asked. "Can hear it in your voice,"

Sarah weakly smiled. "You don't sound like a former Officer at times,"

Theo was falling for this amazing woman more and more with each passing second. Clearly this woman was trained very well, most people rarely recognised that he was former MI6 these days, but this woman clearly knew him a lot more than he would like to admit.

Not necessarily a bad thing though.

"Want to know why I left?" Theo asked.

Sarah laughed. "I already know why. Everyone leaves for the same reason. You left because you wanted the freedom to do what you wanted in the name of Queen and country and most importantly you wanted proper equipment and pay unlike the cheap government

262

things MI6 gives you,"

Theo just stared at Sarah's amazingly kissable lips. She didn't sound like she bought or accepted the reason at all, but at least she had been willing to listen to other people say it. Most of Theo's former friends had banished him, kicked him to the curb and just wished him dead when he had told them he was leaving for a private company.

This sexy woman seemed to be different.

"This way," Sarah said pointing to the bottom of the sand dune they were standing on.

Theo and Sarah started to walk down the dune together and Theo asked about why they were heading in this way. Even if the woman wasn't into him, he at least needed to learn from her for future missions,

"When an atomic bomb goes off or is tested, imagine the extreme force that is created. It creates trinitite which we're looking for. But it would also create a shockwave that would destroy old dunes and create new much taller sand dunes,"

Theo looked at what they were walking on for a moment. Now he actually gave the idea the time of day, it seriously made perfect sense why the sand dune they were walking on was strange and out of place. It was much larger than most of the other sand dunes.

In fact this had to be at least another five metres tall that the other sand dunes in the area. And considering the winds and extreme heat of the local desert that was a very strange fact indeed.

But at least one of the benefits of walking down an extremely tall sand dune was that it created a lot of shade one side, and thankfully Theo and Sarah were walking down that same side.

Theo loved the delightfully cool shade for a few more moments until they reached the bottom of the dune.

"Now we start looking?" Theo asked.

Sarah simply smiled almost like this was some kind of amazing treasure hunt. Theo wasn't exactly sure how amazing it was going to be.

But he was definitely excited about the treasure hunt.

And he was a lot more excited about spending time with Sarah than he wanted to admit.

A lot more.

***

Classified Date, 2022

Kavir Desert, Iran

After a few hours of searching, resting in the shade and drinking plenty of water, Adeline and Theo were just about to give up this utterly ridiculous mission by walking over to another very large sand dune that was almost a hundred metres away from the dune they had walked down earlier, when Adeline felt something under her feet.

Given how they had both been walking, getting to know each other and resting for the past few hours, Adeline absolutely hated to admit it but she knew what the horrible desert felt like under her feet. The desert always felt hot, made her feet sweat and it felt like a constantly moving ocean of sand particles.

But this felt a lot more solid.

Adeline stopped dead in her tracks and she actually didn't care about the boiling hot sun beaming down on her as she looked at insanely hot Theo.

He didn't seem to understand what she was getting at as she smiled at him. But his lack of understanding didn't make him look bad in her eyes, over the past few hours this hot sexy man had told her about past missions, his family and life. Things that no spy was ever meant to talk about, and he included such little details that no background story ever included.

He had been telling her the truth.

As Theo knelt down and started to dig around in the sand, definitely smiling at the coolness of the sand under the surface, Adeline just focused on him.

She had come on this mission because she had been told to and she had hated it from the start. She hadn't wanted to be in this Queen-forsaken country, hunting down Trinitite and the rest. But she had instead found a beautiful man that she felt amazingly comfortable with.

"Down here," Theo said.

Adeline knelt down and hissed as the sheer intense heat of the sand shot into her knees and she started digging.

It didn't take too long for them to dig ten centimetres under the boiling surface to find a massive cool chunk of glassy-rocky Trinitite.

The discovery slammed into Adeline like a ton of bricks. This confirmed every single person's worse fears about the Iranians and that they were not only building nuclear weapons but testing them.

And for the soil to get superheated enough to form Trinitite then that meant that these weapon tests were very, very successful.

Adeline watched Theo as he broke a large chunk of Trinitite off and handed it to her. She hesitated for a moment and then she just stared into his amazingly soft eyes.

The rest of the chunk of Trinitite was far too thick and chunky to break off another piece without the right equipment. You would certainly need a sledgehammer to break it up anymore.

Adeline was amazed that Theo had just given her the key to both their missions. Theo was allowing her to go home a hero, but he would go home a disappointment.

It wasn't logical in the slightest but a simple chunk of Trinitite highlighted the trouble with spies and relationships. There was no winning for a couple.

Even if Adeline and Theo did start a relationship, they worked for different people and it was no secret that MI6 and private companies hated each other. The relationship would never work out and neither one of them was going to leave their jobs.

Adeline took out her gun from her rucksack. Pointing it at the chunk of Trinitite.

"What are you doing?" Theo asked.

Adeline smiled at him. "The bullet should be strong enough to break the Trinitite in half so we can both return as heroes. There are no enemies in the area and even if there were my extraction would be here before they arrived,"

Theo frowned. "Exactly. *Your* extraction,"

Adeline gasped as she realised what she had done. It was just training and her training had always taught her that herself and her mission was always the most important. Even when she had worked with MI5, CIA and FBI in the past, *her* mission was always more important than the joint mission.

She just didn't want it to be this way with Theo, the sexy man she had actually dared to open her heart to.

"Come back with me," Adeline said. "My boss will go mad. Your boss will go mad. But I'll be happy,"

Adeline hadn't meant to say it but it just felt so natural and true. And truth was a rarity in the spy game. Adeline needed Theo to make her happy, at least that's what she wanted.

The distant sound of motorbikes and 4x4 jeeps echoed against the silence of the desert.

"What do you say?" Adeline asked as she smiled.

She would love to get into a firefight with the Iranians but this wasn't the time. Not with the Trinitite mission coming first and she couldn't risk putting her Theo in danger.

Theo whipped out his gun and pressed it against the Trinitite. He fired. Breaking the Trinitite in two.

Adeline wanted to smile but she grabbed the Satellite phone from her rucksack and entered the phone number to summon her extraction.

Adeline picked up her piece of Trinitite and Theo did the same then they ran out away from the dune so the extraction plane could easily see them.

The sound of 4x4 jeeps and motorbikes got louder and louder. Clearly the Iranians were back to check on their experiments.

Adeline saw little black dots move in the distance and come over dunes and ridges and she knew that time was running out.

A massive roar screamed overhead as a massive black military transport plane descended.

Adeline and Theo prepared themselves to jump onto the descending cargo ramp as the plane itself descended.

Gunshots echoed around the desert.

Adeline climbed onto the cargo ramp and pulled herself up.

The pilot started to take off.

Adeline panicked.

She reached down to get Theo. Theo grabbed her hand.

Bullets smashed into him. Theo screamed.

Adeline pulled him up. Theo's blood dripped out.

"Get us the fuck out of here!" Adeline shouted.

***

Classified Date, 2022

Top-Secret Location, England

The sweet fruity smells of apples, pineapples and limes filled the air from delightful cleaning chemicals as Theo awoke in a bright blue hospital bed barely covered up by its pathetically thin sheets.

Theo hadn't been in a hospital room for ages but he definitely knew this was an expensive one with its smart TV hanging on the wall, bowl of fruit on the bedside table next to him and a very nice vase of roses that looked brand new.

There was a window on the other side of the room but Theo didn't care to look. He was just glad to be alive for a change, but he was definitely going to miss whatever pain medication the doctors had him on. He had once been shot in the chest and stomach and a local Afghan doctor who was helping the West had stitched him up and hid him for four days.

Those were the worse four days of his life, but those Afghans were amazing people.

"You're awake then," a familiar woman said.

It took Theo a few moments to notice that beautiful Adeline with her stunning sapphire eyes was standing and looking out of the window.

"Good view?" Theo asked.

Adeline didn't even turn around. "I would like the view behind me, but I'm currently watching some Royal Air Force Pilots argue about something. It's rather interesting,"

Theo just smiled. He didn't know why in the slightest but she was just such an amazing woman. He loved how she was so strong, capable and she had saved his life.

He had no idea what the MI6's and his company's reports would say later, but he knew the truth. The truth was *Sarah* (he had to find out her real name) could have simply dropped him and let him fall to the desert below when he had been shot.

That was actually protocol and what you were meant to do.

But this amazingly intelligent, stunning woman had taken a risk for him by helping him onto the plane. That took some guts considering how snobbish her bosses were probably about letting an "outsider" into their ranks.

"You were out for three days," Sarah said. "I admit I wasn't always here during the day. I had to meet your boss, my boss and talk to our UN Ambassador,"

"Did we find the Trinitite?" Theo asked.

Sarah came over and leant over Theo's bed. He felt his hands turn sweaty and sticky and his stomach filled with butterflies.

"Yep. The lab reports confirmed and now the West is leading sanctions against Iran, and even Russia and China are sanctioning Iran without any conditions,"

Theo smiled that was beyond strange, but the reason was clear enough to anyone who studied geopolitics. At the end of the day, Russia and China only wanted themselves to be the nuclear superpowers so whilst they struggled to get the UK, USA and the rest of Europe under control, those two states would have to be happy with stopping Iran from becoming a true nuclear power.

Theo took Sarah's hand and rubbed it gently. He was surprised at how smooth it was and he really loved the amazing chemistry that flowed between them.

"What did our bosses say?" Theo asked.

"Well your boss is a sexist dick so I broke his nose when he copped a feel," Sarah said.

Theo was hardly impressed but he was equally hardly surprised. There was a reason why there were so few female intelligence officers in his company.

"And my boss wasn't exactly pleased we worked together but he admitted it was clear we got results. And he was impressed I handled your boss and our UN ambassador so well,"

Theo tried to lean closer to her but pain from his bullet wounds pulsed up and down him in a momentary wave of agony.

"What's their proposal?" Theo asked.

He loved the sound of Sarah's laugh and they both knew how spies agencies worked a little too well.

"If you're willing they want us to work together," Sarah said with an amazing smile.

Theo just nodded without any hesitation. He would love getting a chance to know, work and maybe even love with this amazing woman.

"Brilliant," Sarah said with a lot more enthusiasm than Theo reckoned she was used to.

Theo was surprised by Sarah's hug and then her nose touched his and she just smiled.

"Adeline," she said.

Theo shrugged. Was that the name of their new target? Code name? Mission?

"My name is Adeline," she said.

Theo felt his heart skip a few beats as he realised how impossibly hard that must have been for her, and he was so grateful she trusted him enough to share it.

Working with her was going to be amazing fun.

***

Classified Date, 2022

Top-Secret Location, England

A few months year after travelling to China, Russia and the Middle East again, Adeline was so amazed and in love with her insanely hot sexy man. Adeline was amazed at how smart he was, able to pick up and blend with different cultures and languages so seamlessly that regardless of his skin colour he could be a local anywhere in the world.

They made a perfect team. Adeline loved not only Theo's smarts but also how he carried himself with such ease and confidence that he never looked out of place. It was the perfect partner for her own deadliness and passion and playing cat-and-mouse with foreign agents.

It was certainly a different pace from chasing down terrorists in the middle east but Adcline was more than glad sexy Theo was adapting quickly.

So as Adeline sat on a very uncomfortable plastic chair in a large metal hangar in a top-secret airport waiting for their plane to arrive to travel off to another mission, Adeline just felt so alive.

Her beautiful Theo was talking with their handler about the next mission and he really did look so special. After being alone for a decade and hunting down the Queen's enemies by herself, Adeline never believed she could work with someone.

But as Theo smiled at her, a true loving smile, Adeline was so glad she had found him because spy work was a lot more fun, exciting and interesting with a partner.

And no matter what the future threw at them, Adeline knew she would be fine and safe and loved, because she had Theo by her side. And he had her by his.

And Adeline was still surprised that it was all only possible because of some silly Trinitite and a boiling hot desert.

Definitely about as spy-like a meet-cute could get, and Adeline loved it.

SPYING FOR INDEPENDENCE

MI5 Intelligence Officer Nick Blackford stood in one of London's massive ancient libraries with immensely beautiful floor-to-ceiling bookshelves, a dark and rather stunning hardwood floor and Nick really enjoyed the small crystal chandeliers that looked like they were floating down from the ceiling every ten metres. The entire library was a stunning array of engineering and as much as the English hated to admit that a Scottish person designed it, one did.

Nick loved looking through the great books on the shelves because this place wasn't exactly a public library because it was mainly reserved for lawyers, governmental people and other civil servants. Yet it was interesting to say the least how many erotica titles were on the shelves in amongst hardcore romance, spy novels and political thrillers.

Of course there were other so-called more important books in the library but Nick was only interested in the fiction part. That was thankfully where there were so few people walking about, there were only three people in the section that seemed to stretch on for a good twenty metres. Nick would have loved to count how many erotica titles there were in this aisle alone.

But he didn't have the time, or the inclination.

The other three people in the isle were only civil servants, wearing black suits, trousers and all of them had their white ID cards hanging around their neck, working for the UK government so they were hardly a threat, and Nick just needed somewhere local to meet a target and hopefully hack their phone to hopefully stop an awful terrorist attack against the nation of Scotland.

Just like all the other Scottish people, Nick had no problem with the English. The English were kind, helpful and even their weird tea obsessions didn't bother Nick and his fellow Scots, but he just didn't want to be ruled by them.

Nick had wanted Scotland to have its own government that could actually do whatever it wanted in the interest of its people instead of being told by the UK Government what it is was and wasn't allowed to do.

Nick really loved the smell of old libraries because they always had that sensational musty book smell about them, but this also had amazing scents of flowers, lavender and more fruity scents that were presumably coming from the civil servants' aftershaves and perfumes, leaving the wonderful taste of pizza like he had on hot summer evenings with his family a few years ago on his tongue.

When Nick had been working for MI5 yesterday looking through all the buried intelligence reports, the sort of reports that were deemed serious enough to keep a tab on but not serious enough to actually act on, Nick was rather surprised to see three analysts had picked up chatter about a probable terrorist attack against the Scottish people.

But it had been buried.

Now Nick had worked for MI5 for twenty years, he had stopped assassination attempts, he had protected the Welsh, English and Scots from various threats. Nick had never really done much for the Northern Irish but that was just because he had never got those cases. And never in those twenty years and hundreds of cases had Nick ever seen a terrorist attack getting buried.

And it was even worse that the disappeared file had implicated a Supreme Court Justice as one of the people supporting the terror attack.

Nick mentioned it to his supervisor of course, but she dismissed it as him making things up and when Nick went back to his computer the file and report and all remaining evidence of the plot had disappeared.

Nick was just grateful to have a photographic memory so he knew that the source of the chatter was a Supreme Court Justice and that's where things got very complicated apparently according to his Scottish-hating, English Patriotic work "friend" George Ashley.

Apparently MI5 was never going to contact or interview a Supreme Court Justice no matter if terrorist chatter mentioned them as a source, the donator to the terrorists or even helping the terrorists in any material way. All of that was of course illegal but apparently no one at MI5 actually cared about that.

Nick wasn't going to say to anyone outright that his boss and work "friends" at MI5 were trying to cover up something or play down the threat because they would rather deal with a more "important" threat, but he was certainly wanting to.

And at the end of the day, what were a few Scottish lives compared to English ones?

Nothing.

Nick really wanted the Supreme Court Justice to turn up to the library soon because Nick just wanted to get to the truth.

Whatever it was.

***

Michael had no idea his life would be changed for the better today.

MI5 Intelligence Officer Michael Ratlings went into the library that was reserved for only the finest civil servants, other governmental workers and lawyers in all of London. It was just amazing to Michael how massive this place was, of course it was a complete waste of space, money and manpower because Michael had no idea why these people couldn't use public libraries, instead of sapping public money away from more important things. Like hospitals.

But that was life.

Michael had to admit that the library did have beautifully long bookshelves that stretched right up to the ceiling and seemed to go back tens of metres. When he had been in law school he would have loved to have a library like this one, especially as this particular library had a copy of every single government Act that the UK Parliament had ever passed.

That was a lot of legal knowledge, power and resources in one place. And Michael really would have loved this when he was younger.

There was a small group of very young men and women standing over a massive ancient book, dressed in black trousers, shoes and very flattening dresses, and they were gasping about the content and everything. That was a great thing to see and Michael actually smiled at it.

After working as an intelligence officer for over twenty years, it was amazing to see that the youth of today were still interested in learning, growing and reading as much as he had been when Michael was that young.

Even the smell of the library was sensational with the musty smell of real books but he definitely didn't like the scents of cloves, coffee and other spices from people's aftershaves and perfumes. That was just wrong and it felt like they were invading the precious library space.

As much as Michael wanted to stay and look and read at all the books in the library, Michael had a job to do because he had to stop a rogue MI5 agent from doing something stupid.

Nick Blackford had gone rogue today after deleting important terrorist files that would help protect the UK Government and UK Prime Minister. Michael's bosses had already told him that Nick was an extremist that had already infiltrated the very top levels of UK government security.

And that was just typical of Scots.

Michael didn't have anything against Scottish people but most of them were bat crap crazy. Because Michael just couldn't understand why the nutters wanted independence from the UK, the UK might not have been a powerful country anymore, had massive political problems and was entering a massive recession, but to breakaway was stupid.

The Scots had joined the United Kingdom 400 years ago and there was no reason to change that.

But clearly this particular nutter didn't agree, so if what his bosses said was true then this Nick Blackford was going to assassinate a Supreme Court Justice, which made sense because the UK Supreme Court Justice was set to make a legal ruling tomorrow saying if the nutters could have yet another referendum on Independence.

Michael slowly started to make his way through the library, passing aisle of bookshelves after bookshelves. There were so many people inside the library with their different business clothes that it was impossible to see who was who.

But Nick Blackford was hunting down a Supreme Court Justice so that was who Michael had to find. He couldn't let the terrorist kill an innocent person and it was a terribly kept secret that all Justices loved erotica.

So Michael went over to the Erotica section and... oh, Michael realised he was in a lot of trouble.

Michael's heart pounded faster. Michael tripped over a little. Michael's throat was as dry as a desert.

All of this morning Michael had studied every single little piece of information about Nick Blackford, and Michael had looked at his picture plenty of times, but to actually see Nick Blackford in the flesh that was unreal.

Nick Blackford was just standing there reading a book in a long sexy black overcoat that made him look so stunningly beautiful. He was wearing a very well-fitting black suit underneath it that made Michael know that he was extremely fit and not packing a gun.

But he was certainly packing a lot of other goodness.

Michael bit his lip because it was just a shame that the terrorists were always the hot ones.

And this terrorist needed to be dealt with just like all the others.

Michael carefully took out his pistol, went over to Nick and forced the pistol into his side.

And this just felt so so wrong.

**

"Don't move," a man said.

Now Nick had been tortured by Russians in London, the Chinese in Wales and even some extreme versions of the Irish Republic Army in Birmingham, but never ever had been he been held at gunpoint in the middle of a semi-private library in the heart of London with three civil servants just next to him.

It was clear as day that this man was MI5 so Nick was a lot more interested in what lies this man had been told about him and what he was up to. Nick knew he shouldn't have taken a day off work to go hunting on this project but he was never going to let hurt innocent people, regardless of their nationality, to be hurt.

Even if the English wanted that to protect their own.

"Don't move," the man said again as Nick put his book down back on the shelf behind him.

Nick really looked at the man and he was hot, that was a definite truth. Nick really liked the man's strong sexy jawline, smooth radiant skin and the man was tall, seriously tall.

Nick had had a lot of boyfriends in the past, some Scottish, some French and some English. But they had never been this tall before, the man had to be at least 7 foot tall and he was seriously hot because of it.

And judging by the man's accent he was certainly from around London, and whilst Nick had lost his accent and Scottish dialect because it was the only way to make the English and MI5 take you seriously, Nick just knew that he had to be extremely careful.

"What lies did they tell about me?" Nick asked.

The hot man grinned a little, a very cute one at that. "They didn't lie. It is you that have lied you Scottish terrorist. You are a threat to the UK and I will not let you kill the Justice,"

It was amazing how much of an open book this MI5 hot man was. Clearly he didn't like the Scottish that much was clear from his voice, clearly he thought Nick was a terrorist and that the Justice was an innocent person which made sense because of the rigged ruling tomorrow but Nick couldn't understand why his bosses at MI5 would lie.

"Listen mate," Nick said, "I am not a terrorist. Yesterday I found a buried terrorist attack report saying that Scottish people would be bombed. I told my supervisor and she dismissed it. I go back to my office and the report is missing,"

The hot man laughed and as annoying as the laughter was, there was just something rather magical about it. And Nick really wanted to listen to it again.

"Liar. MI5 doesn't bury terrorist attack reports and I've already searched the databases and your computer for this so-called report. It isn't there,"

Nick hated the feeling of the gun pressing harder against him.

"You are a liar and a terrorist. Come with me or I will have to deal with you in front of these people," the hot man said.

Nick looked around and the three civil servants were all together now flicking through some new erotica title. They didn't even seem to be interested in what was going on here.

Nick had to protect them. If this hot man fired and he missed then those people could get hurt.

"How about I prove it to you?" Nick asked. "You said you've gone through my computers right?"

The hot man sneered and nodded.

"Then did you find a computer file by the case number of #20221109ab?"

Nick loved it how the hot man didn't look sure or anything. "And you also would have searched and gone through all my previous cases to get a sense of the man I am?"

The hot man nodded. "You are still a Scottish terrorist,"

All Nick wanted in that moment was to really shout at this sexy man that he wasn't a terrorist but he also really wanted to look at this hottie's beautiful ocean-blue eyes.

It was a silly thing to want but if Nick was about to be arrested for a crime he didn't commit then he at least wanted to remember this hottie.

"Look me in the eye and answer me this, with all my experience, decades of service and all the English people I have protected. Do you seriously think I'm a terrorist?"

When Nick noticed the three civil servants looking at him now Nick just knew that if he didn't convince this hot man that he was innocent sooner or later then he was done for.

And so many innocent people would die in that terrorist attack.

***

Michael had to flat out give it to this Nick Blackford, not only was he extremely hot and sexy but he was also very, very good at making good points. And he actually didn't dare look into his beautiful whiskey-coloured eyes.

And Nick sadly had a great point.

Michael had spent hours reading, rereading and really trying to understand how Nick's mind worked, and besides from him being a Scottish Nationalist he didn't seem like a bad person.

In his spare time, Nick liked to donate his time to children hospitals where he would read stories to the sick children, he would also do charity fun runs and he would spend a lot of time posting on social media things in favour of Scottish Independence.

Normally Michael hated any man that wasn't local because it just made relationships really hard and Michael wasn't into gay hook-up culture, but Nick was beautiful and Michael's stomach filled with butterflies.

There was something more to this beautiful man than met the eye.

And now Michael was really thinking about it, some of the things made sense. Like it was unfair the Scots were forced into Brexit against their will, they didn't have a right to do whatever they wanted even if the UK Government was doing something stupid and they were always a slave to England.

But Michael wasn't going to let this hot sexy man interfere with his mission.

He had a job to do.

"I won't allow you to influence me," Michael said focusing on Nick's chest that was actually a mistake because his black suit made his chest seem very seductive and muscular.

Nick laughed. "Why am I influencing you? I just don't want to get arrested over some lies from MI5. And you haven't answered my question?"

Damn it. Michael really wasn't sure about Nick. He was hot and beautiful and his service record was amazing but his bosses didn't lie to him.

"Excuse gents," an elderly man said and out of instinct Michael hid the gun by his side but the elderly man wearing the long red cloak of the Supreme Court Justices kept looking at him.

Michael let instinct take over and he kissed Nick.

Michael moaned a damn slight louder than he meant to as he was shocked at how large, soft and delicious Nick's lips were.

Out of the corner of his eye, Michael watched the Justice smile to himself and he went to over to the erotica bookshelf.

Michael broke the kiss and just looked at Nick. He looked so adorable with his big wide eyes, cute little grin and his amazing black-suited body.

"You don't think I'm a terrorist?" Nick asked.

Michael stomped his feet gently on the ground. "Damn you. I don't think anything at the moment but tell me what you were apparently going to do to the Justice if you aren't a terrorist,"

"I am not a terrorist," Nick said.

Michael shrugged like he didn't believe him but that sort of felt like a massive lie to him. Michael had hunted hundreds of terrorists on UK soil for the past twenty years and sadly Nick just didn't feel like one.

Michael tensed a little as Nick got out a very small black device that Michael knew was a phone-cloner and he turned it on.

"I was going to clone the Justice's phone and leave. That's the truth," Nick said.

Michael wasn't sure if he believed him but Michael took the cloner off Nick. "I'll make you a deal. If you agree not to run off or commit any terror offences, I will clone the Justice's phone and we will review the data together,"

Beautiful Nick didn't exactly look sure but Michael really wanted him to take the deal because it would still allow Michael to spend time with him (and he only wanted to do that to keep the criminal in sight, of course) and hopefully Michael could learn a little more about this utterly beautiful man.

"Fine," Nick said.

It took every little gram of willpower that Michael had not to jump up and down in the air. But he didn't want to look stupid and he also didn't want the Justice to be scared away.

Michael went off.

He had a phone to clone and a beautiful man to get to know a little better.

***

Nick seriously hadn't expected to basically be a prisoner in all-but-name and standing at the very beautiful fake-marble kitchen island in the middle of Michael's flat. Nick had to admit that the flat was stunning and it felt so nice to be in Michael's flat with its massive black sofas and armchairs, very modern and cosy kitchen and the very impressive wine collection.

Nick had only heard of some of the wine brands that Michael had, let alone actually seen them in real life. He might have been Scottish but Nick did love a good glass of wine.

Michael had set up his very secure laptop on the kitchen island and Nick stood behind the hot man that he was falling for more and more with each passing moment.

"I'm just sorting through the data now," Michael said.

Nick was surprised at how well Michael was taking this, Nick was fairly sure he would be dead or in handcuffs by now because Michael seemed to be the sort of intelligence officer that followed orders without thinking about them.

Nick had no problem with those sort of officers but sometimes orders and intelligence needed to be questioned because it was the right thing to do and it needed to be.

And Nick seriously hoped that the information they got from the Justice's phone would be good.

At the very least it would buy Nick a little more time to make a decision about what he needed to be and maybe, just maybe it would convince Michael that he was innocent.

But he wasn't holding his hopes up very high.

As beautiful, sexy and hot as Michael was, he was an Intelligence Officer first and foremost and Nick just had the sense that he always followed orders no matter what or if they were right.

So Nick was half-planning on how to make a good escape.

"Here," Michael said. "I think this is what you were looking for,"

Nick leant over hot Michael and got so close to him that Nick got to feel hard Michael's perfect body was and Michael pressed slightly against him.

"You shouldn't be doing that," Michael said seductively.

"You shouldn't be letting me," Nick said resting his head on Michael's shoulder.

Then Nick realised that Michael was showing him the recent call logs and bank transfers from the Justice's banking app to a number of international accounts.

Of course there was nothing strange about that at all but considering all the transactions were to countries and accounts that were hostile to the UK that seemed just a tat weird.

"Running the accounts now," Michael said as his laptop screen changed to show a map of the world with dots flying all over the screen.

Nick was impressed that Michael's first thought had been to

track the endpoint of the money and not the account name itself. That was a great idea that Nick wouldn't have thought of alone.

It was times like that Nick really loved working with other officers.

"Why go out on your own?" Michael asked.

Nick was expecting to get a lecture on protocol, rules and all the other stuff that he really didn't care about when innocent lives were at stake. But there was just something in Michael's stunning eyes that made him realise Michael was asking about *his* reasons.

Michael actually seemed to care about what *Nick* wanted and that was rare in Nick's life.

"Because I joined MI5 twenty years ago to help protect innocent people. At the time I didn't care about protecting the Union, Scotland or any single country or government. I only cared about protecting the innocent,"

Michael slowly nodded. "And now?"

Nick laughed because to him the answer was clear as day. "And now all I want in the entire world is for every single innocent person to be safe at night,"

Michael's mouth dropped.

"None of us in Scotland give two craps about nationality. I don't care if a person is Afghan, French, Albanian or any of the other nationalities around the world that the English propaganda tries to make out are evil."

Michael actually seemed lost for words.

"I only care that innocent people are safe. That is what twenty years of intelligence work has taught me," Nick said.

"Thank you," Michael said still looking shocked.

Nick shrugged. "That was nothing. It was the truth,"

Michael rubbed his forehead. "I know it was. I just wanted to hear and, I just wanted to hear something refreshing and someone remind me why I joined,"

Nick nodded because it was great to see that Michael was the great and wonderful man that he had pegged him for.

Michael's laptop beeped.

Nick just laughed hard when he looked at the laptop and saw all the money that the Justice had sent out had all returned to the UK. And eight other names popped up including three very high-up people in MI5, two Justices in the UK's Supreme Court and some other people that made Nick's stomach twist.

Nick just couldn't believe how far this corruption spread and it was flat outrageous that a Justice was involved with such criminal activity.

This is not what Nick wanted at all.

"We have to report this," Nick said. "We have to get these people arrested and the terrorists stopped,"

Michael shook his head and double-checked the Justice's messages and Nick laughed again.

He could read every single message between the Justice and his and Michael's bosses at MI5 as they all showed the Justice instructed his bosses to bury the terrorist chatter and get rid of whoever found it, if it was ever found.

"Okay," Michael said standing up and grinning. "I believe you,"

Nick threw his arms up in the air. "So only now you believe me. I have always been honest with you,"

Michael grinned like a little schoolboy at Nick. "I know but this is proof. You won't go to jail or die,"

"Why the hell do you care?" Nick asked.

Michael hugged him. "Because it means I can ask you out!"

Nick just broke the hug and just looked at Michael. Nick had been asked out before by a rather varied range of hot men but none of them had ever asked him out quite like this before.

"So we just met, you threatened me with terrorism charges and now you're asking me out," Nick said.

Michael hissed a little as he probably realised how weird that sounded.

"I'll think about it," Nick said. "Let's just expose this corruption,"

Nick went to grab the laptop when Michael put his hands in Nick's. "Actually you might be Scottish and you might have different ways, but these people are English targets. So we're going to treat them the English way,"

Nick just shook his head because Scotland was all about justice, peace and doing what was ethical. And if his time in England had taught him anything, it was that those rules didn't apply to the rich and powerful.

And all the 8 people identified were very rich and extremely powerful.

***

Michael was extremely glad when hot beautiful Nick had agreed to his idea about confronting their former boss. And after they had both showered (sadly not together), Michael was seriously amazed at how sexy Nick looked in a crisp white shirt, black jeans and black shoes.

It was definitely taking every single gram of willpower Michael had not to ask Nick to have sex with him right there and then.

"What do I owe this pleasure?" a woman asked wearing a very tight and ill-fitting black business dress and thick black glasses.

Michael, with sexy Nick behind him, went into a very small but posh office with great brown walls, a glass cabinet filled with whiskey to the left and a very dusty bookshelf to the right.

"I see you got me the terrorist," she said.

Michael just smiled as he took out his laptop and placed it in front of his boss.

"Now, what is this?" she asked.

"This," Nick said failing to hide the anger in his voice but that only made him cuter. "Is proof that you were paid a lot of money by a Supreme Court Justice,"

Michael's boss nodded like this was nothing new.

"And these," Michael said, "are the messages between you and the same Justice to bury a terrorist report and frame whoever found it,"

Michael loved seeing the flash of concern dance across his boss's face.

"This is very interest but-" she said.

"But nothing," Michael said. "This is proof and we know 7 other people were paid the same amount,"

The woman got up and went over to her glass cabinet, studying it like this was her last ever drink choice.

"We know these are all extremely powerful people," Michael said, "and I have convinced Nick here to not attack you if you agree to do something most English with us,"

The woman turned and grinned at Michael. "You want to make a deal with me so I am innocent and the other 7 people and the Supreme Court Justice are found guilty,"

Michael hated hearing Nick hiss behind him. It was completely wrong that their boss was going to get away with everything but this was the only way.

"Yes," Michael said. "It would be too impossible for my liking to investigate and find evidence of all of your corruption and your corrupt friends. So you give us the evidence, they get arrested and charged and you walk,"

The woman went back over to her desk and sat perfectly straight because she knew she was in full control of the situation.

Michael leant on the desk and tried to look as scary as he possibly could. "And you drop any hate against Nick and no terror attack against the Scots,"

The woman laughed. "Oh darling Michael, his punishment will come tomorrow and hell, all of Scotland will be punished tomorrow so my hate is meaningless,"

Michael really didn't want to know what she meant by that.

"I agree to your terms and I will get the arrest warrants for everyone and the evidence into MI5 custody, anomalously of course, by the end of the day. You have my word and I promise you both I will not come after you for this,"

Michael just shook his head. "Only because you'll get a

promotion or two out of this,"

The woman grinned again as she left her office and Michael just hoped that she would stick to her word but as Nick had explained plenty of times over on the way here, when it came to the rich and powerful they only kept their word when they got even richer.

Nick came up behind Michael and hugged him. "You didn't have to do that. There were other ways,"

Michael turned around and smiled at the beautiful man and his lips that were only a few centimetres away.

"Maybe," Michael said, "but sometimes you need to make deals with the devil. The UK functions on corrupt deal after deal. If we arrested every corrupt person in the UK then there wouldn't be a government left,"

Nick weakly smiled. "I know and that's what my country wants to change,"

Michael laughed at himself because if Nick had said that a few hours ago he might have gotten defensive and moaned at Nick for being silly but now, but now he actually wanted to hear more and just understand Nick a little more.

Definitely not for political reasons because Michael doubted he would ever believe in the same things as Nick, but because Nick was a beautiful, clever man that had really grown on him the past few hours.

And after twenty years of intelligence work, Michael would have liked to believe he was great at knowing what people were like, the sort of person they were and if he could trust them with his life.

Michael wouldn't trust a single person at MI5 but he would trust Nick. The beautiful, hot, clever man that he was seriously falling for.

And a very beautiful man that Michael didn't want to say goodbye to just yet.

"Let me buy you a drink," Michael said.

***

Nick never ever would have imagined last night being quite as magical, perfect and spellbinding as it had been when Michael had taken him out for the most wonderful dinner he had ever had. They went for French food at a local posh restaurant, where they had laughed, joked and had amazing fun.

Then they had gone to some dance clubs and kissed a little and really had some fun last night.

Nick stood in front of a large glass window in Michael's bedroom with hot sexy Michael still in bed empty behind him. Nick had to admit that Michael had a sensational flat and a very nice bedroom with black silk bedsheets, very supportive pillows and a built-in wardrobe.

The morning air was crisp, cold and cosy. Nick was really looking forward to when Michael woke up because Nick wouldn't mind a round two after last night and it would just be great to chat more.

In his past relationships Nick had never really been one for talking because he had never been able to talk about work, his missions and his kills before, but this time was different.

All last night and when they been feeling together, Nick had had the strangest feeling in the world and Nick was only realising now what it was. It was the feeling that being with Michael was very natural to him.

When they were at dinner, the dance club and even in bed, there had never been an awkward silence, a moment of boredom and everything just went so smoothly. Nick had never had that with a man before, there had always been strange moments that killed the mood because conversations stopped or something.

With Michael that never happened.

Nick looked at Michael as he started stirring, they both blew each other a kiss and then Michael checked his phone a little. Nick was hoping he would confirm that their boss did do as she said she would, because Nick had only checked the Supreme Court's ruling on the independence case. Which of course they rejected, the precious Union wasn't going to let Scotland go without a fight.

But Scotland would be free one day that was a promise.

"She did it," Michael said as he got up in only his pink boxers that somehow managed to make him look even hotter.

Nick kissed him and Michael just looked into his eyes with an expression that wasn't quite sad or happy, it was something in-between.

"What?" Nick asked.

Michael kissed Nick again. "I don't know. I like you. I like you a lot but is this going to work? We don't agree with politics, we don't agree on backroom deals and we don't agree on-"

Nick just kissed him. "I believe in this. I have never felt as good with a man as I have with you. I want to see exactly where this relationship goes because I know it will go far,"

Both men smiled like teenage boys at each other and Nick kissed Michael again and again. Then Nick pushed Michael away gently when he started getting a little too excited.

"But if you really doubt any of this relationship then I'll know. We both have to go to work today and tackle a new case," Nick said.

Michael nodded.

"So I'm going to take a shower and if you want this relationship then join me. If you don't, go to work and I'll know what I mean to you," Nick said.

As soon as Nick said the words he wanted to take it all back because he didn't want to give Michael an excuse not to come with him. He wanted, needed a relationship with Michael more than anything else in the world.

Nick would have happily given up being an intelligence officer if it meant spending another day with Michael.

That was exactly how much he cared about Michael.

"Okay," Michael said weakly smiling.

Nick went off to the shower and closed the shower door, stripped down and started having a shower. He really wanted Michael to join him and he seriously wanted their relationship to last forever but he knew there was a minor chance that it wouldn't happen.

Moments later the shower door opened and Nick felt two very

strong manly arms wrap around him and beautiful lips started kissing his back.

And Nick immediately knew that their relationship was going to be fine, would probably last forever and Michael was just as into Nick as he was into him.

Nick and Michael were late to work after a quick round two. And that was perfectly fine with both of them because they would both always love, protect and treasure each other for the rest of their lives.

DEMOCRACY WORKS

MI5 Officer Finley Boddy had always loved how amazing democracy was. It gave the amazing, wonderful people of a country the chance to have their say, choose their leaders and actually have an input into how they wanted their rulers to impact their lives. It was just such an amazing way to run a country and Finley seriously felt sorry for any country unfortunate enough not to have their absolutely brilliant governance system.

And Finley was going to do anything in his power to keep UK democracy working.

Finley sat in his little black car with the heating on full blast to keep himself warm and toasty and ready for action. He had parked his little car on a long wide road filled with potholes, broken street lamps and overflowing rubbish bins, but Finley wouldn't have it any other way.

As he looked at all the abandoned warehouses that lined the road with their wire fences rusting away and getting broken into more times than not, Finley was so excited to be here.

The road thankfully wasn't completely empty as there were about ten other cars parked on the road but all of those had smashed windscreens, stolen hubcaps and some even had their cars stolen. Yet that was all good because at least it sort of gave Finley a little bit more camouflage in case anyone in those warehouses and so-called abandoned factories saw him.

Tonight was a perfect night for intelligence work with it being pitch black, icy cold and there was no one about. Finley could probably run, dance and scream down the road without anyone paying attention to him or even noticing he was here.

But that was too much of a risk.

Finley might have preferred to be at the gym tonight working on his body (to make sure he had the strength required for his job, not for vanity reasons) but he had had a leg day yesterday, or maybe he could have been working on his amateur gymnastic routines which he was amazingly good at, or maybe he could have gone to some gay clubs in London or Kent to meet a cute boy.

But he loved intelligence work and democracy far too much for any of that to stop him coming out tonight.

And Finley was really glad that his vegan chia latte was sending beautiful hints of cinnamon, bitter coffee and sweet sugary scents into the air and it made the delightful taste of cookie form on his tongue. It was so nice to smell something good for a change considering how bad the car stunk when MI5 had first given it to him.

It was so cold outside that Finley was surprised that the little black car that MI5 had given him for this mission hadn't frozen or failed to start because it was so icy. Finley had been concerned about the engine coolant getting frozen but he had to admit that MI5 was better than that.

Even the icy cold silence of the road Finley was watching was a great change from all the constant noise, chaos and business of London and the other cities that Finley normally worked in.

But Finley just couldn't help but feel this was nothing more than the calming silence before the storm.

And Finley was so excited about this mission because it combined everything he loved about the UK.

Because with there being a general election tomorrow to decide who would be the next Prime Minister for the next four years (or matter of weeks as that was the trend these days) MI5, 6 and all the other UK intelligence agencies weren't officially allowed to get involved in politics, but for the sake of democracy they were running a very covert op.

Finley had jumped at the chance to be here tonight because one of these warehouses was meant to be a Russian computer centre where they created fake news, uploaded it straight into the UK critical infrastructure and fed all their hate, despise and propaganda into the UK media for the people to consume.

Finley seriously hated the Russians with all of his heart because they were the massive threat to his beloved democracy and they were a threat to everything he had fought so hard to protect over the years. The Russians were just foul, disgusting and outrageous people that needed to suffer for their crimes against democracy.

Finley had been sitting in the car for about two hours now and he just couldn't get the horrible crimes out of his mind. It was too disgusting to imagine that inside one of these warehouses, the Russians were doing such awful things to his democracy and chances are the current government would stay in power.

And Finley fully respected that some in MI5 thought that was a good thing, but everyone in the intelligence community had seen the leaked documents about how much further right the government was going to move, and their new election campaign promised three simple things.

The repealing of gay rights, repealing benefits and giving all illegal immigrants a life sentence of hard labour.

Of course under international law a number of these three things were illegal and Finley was just concerned about himself more than anything else. He had read plenty of stories from his fellow gay friends in other countries, he didn't want to be illegal just because he loved another man and Finley seriously hated the whole anti-immigrant stance of the UK.

Finley had checked the data recently at MI5 and it was just amazing how 84% of whoever came to the UK was legally allowed to set here because they were real immigrants and they wanted to work and pay tax. But clearly politicians didn't like data and real numbers but that was why this mission was so important.

Because so many lives, lifestyles and democracy itself rested on Finley helping to make sure the current government failed.

And Finley seriously didn't want to be illegal like all those that came before him had to suffer through.

***

Private Security Contractor and Former GCHQ Officer Hunter Muffin was so glad to finally be rid of bloody GCHQ, the UK's version of the US's NSA, because during the five years he had loyally worked for them, he had seen so many attacks, cyberattacks and disinformation campaigns than he ever cared to think about, and all GCHQ could do was sit on their backsides and protect the UK through computer work. Which was extremely useful and Hunter loved his fellow geeks for that but sometimes action and gunfights needed to happen to really protect the UK.

And Hunter was just glad he could do it.

Hunter stood on the edge of an icy cold alley with dirty brick walls either side of him with ripped down posters of something or another and bins were overflowing but he was more than glad the alley didn't smell at all.

In fact Hunter had made sure he had picked a hiding spot that didn't smell awful, and at least the air was damp, crisp and almost refreshing instead of smelly. That was something Hunter really didn't want to have to deal with.

Out ahead of Hunter was a long dark road that was mostly illuminated only by the moonlight as all the streetlamps, that were an even ten metres apart, on road were broken and he wouldn't have been surprised in the local council had cut the power to this area years ago, maybe even a decade. That was how unloved the area looked.

Thankfully with the rather wonderful moon being full tonight, it gave Hunter plenty of light to study his surroundings and formulate a plan. All Hunter could focus on was the massive rusting warehouse in front of him because that was his target.

The warehouse from the outside looked to be completely rusted and wrecked with massive chunks of the metal cladding on the outside being torn away in the wind, rain and the roof hardly looked any better.

But Hunter had seen people coming and going for days and nights and even takeaway deliverers (which Hunter had posed as) were receiving plenty of orders. When Hunter had been inside, he was surprised to see that everyone was English in the warehouse and it hardly seemed like any foreign powers were involved, that was surprising considering it was almost always Russia who was behind these sort of misinformation campaigns.

Hunter hated the silence of the road. It wasn't natural and Hunter seriously preferred the nosiness of London and the other cities that his private contractor firm had sent him to, Canterbury in the south of England was probably his favourite but the silence here was just annoying.

The only good thing about the silence was that at least he could be able to hear if anyone was sneaking up on him.

Hunter edged forward slightly and focused for a moment on the eleven cars that were parked on the road. Normally he would have been glad to see so many parked cars with broken windscreens, stolen hubcaps and some had stolen wheels but Hunter knew that a car had joined this lot since yesterday.

And that was so annoying and very dangerous.

Hunter already hated the people inside this warehouse enough because they were trying to divide democracy, people and keep the ever-moving-further-right government in power. Something he seriously didn't want as the government was coming after gay rights next then ethnic minorities and then women.

It was just utterly pathetic that even in the 21st century people still believed that the morals and laws of the 19th century were still perfectly okay and we had to return to them to protect the "fabric" of society, whatever the fuck that meant.

But Hunter didn't entirely blame the politicians for this mess.

Hunter really blamed democracy for it all because whilst it was always far, far better than the alternative of a dictatorship. Democracy was far from perfect because to Hunter it just seemed like people were choosing politicians over their personality and how outrageous they were. Instead of what was right for themselves, their families and the country.

Maybe it had always been like that but Hunter just hated how people were voting for politicians who wanted to destroy groups just because they were white, straight, rich and powerful.

Hunter shook his head because he couldn't focus on his mild distaste for democracy because there was a mission to do, a country to save and a disinformation campaign to stop.

A car door slammed shut.

Hunter crouched down and focused on the long line of cars that were parked on the road. He saw a man start to walk towards him but the moonlight was far too poor to let Hunter see his face.

Hunter was going to have to grab him. If it was an innocent person then Hunter would just let them go, if it was an enemy Hunter would knock him out and arrest him later and if it was another UK intelligence agency, then Hunter really didn't know what he would do.

As far as Hunter was concerned all the UK intelligence agencies were as weak as each other when it came to protecting the UK's integrity. All the agencies knew the challenges and risks and dangers the government posed to the UK but because they were "elected" no one wanted to do anything about it.

Yet another drawback of democracy.

Hunter stood up and pressed his back against the icy cold brick wall of the alley and waited for the person to walk past.

Hunter heard the man's footsteps get closer.

The man walked past.

Hunter grabbed him. Slamming the man against the wall. Covering his mouth with his hands.

Hunter slammed his arm against the man's throat and looked at the... wow.

The man Hunter was currently pinning against the wall was actually really beautiful, gorgeous and damn well attractive. The man was wearing a very well-fitting black overcoat that highlighted how fit, sexy and toned he was and Hunter was so tempted to give him a little pad down to cop a feel, but he forced himself not to.

The gorgeous man also looked so cute with his smooth white face, pointy chin that only seemed to make him seem even cuter and it was actually like the gorgeous man's face was a perfect seductive blend of masculinity and femininity.

That perfectly seductive blend was only accented wonderfully by the man's longish black hair that was going curly and cute and really made the man seem so innocent.

Hunter accidentally kneed the gorgeous man and he instantly felt the cold hard impression of a gun at the man's waist.

Now Hunter was just wondering why the hell was such a cute man creeping about abandoned warehouses with a gun late at night?

And whatever the answer was it just concerned Hunter a lot more than he ever wanted to admit.

***

Finley actually had no problem whatsoever with being thrown about by cute sexy men, it was something that his ex-boyfriends had done plenty of times before but there was just something about this man that seriously captured Finley's imagination.

Finley was even a little turned-on by the fact the hot man had his arm across Finley's throat but he was pushing against it and with each passing second the pressure seemed to be getting less and less.

Even the icy coldness of the brick wall behind him and the entire dirty alley wasn't too bad and now there was a hot man involved this was nowhere as bad as it could have been.

As the hot man took his rough hand off Finley's mouth, he just smiled at the hot man because he really was hot. The man didn't look like a Russian or anyone who would want to harm wonderful democracy and he clearly wasn't the fighting type.

Finley seriously doubted he was even a real intelligence officer because Finley didn't see any indication of toned muscle judging by the outline of his skin-tight hoody, black jeans and hiking boots. There clearly wasn't any fat on the hot man's body but he wasn't muscular either, something he had learnt to expect from intelligence officers.

But Finley was a lot more interested in the hot man's handsome face with his short brown hair cut in a crewcut style that really worked on this hottie, and Finley couldn't look away from the hottie's strong jawline, round chin and very beautiful emerald eyes with little flecks of sapphire mixed in.

"Who are you?" the hottie asked like the very act of speaking was painful for him.

Finley was more than grateful his throat had dried up but he was a little annoyed that sweat was dripping off his back. He just hoped this hottie wouldn't notice.

"MI5 Finley Boddy," he said.

Damn it that was such a stupid thing to do Finley realised, he never should have identified himself and normally he never did. He especially shouldn't have said that when the hottie was still pinning him against the wall.

What the hell was this hottie doing to him?"

Thankfully the hottie released him and Finley vowed not to keep doing stupid things in front of the insanely hot man.

"I didn't think MI5 and the other agencies were bothering with this threat," the hottie said.

Finley smiled. "Some of us are even if it is illegal and outside of our remit,"

The hottie slowly nodded and Finley could tell he was a little confused but glad about him being here at the same time.

"Who are you?" Finley asked, really hoping this hottie wasn't a foreign agent or something else that would only complicate matters.

"Hunter Muffin, former GCHQ and now a private contractor," the hottie said.

Finley smiled because he had been sure this guy definitely wasn't a real intelligence officer and that really made him feel good if this man was a danger to his precious democracy then there was a good chance Finley could take him.

Finley looked over to the warehouse that he had been walking to when beautiful Hunter had grabbed him.

"There's no security on the outside," Hunter said. "I don't see any cameras and there was more than enough holes in the wire fences for us to go through,"

Finley nodded and it was clear that Hunter had been here for a while if he was able to get this much information. "How long?"

"Two days really maybe three," Hunter said. "The company I work for learnt about the threat and I was assigned to stop it before the *election*,"

Finley looked at Hunter a little more as he said *election* with such disdain.

"You don't like elections?" Finley asked knowing it was impossible for people not to like them.

Hunter laughed and Finley's heart skipped a few beats, Hunter's laughter was so sweet, beautiful and lyrical. Finley really wanted to hear it again.

"I suggest we work together on this," Hunter said. "What backup do you have or equipment?"

Finley's mouth dropped a little at how bad he felt whenever he spoke to private contractors because they always had the private money, investment and research and development departments to get all the cool gadgets.

Finley just got out his gun. "That's my backup and that's my only equipment,"

Hunter looked like he was about to laugh, which Finley wanted so badly, but Hunter only nodded his head slowly.

Now Finley felt like such an idiot again because this damn beautiful man was bringing out all of his insecurities about his work.

Smoke bombs rained down on them.

Finley heard heavy footsteps come at him.

Someone grabbed him.

Finley punched them.

He hit body armour.

Finley jumped into the air.

Kicking out his legs.

He cracked a helmet.

More people charged at him.

Finley hated the smoke.

His eyes watered.

Smoke was clawing at his throat.

Someone grabbed Finley.

Throwing him against the wall.

Finley's head slammed into it.

Finley's world went black.

**

Of all the ways how Hunter wanted to spend his night, it certainly hadn't been stripped naked and tied to a stunningly beautiful man he had only just met. Now this wouldn't have been all bad but Hunter had been tied to sexy Finley with their fronts and wayward parts touching.

Hunter had only just woken up but it was very annoying because he was seriously enjoying the breath-taking view of Finley's very toned and hot and insanely beautiful body but Hunter's wayward part was trapped against something and he was in a little bit of pain down there.

Hunter managed to look around to see there were in the middle of a massive warehouse that was easily a hundred metres long and wide and there were a group of people typing, swirling and shouting at computers around them.

"Complete the data transfer," a man with a deep voice said.

But what really concerned Hunter was that the computers the people were sitting at were all leading to hundreds if not thousands of servers and that reminded Hunter of why he had really wanted to come on the mission.

Part of GCHQ's mandate was to protect the UK's critical infrastructure and right under this warehouse was a massive superfast internet cable transferring insane amounts of data from mainland Europe to the UK and right into the heart of London.

It was clear as day as the groups of people were using these computers to pour information right into cables and feed it into the UK internet framework. And Hunter just knew if the criminals really wanted to then it wouldn't be difficult for them to feed so much data through the cables to cause an overload and cause all of the UK's internet framework and infrastructure to shut down.

As beautiful Finley started to stir, Hunter just hated these bastards for attacking them like that and risking sexy Finley's life. And why the hell these criminals had stripped them both naked was beyond him but out of the corner of his eye Hunter did manage to see their clothes in two neat piles.

"Good to see you both awake," the man with the horrible deep voice said.

Hunter smiled weakly at Finley as he woke up and Hunter laughed a little as he felt Finley's wayward parts spring to life too.

They were clearly both into each other and Hunter really wanted to ask this cutie out on a real date.

"Why strip us?" Finley asked.

"Because I like hot men," the man said, "and my workers deserve a little show after all of their hard work, and thank you for tipping me off Officer Boddy with your door slamming,"

Hunter just looked at Finley and he could tell how guilty he felt.

"What work are you doing here?" Hunter asked looking around to see if there was a way out.

"I thought you would appreciate what I'm doing Former Officer Muffin, you do hate elections, democracy and politicians after all,"

Hunter looked at Finley and he was amazed as Finley looked horrified at him and like he was the worst person in the entire world. And even though Hunter had never ever felt guilty for his views before, he felt like utter shit because the last thing he ever wanted to be was a monster in Finley's eyes.

"I don't hate democracy," Hunter said. "I just hate how people keep voting us towards damnation,"

Hunter was so glad that Finley sort of nodded.

A loud humming sound echoed around the warehouse and Hunter found him and Finley were being lifted up and turned to face the man with the deep voice.

Hunter instantly spat at the man's feet and he hated the middle-aged man with his baggy jeans, white crisp shirt and black Chelsea boots.

"I don't care why you do or don't," the man said. "I hate the UK too and that's why I keep steering it towards damnation and the best thing about it all is that you're right. The people do just keep voting for what I want them to do,"

Hunter felt Finley's sexy body shiver with fear.

"The people don't question the information they see. They don't care if politicians are honest or not. You were right the entire time Hunter. As long as people see a big personality that shouts and screams at so-called weaker people then they get their vote," the man said.

Hunter hated how this man knew exactly the point he had raised in the past to his friends and family about the failures of democracy but also the immense benefits.

"How long have you been watching me?" Hunter asked.

The man shrugged. "Maybe four years. You have given me a lot of good content to frame you with,"

Hunter and Finley's eyes just widened and they both instantly understood what this idiot was planning. Hunter couldn't believe the man was going to frame him for all of it.

Then Hunter focused on all the massive computers, small groups of people and all the electronics that could possibly burst into flames and cook them both alive.

If these people were smart enough to pour fake news and

information into internet cables then it wouldn't have been hard for them to tell the computer's cooling fans to turn off. Then it could only be a matter of time before the computers caught alight and killed him and beautiful Finley in the process.

"How much longer until the data transfer is done?" the man asked.

"Done in two minutes boss. The transfer is fully automated. Can we go now?" a young woman asked.

"Of course," the man said.

He whipped out Finley's gun. Shooting all the other people in the head.

Hunter hissed. He hated he was chained up and locked in a warehouse with a madman with a gun.

"You see cuties," the man said. "I have laid out all the evidence to show that you Mr Muffin were behind the attack itself and the cyberattack that is going to cripple the opposition's computer systems and pump out so much hatred that all the stupid left-wingers and centralists will have to vote far-right because it will look like the only sane option,"

Hunter spat at this idiot again.

"And it will look like you Mr Boddy have killed all your workers to hide your tracks and all this evidence of mine will be released at the same time as the cyberattack,"

Hunter just looked at beautiful Finley. They didn't have a lot of time to escape, kill this madman and stop the cyberattack.

And that was all against the ticking clock of the computer fans being turned off and catching light.

"Before I go," the man said going over to one of the computers.

The computer exploded.

The man screamed. His face was engulfed in flames.

Seconds later his corpse slammed onto the ground.

More computers exploded. Flames roared in the distance.

Hunter and Finley had to escape now. There was no more time to mess around.

***

Hunter absolutely hated that stupid pathetic man who was so stupid that he was now nothing more than a smouldering corpse behind them.

Hunter had to escape before the burning computers cooked him and beautiful Finley alive. Or choked them to death on the toxic fumes now filling the air.

He really focused on what was tying him and Finley together. Hunter had been caught on being tied to such a beautiful guy before and that disgusting middle-aged man but now Hunter had to focus.

Their legs were tied together with rope that wasn't too thick or thin. Ideally they could snap the rope with their leg muscles but Hunter wasn't strong enough for that.

Their chests and stomachs were tied together with the same sort of rope but it was a lot thinner.

The real problem was Hunter and Finley's arms were pulled up over their heads and tied to some kind of pulley above them using very thick rope. Hunter was certain they could break that.

Another computer exploded.

The rope around their legs snapped.

"Thank God yesterday was leg day," Finley said.

Hunter wanted to kiss this hot sexy man more than anything.

"How are we gonna get rid of the stomach and chest ropes?" Hunter asked.

"You need to stay perfectly still for me," Finley said.

Hunter had no clue what Finley was talking about. More computers bursted into flames. Choking black smoke filled the warehouse.

Finley jumped up and jammed his knees against Hunter's knees and he started to move up and down.

Hunter quickly realised Finley was using his core strength to push his legs against Hunter making the rope stretch and hopefully snap.

The chest and stomach rope snapped.

"Excellent body by the way," Hunter said.

Finley grinned. "Not so bad yourself,"

Now they were free Hunter pulled his biceps to pull himself upwards so he could look at the pulley they were tied to.

The smoke was getting thicker and thicker. Hunter could barely see it.

Hunter's biceps hurt. They felt like he was being stabbed.

Hunter just didn't want to even imagine how close the cyberattack was close to launching.

"Let me," Finley said.

Hunter just watched as the beautiful man pulled himself upwards like a gymnast and wrapped his feet around the metal cable the pulley was hanging from.

Finley pulled himself up so he was artfully hanging from the metal cable and he smashed his fists into it.

Hunter dropped to the floor with a thud.

Finley screamed.

He fell to the ground.

He didn't move.

Hunter rushed over.

More computers exploded. Popped. Banged. Hunter checked Finley was breathing. He was.

Only just.

Hunter wanted to just run out of the warehouse with him.

He had to stop the cyberattack first.

The black smoke was so thick now. The roar of flames was deafening.

Hunter felt the flames lick his flesh.

Hunter went forward. He found a massive computer still working. It was showing 98% on the screen.

He rushed over to it. Hunter looked for an abort function.

There wasn't one.

The computer burst into flames. The glass screen exploded.

Shards sliced into Hunter's stomach.

He just knew that wouldn't stop the attack and get him arrested.

Hunter quickly rushed round the back of the computer. It was connected to a strange black box device with massive cables pouring out of it.

It looked like something someone would use to attach the computer to servers.

Hunter realised the servers weren't connected to the massive cable connecting Europe to London. It was the computer and the servers were feeding the information to the computer through the black box device.

Hunter went over to it. He grabbed it. It was burning hot.

He screamed in agony.

Hunter threw it to the ground.

He smashed down on it.

Shattering it.

The burning hot material melted onto his foot. He screamed.

Hunter wiped as much as he could away.

Hunter had to get out.

He charged over to Finley. Scooping him up in his arms.

Hunter rushed towards the exit.

There was no chance to find their clothes. It was too late.

As Hunter just charged as fast as he could out of the burning warehouse Hunter really hoped the cyberattack was over and most importantly the beautiful man in his arms was alive.

***

It was four hours after the polls had closed the next day so it was two o'clock in the morning as Finley sat with the most beautiful guy he had ever met before. He was so glad that he hadn't inhaled too much smoke and besides the minor burns to his body and the cuts from the fall this little incident shouldn't have any lasting impacts.

But as Finley wrapped his arms around beautiful, hot, sexy Hunter, he really hoped this little incident would have a lasting impact on both of them, as they both sat on the icy cold edge of a glass balcony in one of London's tallest buildings.

From Hunter's wonderful apartment that the balcony belonged to, Finley could see the breath-taking skyline of London with all of its skyscrapers, weird buildings and bright stunning lights that really made London so beautiful, perfect and very, very precious.

Finley could even see the River Thames coursing through the darkness below them, and it really had been a wonderful night between them both. As soon as Finley had got out of hospital, he had phoned Hunter and wanted to meet, Hunter had cooked them both the most amazing mouth-watering meal of juicy crispy vegan chicken burgers, golden chips and creamy vegan vanilla ice cream Finley had ever had. Then they had spent the entire night talking, hugging and really getting to know each other.

But they hadn't kissed, spoken about the future or even the election that was currently being counted. Because if what the madman in the warehouse had said was true about Hunter then Finley really didn't want to spoil tonight by talking about it.

Finley hugged Hunter even more and Finley loved the feeling of Hunter's thin body under his black hoodie and Finley really felt like a teenager again, that was something he hadn't felt for a long time.

And it felt utterly wonderful to have that feeling back.

"Who was that guy in the end?" Hunter asked quietly as he turned to look at Finley, and Finley really loved staring into Hunter's large adorable eyes.

"You knew I would have MI5 look him up," Finley said. "His name was Jude Griffins a former MI6 operative from the 80s and someone who learnt very quickly that the intelligence agencies of the UK were a little thick and the UK had betrayed him a total of five times and Jude had finally had enough,"

Finley really didn't want to get into the horrific details about how the UK had allowed the Iranians, North Koreans and Russians to capture Jude and torture him before they released him. but judging by Hunter's frown he ready knew or could guess what had happened.

"And then he wanted to destroy the UK and torture it like the enemy tortured him," Hunter said.

Finley just nodded because he sort of felt like Hunter wanted to make a point. "You can say it,"

Hunter smiled at him and Finley seriously couldn't get enough of his perfect smile. "I won't make me point, but why, why do you love democracy so much to the point of obsession? I like it, I do, but I accept it has massive weaknesses,"

Finley pulled Hunter closer to him. "So do I but without democracy what the hell are we? We're no better than China, Russia or the people we fight every single day to stop,"

Hunter slowly nodded.

"And I choose to believe no matter how stupid some of these governments are that get into power. Reason, rationality and hope will prevail. Like the current government, sure they will get in again but not with as much power as they did before. And that is only possible because…"

Hunter laughed his beautiful laugh again.

"Because of democracy. Some people realised this government is stupid and not serving them so they will vote for someone else,"

Hunter slowly nodded. "But how much damage will this government do before they're voted out for good? That is what I despair about,"

Finley ran his fingers through Hunter's wonderful hair and wanted so badly to kiss him. "I don't know but democracy will prevail and sooner or later they will be gone for good. Just you wait,"

Finley laughed his beautiful, sexy, lyrical laugh again and Finley's wayward parts sprung to life.

Hunter bit his lip. "I love your optimism. I like you a lot. And I seriously like your body,"

Finley shivered in delight as Hunter carefully ran his fingers down Finley's clothes and stop just short of his belly button.

"You're such a tease," Finley said getting so close to Finley that their noses touched.

"Why don't you show me some of your gymnastic skills in my bedroom and we'll see what happens from there?" Hunter asked.

Finley just kissed him.

And moaned in sheer delight and pleasure and attraction as he felt the strength and wonderful passion behind the kiss. Hunter was really into him, and Finley was seriously into Hunter.

As Finley jumped into the air, wrapped his legs round Hunter's waist and Hunter carried him off to the bedroom, Finley just knew tonight and tomorrow were going to be utterly amazing.

And he really knew that they were going to be seeing each other for a long time after tomorrow. He just had an amazing feeling.

And as much as Finley knew Hunter would hate to admit it, they only met, fell in love and were together because democracy worked and that was far from a lie.

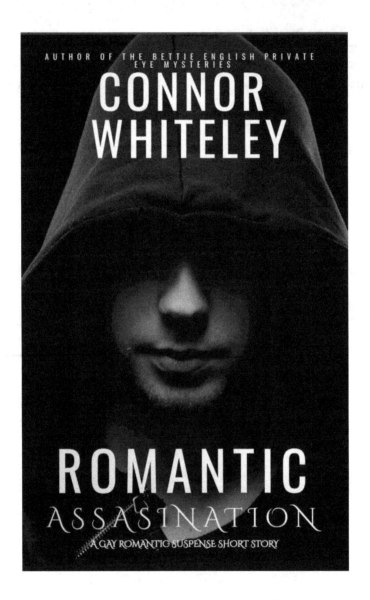

AUTHOR OF THE BETTIE ENGLISH PRIVATE
EYE MYSTERIES

CONNOR WHITELEY

ROMANTIC
ASSASINATION
A GAY ROMANTIC SUSPENSE SHORT STORY

ROMANTIC ASSASINATION

As I, Richard Birch, started to slowly walk down the long sterile white hospital corridor of Kent General Hospital (a pathetically creative name for a hospital) with little wooden fire doors lining the corridor with small and large hospital rooms shooting off from them, I had to admit that I do love a good killing.

There were tons of people walking up and down the corridor. The vast majority of them were young families, adult children and even the odd elderly person as they went to visit friends and family members in hospital. I really hoped whoever they were going to visit would be okay.

I might kill bad people but I am far from a monster.

There was a particularly hot man and woman wearing matching Easter jumpers, blue jeans and blue trainers walking down the corridor hand in hand. They were cute but it was just a shame that they were straight.

The little hospital lights in the sterile white ceiling flickered a little, then popped, banged and vibrated so some of the lights were off with a few seconds before new ones turned on.

That was just typical of hospitals in the UK at this point and I was just glad that I had more than enough money to go private at this point. Which was rather fun at the moment because even though I never used the UK's free service, I always killed politicians that wanted to tear it all down.

Like I said, I might kill people but I am no monster. Innocent people rely on free healthcare so I have to protect it.

The entire corridor smelt of jasmine, cloves and lemon-scented cleaning chemicals that were getting stronger and stronger with each passing moment, and it left the most disgusting taste of blueberry pie on my tongue because my sweet mother bless her, she just couldn't tell sugar from salt, and cloves and cinnamon.

Her cooking was absolutely awful, and somehow I survived.

With everyone talking, music playing in the background and new orders for doctors in the background, it was rather loud in the corridor but that was perfect for me as I continued to go down the corridor where I was hoping to kill a very bad woman indeed.

I only had to kill her in secret.

And not get caught.

You see when someone pays me three million pounds to kill a Mrs Clarice Zouch, I do three simple things. I donate one million to the hospital that I'm about to kill at, I donate another one million to my favourite cancer research charity and I do a hell of a lot of research on the target to make sure she actually deserves to die. Because believe in me, I get hired ten times a year to kill school teachers at private schools because the snobby nobs called parents wanted to punish the teacher for failing their precious little teenagers.

Maybe if the little teenagers actually tried at school and didn't grow up thinking mummy and daddy will always provide for them, then maybe they wouldn't fail.

Anyway, sorry about that, I just hate those snobby nobs.

Clarice was not a school teacher in the slightest because she had run a UK-wide human trafficking organisation that smuggled vulnerable men into the country with the promise of shelter, food and money for their families. But as soon as Clarice got them they were handcuffed and turned into slaves.

Then if one of them tried to escape or even spoke about escaping three families' would *disappear* from the face of the earth. All these people wanted was to live a better life in a "good" country (but I couldn't call the UK that for ages yet each to their own) and even though the police had thankfully shut down her organisation and destroyed her ring, and sadly deported all of the slaves, which half of them were dead now in their own countries (well done UK Government) Clarice had been clever enough to not leave any evidence of her involvement.

So she was free and in hospital after surviving a very rare form of cancer.

Well now I was going to kill her anyway.

***

Assassin Charlie Allen just sat there in the cold wooden hospital chair in Clarice's room and watched her sleep peacefully. He had always hated Clarice. She was a stuck-up bitch that prayed on the weak, vulnerable and dim-witted to the predations of her foul kind.

Charlie was a little surprised that Clarice had cared to go to a free public hospital instead of a private one with much better security. All Charlie had had to do was walk into the hospital, pretend to be her boyfriend and cry the entire way with the nurse escorting him.

Charlie didn't like the massive white sterile walls that were so lifeless and dead and dull, just like how Clarice was hopefully going to be in very short order.

Even the hospital bed that was nothing more than a thin metal thing with even thinner sheets wasn't that impressive, but maybe Clarice had wanted the secrecy and to keep a low profile. This was certainly the lowest profile Charlie had ever seen a criminal mastermind keep, but this was also just sort of sad that Clarice, the enslaver of innocence, was going to die in a small little hospital room in a backwater hospital in a backwater county that no one cared about.

At least this way Clarice wouldn't hurt another single person ever again.

The constant sound of people talking, walking and rushing about outside made Charlie pleased that even if Clarice screamed her head off there wouldn't be too much of a chance of someone hearing and rescuing her.

Charlie had already bought himself a new dagger just for the occasion and he had planned three different escape routes, so hopefully that would all work out so Charlie stood up and went over to Clarice.

Charlie had to admit he was bisexual and always tended to leant towards men, but Clarice was beautiful and very hot. Charlie would have been interested in knowing exactly how she had seduced her slaves and her criminal employees but that didn't matter now.

Charlie was going to get revenge and complete the mission that his boyfriend couldn't do six months ago when Clarice had killed him in front of CCTV cameras but the police weren't bothered. Apparently, there was no point arresting her for murder when she still hadn't revealed the extent of her network to the police.

It was disgusting but Charlie also understood it. His boyfriend was one life against the hundreds of innocent lives that were being beaten and tortured every day for Clarice's enjoyment.

Charlie took out his dagger and enjoyed the warm heavy feel of the bone handle against his hand and he went to spilt her throat when the wooden door opened and someone quickly shot inside.

Charlie just smiled like a little schoolboy when he noticed a man had come in and he was holding a gun with a silencer. The man was very tall, easily seven foot, with a long black overcoat, sexy tight black trousers and black trainers that sort of gave him the smart-casual look that Charlie really loved on people.

The man didn't seem threatening or scary towards Charlie and Charlie respected that. At least he was dealing with a pro-assassin and not some baby amateur that was going to kill him out of fear.

But all Charlie could really focus was on the man's stunning eyes. There were stunning flicks of sapphire and violet in a field of dark emeralds and that only amplified how stunning he was and how perfect the man looked, even though he looked more like a GQ model instead of an assassin.

"Can we kill the bitch together?" the sexy man asked.

Clarice woke up.

Whipping out two guns.

Aiming one at both of them.

*****

Now I have met a lot of hot sexy men in my time but this man has to top the list completely, and in fact he has to be the most beautiful person I had ever seen, and that includes a hell of a lot of men and women.

It was just a shame that I couldn't look at him too much because of stupid Clarice aiming a gun at me and the sexy man. The man was so damn cute and I was flat out not letting pathetic Clarice harm him.

And Clarice was even uglier than I ever thought possible.

"What are you two doing here?" she asked.

I just gestured the gun at her. "I'm here to shoot you and I presume he's here to stab you?"

The sexy man grinned. "I was actually going to paint the walls with her blood. I'm rather artistic like that. I'm Charlie,"

I actually couldn't believe this sexy man was seriously flirting with me over a woman that was aiming guns at our chests, but I could see what he was doing. She was clearly interested in who we were and she didn't want to kill us yet.

If she had we would have been dead the moment she woke up.

"Richard," I said, "and I have always admired the artistic killers in the industry but I just don't have the flare for it. I prefer to kill and go. How do you manage it?"

Sexy Charlie shrugged. "A person is beautiful in life so why not in death?"

Judging by Clarice's face, she was absolutely horrified about the entire conversation and that just proved that she needed to die even more because she was a philistine.

Clarice got out of her hospital bed wearing thankfully a very thick pink dressing gown and she gestured me and Charlie to stand next to each other as she waved her guns around like an amateur.

It wouldn't be hard to take her because I seriously doubted she had actually ever fired a gun before but she was still dangerous.

And she still had to die.

***

Charlie absolutely couldn't believe Clarice was wearing a very foul dressing gown that was pink of all things. Any idea, notion or thought that Clarice was remotely attractive was dead to Charlie now and all he wanted to do was kill her because she was a worthless criminal that just had to die no matter what.

And Charlie really wanted a moment to actually look at the beautiful man he felt more and more drawn to with each passing second.

"Who hired you?" Clarice asked.

Charlie shrugged. "No one. You killed my boyfriend six months ago,"

Charlie was shocked to see Richard punch the air like that was a good thing. That was so tactless of him.

"Oh damn," Richard said. "Sorry. I meant it was good you're single. Sorry about your boyfriend. Let's make her death slow and painful for that,"

"Nice safe," Charlie said, and he really couldn't believe how much he was falling for Richard. There was just something about the hot sexy way that he acted.

"Boys!" Clarice shouted.

"Your victims hired me," Richard said, but Charlie knew that was a lie.

It was clear as day that Richard was a professional so it was impossible for some former slaves to afford him.

Clarice came over to them and Charlie wanted nothing more than to snap her wrists as she pressed the cold metal barrels of her pistols against their chests. It was disgusting that she was threatening to hurt beautiful Richard.

"Liar," Clarice said, raising the gun to Richard's head.

Charlie weakly smiled because this was good and Richard really was extremely clever. If Richard could make her focus even more on him then Charlie was just hoping he could kill her before she knew what had hit her.

Then Clarice focused the gun on him.

"I know you won't tell me but I know your employer will be watching both of you," Clarice said. "And when they find your dead bodies that will serve a clear message to leave me alone,"

The wooden door opened. A nurse popped in.

Charlie charged forward.

Richard did the same.

They bumped into each other.

Nurse screamed.

Running out the door.

Clarice shot back.

Waving the gun round chaotically.

Charlie took her left.

Richard took her right.

They charged at her.

They tackled her.

Charlie snapped her wrists.

Richard snapped her legs.

Charlie grabbed his dagger. He started carving into her stomach and chest and face.

"We need to go," Richard said.

"But my boyfriend. She deserves to suffer," Charlie said.

"His memory will be useless if we're caught,"

"Go. Leave me,"

"Ha. I am not leaving you beaut. It's too rare to meet such a great assassin," Richard said.

Shouting and screaming and running filled the corridor outside and Charlie just wanted to paint the entire bloody room in Clarice's blood, muscles and flesh but sexy Richard was sadly right.

They had to go. Now.

And as Richard exploded open the door shooting as he ran with Charlie close behind him. Charlie was just amazed at how amazing Richard really was.

***

I was more than slightly impressed a few hours later as me and Charlie sat at a little wooden table under a green dark metal roof of an extension as we both wrapped our hands around each other. We were sitting at a little café on a quiet London street that was nothing more than a lot of empty sealed shops that hadn't been opened for decades and the tarmac road was filled with potholes but the little café seemed to do more than well enough to keep the lights on.

After me and Charlie had run and shot our way through the hospital, escaped and then changed clothes ten times before we came to London, I was amazed at how professional Charlie was because most of the time amateur assassins never think about changing clothes, vehicles and IDs about five to ten times before knowing the police would never ever find them.

But Charlie did know that and he was actually surprised that I didn't change clothes and locations another three times but that was a little overkill especially when the only victim was a person like Clarice.

The day had thankfully warmed up, the air smelt amazing with hints of bitter coffee, cinnamon and strawberries because of the delightful pies the café specialised in, and there wasn't a single sound in the street.

It was perfect.

Then I realised that this was the first time all day that I had actually gotten a real chance to see the stunning man I had killed someone with, saved and escaped with. Charlie was exactly my type perfectly but also so much more than a mere type.

I will never deny that I love blond boys that are fit, slim and extremely attractive. I loved how Charlie's face was so smooth and round and perfect in every way. And I was very fond of his stunningly smooth and fit body that I had thankfully gotten the privilege of seeing ten times today already.

Yet my favourite thing about Charlie just had to be *him*, it really was so breathtakingly rare to meet an assassin that was so calm, collected and professional as Charlie. I had met a few assassins over the years and they were always stupid that I had been shot trying to save them.

So I shot them instead so they wouldn't have to suffer in prison and they wouldn't reveal everything about me.

But I just knew as I stared into beautiful Charlie's eyes that I wouldn't have that problem because Charlie was perfect, smart and very attractive.

Of course, I didn't know what was going to happen tomorrow, next week or next month but I knew that just for today, me and Charlie were going to finish our coffee, go out on a real date and surely end up back at my brand new apartment bought under a fake name for some sex and fun.

And then we would see where our relationship would go tomorrow and the day after and the day after that.

But I had a very strong feeling that things were going to be perfectly fine and I was going to savour every single precious moment of this until there were no more moments to savour.

AUTHOR OF THE BETTIE ENGLISH PRIVATE EYE MYSTERIES

CONNOR WHITELEY

SAVING
MR BILLHORN

A GAY ROMANTIC SUSPENSE SHORT STORY

SAVING MR BILLHORN

Now, don't you dare get me, Norman Cole, wrong little person. I am no saint, I am not a traditionally good person and I definitely am not a "pure" person according to the religious nutters, but I get results and most importantly I actually help people. I don't sit in a stone building and pray all day hoping for some magic powder to be sprinkled down from heaven to save lives.

No. I actually go to where people need help and I get the job done. Not always legally, ethically or morally, but I bring home the person in need of help.

And before you ask, I don't really know where my attitude came from but I passed basic and advance military training with flying colours but I never ever got to serve in the military because they really didn't want some fag in their ranks, so they beat me, punished me for beating them and then well... there was a little firearms incident one night.

Of course, *I* didn't kill them, their guns killed them and since the military didn't want a fag screaming about all the discrimination he had suffered. Well, they agreed (and couldn't prove murder) to sweep it all away, I was given a pension, a payoff and I got to keep my weapons.

So now I help people.

It was an awful cold, bitter, icy late afternoon as I hid inside a large green hedgerow in the south of England watching my target red brick detached-house. It might have been damp in the hedge filled with little twigs, leaves and something that I was telling myself was a wet blanket behind me as it licked my fingers (no it wasn't a rat. I wasn't allowing myself to think that) but I needed to be one with the hedge.

The view out from the hedge was a rather wonderful garden with a square-shaped lawn that was covered in icy frost making the blades of grass look like little shiny daggers in the dying sunlight and it really did look magical.

Rows upon rows of baby apple trees, roses and other dead trees littered and lined the garden, I didn't know if the person who owned the house actually liked their garden or not. It was a classic blend of chaos and well-maintained beauty.

It was strange like that.

The air smelt of delightful lilacs, roses and wood smoke, but that had to come from the house behind me because there was no chance whatsoever that this target house was that nice to smell and it left the taste of picnics on my tongue from my childhood. Yet at least the world was silent without a twig breaking, a dog barking or even a car driving past, with any luck that also meant there would be no witnesses to me saving the poor soul I had been paid to.

The house itself was probably the oddest on the entire street because it was made completely from red brick, instead of the classic brown and yellow that made up the rest of the houses on the street, and it was the only detached house. All the others were semis and both houses either side of it were abandoned.

Of course, I couldn't say with any certainty whatsoever that the neighbours fled because of who lived in this house but it wouldn't have surprised me.

From the back garden, the house had a very nice copper-coloured pair of French doors which was perfect because they were so easy to break into. Perfect.

You see I was here because two nights ago Dorrie Billhorn contacted me requesting help to rescue her father after he had been kidnapped by drug dealers because Dorrie's young brother had become a dealer but used all the product instead of selling it, so the gang had kidnapped the father to make the son pay.

Well that was all well and good until the son, aged 22, had been stabbed ten times by a petty thief who had followed the son from the bank to a dark alley.

That was very stupid in my opinion. The son should have had an escort with the money and certainly not gone into any dark alleys but I know it was my job to help save the father from the mistakes of the son. Definitely a new phrase that I haven't heard before and I had managed to track down the father and kidnappers to this house in particular.

I always carried a pistol, a crowbar and a small black bag filled with some other goodies when I do a job because I simply never knew what I was going to need.

"Five minutes," a man said next to me.

I jumped and instantly cursed myself as I snapped a very large twig. A mistake that could kill me in most situations.

"We breach in two minutes," a man said.

I looked behind me and I was just shocked. There was a beautiful man crouching there wearing all military gear, a very hot look, leather boots and the cutest face I had ever seen. He couldn't be any older than me at 26 and he was just perfect.

His face was a little pointy, his eyes were wide and innocent, and there was just something about him. He really was just stunningly perfect, sexy and downright beautiful.

But why was he here?

I was extremely careful in covering my tracks and making sure that whatever job I was on was a secret. It couldn't be traced back to me because if I ever got caught then I was going to die, be imprisoned or I don't know.

"Who the hell are you?" I asked, very quietly.

"Former SAS," the hot man said.

I simply nodded. That meant the man was even more trained than MI6 officers, commandos and basically this hottie was the best of the best, except for the little fact that I didn't believe him. Since why the hell would a 26-year-old SAS officer simply quit or retire?

He was lying.

"Why are you former?"

The hot man grinned. "Because my boss wanted to send me and my friends into a suicide mission. We went. I was the only one that survived and I killed him because he was insane,"

My stomach churned and to my surprise it actually filled with butterflies. I fully admit that this hottie might have killed a man for bad reasons, but I just... I just sort of got the sense that he was a good person at heart like me.

And we both just do things in illegal and criminal ways to get the job done.

I carefully took out my pistol with its silencer attached and aimed it towards the house. "Why are you here?"

The hottie shrugged. "The daughter knew me from school and she told me about her father's problems and I just wanted to meet you. You certainly are cuter in person than on the daughter's phone,"

I just grinned. Maybe this hottie was smarter and hotter than I ever thought possible.

"Breach," the hottie said.

We both silently ran across the lawn.

We both went either side of the French doors. I felt the icy cold brick against my back and I aimed my gun ready to move.

There was a small stone statue next to me. I picked it up. Throwing it through the French door.

The hottie laughed.

Shouts came from inside.

I didn't dare look round to look inside the house. That would have been a death sentence.

Moments later three tall men dressed in black stepped out.

I shot two in the head. The hottie snapped one man's neck.

Three corpses laid in front of the door ready for their friends to see.

I heard two people whispering. They were getting louder and louder.

A man jumped out.

Charging at me.

He was fast.

He kicked me in the chest.

My gun flew out of my hands.

My head whacked the wall.

He punched me.

Again and again.

I blocked.

Jumping forward.

Knocking the man off balance.

The man headbutted me.

He leapt up.

Jumping into the air.

Landing my shoulders.

He wrapped his leg around me.

He squeezed.

He was choking me.

I ran backwards.

Slamming him against the wall of the house.

He screamed.

His grip tightened.

I was really choking.

I gasped the air.

I slammed myself against the wall.

He screamed.

His grip loosened.

I gripped his legs off me.

I threw him by the legs off me.

He flew through the air.

He landed gracefully.

Whipping out a gun.

He fired.

I dived to one side.

I found my gun.

I jumped up.

Shot him in the head.

A loud snap echoed through the entire street as the hottie finished up with his own kill.

I looked at the hottie and he really was beautiful. We had both just been in a terrible fight but he still looked so perfect, seductive and alluring.

There was probably so much history to him, so much past to discover and so much heart-breaking to explore. I so badly wanted to explore all of that and so much more with him because he really was stunning.

But I had to focus on the mission now because there was an innocent person that needed to be saved.

Me and the hottie went through the French doors with our guns raised and I was surprised at how wonderful the dining and living room were.

The walls were painted blood red, there was a large oak dining table in the middle of the room and then down the other end there were some sofas. I really didn't care too much about the mugs on the coffee table but if they were a reliable indicator of the enemy then there would still be two more people to kill.

But the smell was off.

I had rescued a ton of people over the years and I just knew that kidnappers always made their victims wee, poo and vomit over themselves at least once or twice before they were given bathroom privileges. That always left the smell of those things in the air and this house didn't smell like that at all.

The house was perfectly clean and sterile.

"Show yourself," I said.

I loved hearing the hottie gasp as he finally understood it as well.

A moment later a brown wooden door opened and a middle-aged man who was bruised and blackened stumbled into the living room with a pistol to his head, and a supposedly beautiful woman walked in wearing a flowery dress.

A very short flowery dress that was way too short for a cold day.

I heard three more men walk up behind us.

Damn it. This wasn't good at all.

"It seems my distraction plan worked," the daughter said.

I was about to pull my pistol on the hottie but he just shook his head and he seemed really pissed. Like this was the first time he knew that he was being set up.

"She isn't wrong," I said grinning. "You really were stunning and maybe if you weren't here I would have detected this deception sooner,"

The hottie grinned back. "She played us both. I normally pick up on things like this so… you are cute too,"

Only cute? I wanted to talk about that with him then and there but we needed to escape first.

Then the middle-aged man smiled at me and I shot him.

The daughter fell to the floor, kissing her father and checking for a pulse.

"This wasn't a kidnapping. You beat up your own father for show," I said.

The daughter slapped her father's body and stood up. "You aren't wrong. He wasn't in charge of the drug operation but we just wanted to prove a point to my idiot brother,"

The hottie stepped forward. "Let me guess you run a drug business but don't take drugs yourself?"

The daughter nodded. "None of us do. It's a condition of their employment. Drugs destroy lives, they kill people and I value my workers too much to lose them to addiction,"

I just shook my head. I actually did understand what she was saying but she was just so stupid.

I heard the three men behind us take two steps closer.

"Why bring us here?" the hottie asked.

The daughter shrugged. "Because one of my competitors was looking into hiring you both. You two are the only local and effective assassins in the business. No one else dares challenge me,"

Again I could understand that and it was good to know that I had a reputation after all the time but enough was enough.

I shot the daughter in the head.

I jumped to the ground.

Bullets screamed through the air.

I spun around on the floor.

I shot a man in the head.

The hottie hissed.

Two men shot the hottie.

The hottie fell.

He hissed.

I screamed in rage.

I leapt up.

Charging at the idiots.

Their guns were empty.

I leapt into the air.

Kicking them in the head.

One man's neck crunched.

His corpse fell.

The last man got me into a headlock.

He slammed my body against the table.

The table cracked.

He was choking me.

I struggled.

I kicked.

I punched.

Nothing worked.

I felt around his wrist. He had to have a knife or something.

The man screamed.

The hottie fired his gun.

The man's corpse dropped.

I fell to the ground with him.

I slowly got up and smiled at the really hot man that was standing right in front of me. I noticed he was wearing a bulletproof vest and I just really looked at him for a moment.

I admired his large beautiful muscles and the little veins that defined his now-exposed arms, his perfect pointy face that I wanted nothing more than to simply grab, pull closer and kiss, and I really did love his eyes. They were almost like golden whiskey-coloured beacons of light and hope and maybe love in the darkness that was the world I lived in.

It was only then that I realised that my life of hunting down bad guys, saving the innocent and living in the moment was extremely busy. The only time I really allowed myself to have enough free time to have cheap sex was around my birthday in November, how lame was that.

But for the first time in years, in a shot-up house that smelt of vapourised blood, gunshots and oak, I actually felt drawn to a beautiful and very capable man, and even better he was actually into me as well.

"Am I really only *cute*?" I asked, "especially when I said you were *hot*,"

The hottie smiled and took a few steps closer to me. He looked me up and down and smiled. "Well I like what I see and I really like the man I fought next to. We could save a lot of people together,"

I shrugged like that was something I wasn't interested in, even though I was so pretending. "We could explore a lot together too,"

I took a few steps closer to him and pulled at his bulletproof vest and he got so close to me that I felt his wonderfully warm minty-scented breath on my face. He really was so cute.

"No cops are going to come for ages," the hottie said. "We could see what the Billhorn family has in the kitchen. I'll cook and we can... get to know each other,"

I grinned like the little schoolboy I really felt like around him. "Sure but I would at least like to know your name,"

The hottie laughed. "Oh yeah sorry. My name is Hunter Crow,"

As I watched the hot sexy man walk away from me to find the kitchen (and I really focused on his wonderful ass), I simply laughed to myself because that really was the perfect name for a person who hunted down bad people and saved the innocent.

Just like me.

AUTHOR OF THE BETTIE ENGLISH PRIVATE EYE MYSTERIES

CONNOR WHITELEY

ROMANTIC THIEVES

A GAY ROMANTIC SUSPENSE SHORT STORY

ROMANTIC THIEVES

The only idea Art Thief Steve Barker could come up with to get back at his homophobic father was to rob him, steal his favourite piece of art and then burn it. Steve didn't exactly know where the idea had come from but he really, really liked it so that's exactly what he was going to do.

Steve crouched down on the cold white marble floor of his father's massive gallery with ten large pillars of polish black marble lining the walls that were filled with so much art that Steve couldn't tell what the colour of the walls actually were these days.

It had been years since Steve had spoken to his father, mother or the rest of the family. They could have decorated the gallery a thousand times without Steve ever knowing and it wasn't like any of his family tried to talk to him too, because at the end of the day, he was nothing more than a little sissy fairy boy.

The art gallery itself had hundreds of portraits and landscape paintings of countrysides, towns and famous cities and they glowed dimly in the moonlight that came into the gallery through the massive glass roof overhead. There wasn't an access point on the roof thankfully so Steve didn't need to worry about climbing down like he had originally thought and since his family never changed the passwords Steve simply walked through the front door.

Avoiding the cameras of course.

The only major difference in all the years since Steve had left was there was so many fascinating and beautiful sculptures and artefacts in glass cabinets in rows. There were little lights inside each cabinet and that only made each artefact seem even more beautiful and stunning.

The glass cabinet that Steve was crouching next to was of an absolutely stunning pair of golden sapphire earrings from mainland Europe hundreds of years ago. They were stunning and very well protected.

And Steve really didn't want to grab something that he didn't need because that only increased the risk of getting caught, something he had almost learnt the hard way as an art thief over the years.

The entire gallery was engulfed in darkness with only the small lights from the glass cabinets and the bright moonlight providing any light whatsoever, so Steve was going to have to be extremely careful but after stealing for so long it was just second nature to him.

The entire art gallery smelt of harsh cleaning chemicals with the absolutely brilliant aromas of orange, cranberry and lemons filling the air. It was such an outrageously good combination that Steve loved it, and it left the taste of Christmas cake on his tongue.

The art gallery was silent so Steve poked his head up and he just smiled at the treasure that he wanted to steal more than anything else in the entire world. He wanted to steal the portrait of him and his two brothers that his father still loved for some reason.

But something was wrong with the painting as it sat there right in the middle of the gallery on a little painting easel.

Steve always remembered how damn hot the day was when the painting was done, and Steve had been on the outside with his two brothers to his left. Now the painting that Steve had heard his father constantly talk about and show it off to visitors was missing him. His father had actually cut the painting to cut Steve literally out of it.

That was outrageous.

And now Steve was even more determined to steal the damn painting. All Steve had heard from his father before he had run away was how wonderful his two brothers were because they were straight, had wives and were going to produce the most perfect offspring imaginable.

Steve had already hacked into the security company that his father used for the art gallery and found out there was very little security in the entire gallery. The only pieces of security were in the glass cabinets, roof and walls themselves.

Steve stood up and silently started walking over to the painting.

"Hello?" an elderly man said in the distance.

Someone grabbed Steve's ankles.

Pulling him to the ground. Dragging him behind a glass cabinet and slamming a hand over his mouth.

Steve just looked at the utterly gorgeous man who had tackled him. Steve had never seen a more beautiful man in his entire life. He had broad strong manly shoulders, a very cute smile and a short blond beard.

He was extremely hot and sexy and stunningly beautiful.

But why on earth was he here?

***

Art Thief Joey Grace seriously hated when he tripped a security alarm as he was breaking into the estate. Damn those security people and their dodgy records and damn himself for not expecting it.

Joey currently laid on top of a downright sexy twink of a man that was beyond gorgeous. He was so damn hot with his long brown hair, tight black jeans and black t-shirt. He was so cute and he was so warm.

Granted Joey could have sworn he felt something long and hard almost stabbing him but he was even more surprised at how professional this man was. He wasn't struggling, making a sound or anything which was brilliant considering there was a security man coming into the art gallery as they were hiding behind a glass cabinet.

It was only a matter of time before the security man found them so there wasn't a lot of time to get the ancient Greek earrings that he needed and escape and hopefully this hottie would help.

Joey wasn't exactly sure if this hottie was friend or foe for now but he didn't have a lot of options if he didn't want to go to jail. And he just wanted to escape the disgusting aromas of cranberry, oranges and lemons, it was a foul combination.

In fact this entire damn art gallery was rather foul in a way because Joey always stalked his targets for a while before he robbed them and it was disgusting how the family spoke about a man called Steve. It seemed that the two brothers wanted to get in contact with him to make up for their parents' mistakes but the parents threatened to cut them off if they dared do that.

This entire family seemed absolutely pathetic.

But what they lacked in parenting skills they definitely more than made up for with their art tastes.

Joey slowly took his hand away from the hottie's mouth. "Art Thief Joey. After ancient Greek earrings,"

The hottie smiled. "Steve. After revenge on my father. After painting on the easel,"

"Hello? Anyone in here?" an elderly man said.

Joey watched sexy Steve silently crouch like he was a gymnast, a very hot one at that, and they both carefully watched an elderly man walk into the art gallery.

Joey was surprised the man wasn't tall, but he was carrying a Glock-17 pistol, wearing black shoes and a green bulletproof vest. He was serious.

"We need to deal with him," Joey said almost silently.

"Bigger problems. My father always told his people to get help. There's probably another ten security guards en-route,"

Damn it. Joey really liked this hottie so close to him but he had to focus on the mission and the job.

"We need to knock him out," Joey said.

"I hear you!" the elderly man said.

Joey felt Steve lean over him and it felt great to have his body so close to him.

A bullet screamed through the air.

A glass cabinet on the opposite side of the gallery shattered.

A deafening alarm went over.

"Got you?" the man said on the other side of the gallery.

Joey couldn't believe how silly this security man was but he was still a man with a gun. A gun that could and would kill them both.

"Make a distraction," Steve said.

Joey was about to protest when Steve silently ran off and pure excitement filled with Joey because Steve was clearly a very crazy, fun and clever man to be around.

And his amazing body didn't hurt either.

***

Steve was so excited as he silently ran to the other side of the art gallery, past glass cabinets filled with ancient treasures and the aromas of orange were growing even stronger now. The entire art gallery was silent except for the heavy footsteps of the elderly male security guard as he tried to hunt them down but he was certainly a bad guard.

Steve supposed that sexy Joey, who was insanely hot, had tripped an alarm or something that was definitely the sign of an amateur thief but he was hot so that sort of made up for it.

Steve's biggest problem and the thing he couldn't believe was that the stupid security guard was actually interested in shooting them. Steve knew for a fact that his father hated guns, shooting and death so it was strange that a security guard would be interested in shooting them and not tasering them.

Unless this wasn't a security guard.

Steve just couldn't believe it had taken him so long to realise this was another thief. A very armed and dangerous thief.

"Where are you two?" the armed thief asked.

Steve now couldn't understand how the man knew there was two of them. He silently crouched behind a glass cabinet as he noticed sexy Joey was standing up.

Joey went out into the middle of the art gallery and clapped his hands that echoed off the walls and Steve watched the armed thief walk up to Joey.

Thankfully the armed thief stood with his back to Steve so it would only take one single jump to hopefully take down the bad guy.

The armed thief pressed the gun against Joey's head.

"I need you to help me," the armed thief said.

"If you want help then why do you have a gun to my head?"

"Oh," the armed thief said putting the gun away. "Sorry about that I didn't know if you were a security guard or not,"

Steve really couldn't understand this now. Was this a play to make him come out of hiding?

"I need you to tell me where the father's favourite painting is? I'm the artist you see and I want it back,"

Steve stood up and went right in front of the so-called artist and Steve really looked at him.

The so-called artist was certainly older, fatter but he always did have a slight American accent and a very slight interest in guns. And there was something about the nose that reminded Steve of the artist.

"Steve?" the artist asked. "What are you doing here your father will kill you if he finds you here?"

Steve just nodded because this was definitely the artist. The only person who seemed to see Steve as something more than his sexuality.

"It's over there on the easel and I'm here to steal it to punish my father." Steve said.

"Oh," the artist said taking out his gun and aiming it at the painting.

"Wait," Steve said going over to the easel and picking up the painting, surprised by its warm and rough texture.

It was almost strange looking at a perfect painting of his two brothers again after not seeing them for so long.

Steve threw it on the ground and stomped on it. Harder and harder until it was completely destroyed and broken.

The artist laughed. "Well I was going to do the same thing so no hard feelings and I just wanted revenge for your father firing me as his personal artist,"

Steve nodded and then looked at Joey. "What were you after?"

Joey smiled as he went over to the glass cabinet towards the back of the art gallery, and Steve really enjoyed watching his ass from behind as he walked, and he smashed the glass taking out two very small and ancient earrings.

Then he smashed the one next to them but Steve couldn't see what he was stealing out of it.

"Oh," the artist said. "Before we all go, your brothers wanted me to tell you they want to talk with you. Their phone numbers are the same,"

Steve just nodded because he really wasn't sure about that but it would be great to finally have some family again after everything that had happened in recent years.

Then Steve focused on Joey as he came over to Steve and smiled. Steve's legs were weak and he was so desperate to kiss and taste Joey's big, soft beautiful lips.

The sound of police sirens in the distance echoed around the estate.

"Well then," the artist said. "Good day,"

Then he simply walked away and Steve grabbed Joey's hands and they both ran away together with both their missions done.

***

A few days later, Steve sat on a wonderfully warm wooden bench in the middle of a large abandoned park with thick green grass stretching out for tens of metres in all directions, the sound of ducks splashing in the large pond twenty metres away and the smell of nature filled the air.

It was such a beautiful day with the cloudless sky above Steve, and it had been great getting to see and caught up with his brothers again and hear how married life was treating them. There were clearly massive issues to overcome from the past but Steve was excited for the future because he might actually have a family again.

A few moments later the beautiful smell of sexy spiced aftershave filled the air and a strong manly arm wrapped round Steve as Joey sat down next to him. Steve seriously loved the feeling of Joey's firm, hard, warm body against him and Steve kissed Joey's large and wonderful lips.

Since they had escaped into the night together after the theft, they had walked around for hours talking, exploring each other's bodies and really getting to know each other. Steve was surprised that Joey wasn't as much of an amateur as he feared him to be, he had a delightful sense of humour and every moment with Joey just felt so preciously wonderful that Steve never ever wanted their time together to end.

Steve was even starting to think he was falling in love with Joey, but as his dick of a father used to say, when someone meets the right person they just know, and sadly his father might be right.

Joey was stunning.

Steve quickly caught up with his Joey and told him how great it was seeing his brothers again and seeing pictures of his nieces and nephews and kissed Steve again before Joey took Steve's hands in his.

"I got a present for you," Joey said.

Steve couldn't believe that they had only been going out for a few days and normally he didn't even start to think about buying presents until the two months mark, normally later.

Joey took out a very expensive and modern golden necklace with three small diamonds on it and Joey put it on Steve.

He felt so beautiful, stunning and gorgeous that it was a strange feeling to have because he had never been allowed to look like this, act like this and do something even remotely feminine that Steve was really surprised that he liked the necklace so much.

"I took it from the cabinet the other night. I thought it would look perfect on you, and you look even more stunning than normal," Joey said.

Steve just kissed beautiful Joey again because he knew that they would go on jobs together, teach each other how to become better art thieves and they would do a lot of loving in-between jobs. Steve just felt so excited to be with Joey that he wouldn't be surprised if they fell in love in the future and hopefully did a lot more together.

But whatever the future was going to bring, Steve and Joey were going to enjoy every single precious moment they had together and that was exactly how Steve liked it.

AUTHOR OF THE LITTLE ENGLISH PRIVATE EYE MYSTERIES

CONNOR WHITELEY

AULD
ALLIANCE
A GAY SPY ROMANTIC SUSPENSE SHORT STORY

AULD ALLIANCE
6th January 2023
Crete, Greece

MI6 Intelligence Officer Luca Mills had always had a soft spot for the amazing country of Greece because of its sensational food, breath-taking history and wonderful men (Greek men seriously knew how to have sex) so whenever Luca was summoned to Greece on MI6 business, he was hardly impressed and he always wanted to execute his mission quickly and effectively.

Anything to protect the amazing people of Greece, Europe and the UK.

Luca was walking along a very long sandy orange road that was so typical in Crete that all the damn roads just looked the same, without his GPS Luca honestly had no idea whatsoever if he would ever find his way around Crete. It was so massive for starters and it wasn't exactly like there were many signs showing him the way to the beach he was heading to.

And if the roads were bad enough then the endless fields of olive trees and cacti lining the road without any little rock walls was just cruel. As beautiful as the olive trees were with their thin branches, rough bark and gorgeous plump olives hanging off the trees, they too weren't helpful to him.

He couldn't steal any olives because everyone on Crete and throughout Greece was poor now, so one stolen olive to give him strength could mean yet another Greek family struggling to provide food on the table.

It really was that bad sadly.

Immense fiery orange hills made from solid crumbly rock seemed to rise out of the land in the distance, and that was what Luca really liked about Crete in a way because it was a bit of a weird place. It could be a beautiful island filled with olive trees, beaches and hot sexy Greek men but it could also be filled with deadly rock hills and cacti.

The air smelt wonderful of nature, sea salt and sweet olives that Luca was so tempted to steal just so he could have the privilege of tasting some real Greek olive oil but he couldn't yet because he had to focus on the mission, so now at least Luca sadly knew that the amazing taste of olive oil dipped in crusty buttery bread that forming on his tongue, would have to do him for now.

MI6 had sent Luca to Crete for a so-called secret and very simple mission, and Luca supposed that he should have realised instantly whenever a snobby desk jockey who hadn't done field work for ten years said a mission was "easy", it was going to be next to impossible.

And this mission seriously was.

Russian Federal Security Services had infiltrated Crete about two weeks ago and the Greek Government had thrown a lot of might to hunt down the Russians but they all turned up dead.

Thankfully some Greek National Intelligence Service contacts leaked the news about the Russian threat to the international intelligence community and as far as Luca knew the UK was the only country to answer, but even that wasn't correct.

Only Scotland, which was sadly part of the UK, had been the only country to answer so far.

As a proud Scot, Luca had pressed MI6 to let him go to Crete for the past week because it was his duty to stop Russia and help protect Europe. Of course the whole "protecting Europe" argument held no water with the English because as far as they were concerned all Europeans were dirty foul foreigners.

But Luca managed to wear his bosses down enough so they said yes to get rid of him and they seriously wanted to with the rusty gun they had given him and the other equipment they hadn't given him. MI6 had refused to give him a single gadget but they openly gave tons of gadgets to English agents.

Now that really was discrimination plain and simple.

Luca stepped to one side on the long orange sandy road and waved as a banged-up Greek car rushed past.

The car was so beaten, bruised and mostly destroyed that Luca honestly couldn't tell for a moment what make the car was. It was just a sad fact that most people in Greece were so poor that it was all they could afford.

At least using the information that a contact had given him in a local beautiful village in the nearby hills, Luca knew the Russians were located at a beach not far along this road so all that Luca needed to do was get to the beach, kill the Russians and recover any data he could.

Because Russians didn't just infiltrate a nation for the fun of it.

There had to be a plan afoot here and Luca just knew that whatever that plan was, it would scare him a lot more than he ever wanted to admit.

A damn bit more.

***

DGSE Intelligence Officer Pierre Martin seriously didn't know what all the fuss was about with Crete, because he seriously loved the absolutely perfect Greek men, he loved Greek food more than life itself and he was a real sucker for Greek history, but Crete?

As far as Pierre was concerned Crete was just a poor island that had been abandoned by mainland Greece, like so much of it, to suffer and decay into a wasteland.

And as Pierre was walking down a painful long orange sandy road, he could really understand that whilst his French bosses had loved him for going to Crete to help out, they all acknowledged that it was a wasteland and the Russians were stupid for wanting to travel to this particular wasteland of Greece. It was just a shame that everyone in French intelligence knew that the Russians actually weren't stupid and if they were here in Crete then there was an excellent reason why.

Pierre had phoned an ex-boyfriend at Europol to see if there was any top-secret information in Crete that would threaten European national security, and thankfully there wasn't. Apparently, there was something to do with the British on Crete a few years ago but Pierre really didn't care about that.

Not when a group of English people had beaten him up only last year when he was visiting London as a real tourist (not an intelligence officer) just because he was French and the UK Government had publicly said that the French were no friend of the UK.

It was pathetic but that was the world he lived in.

Pierre did enjoy the breathtaking views of Crete because it might have been an utter wasteland with nothing but olive trees, orange rocks and Cacti for as far as the eye could see but it was relaxing in a strange way.

It was even better that the air smelt of nature, olives and sea salt. It was a perfect way to wake up the senses.

And Pierre really knew his senses needed to be fully alert today.

A small dot in the distance made Pierre frown because he knew that someone else was coming towards him. He just knew that someone was travelling on the same road as him and even worse whoever the little dot was they could be a Russian agent.

If that was the case then they had to die.

A few minutes later the dot became visible and Pierre just stopped. His heart felt like it was going to explode. His legs felt weak. His entire body ached.

The man was absolutely gorgeous.

Pierre had just stared at the man who was the dot as he walked towards him. And Pierre was seriously just stunned there was no good way to do justice to the man's beauty. Pierre couldn't believe how perfect the man's longish brown hair was with its beautiful thickness, curls and... it was sheer perfection.

Pierre wanted so badly to run his fingers through the man's hair, and the man's fit sexy body in his skin-tight shorts, white shirt and white trainers only amplified how amazing the man was.

Before now Pierre had had no idea a man could look *this* good in some shorts, shirt and trainers. It was almost like the man was a god in incarnate, like from the stories and myths from the ancient Greece. Pierre even supposed this could be the God Adonis himself.

Then Pierre noticed the black rucksack on the man's bag and he instantly knew it was made by a brand that worked exclusively for the UK Government.

He was a fucking intelligence officer. Damn it. And an English one at that.

Pierre whipped out his pistol.

It took Pierre a few moments to understand why the Adonis wasn't aiming his gun at him, but Pierre just grinned when he realised the hot Adonis was stunned by him too.

"Who are you?" Pierre asked.

The Adonis grinned like a cute little schoolboy for a moment. "Who are you?"

"DGSE Officer Pierre Martin,"

The Adonis nodded. "Good, the French have always been good to my wee country,"

Pierre just looked at the Adonis because his accent was perfectly English just down to the little sounds and ways of speaking unique to each region of England, so presumably this hottie had worked a lot in the southeast, maybe Kent itself.

But the word *wee* sounded like he had said it on purpose, and there was only one country in the entire place that was friendly with France and used the word *wee* like that.

"You're a Scot?" Pierre asked, unsure what to make of that. He had studied at university in history and learnt a ton about Scottish-French historical relations, including the treaty that protected both countries called the Auld Alliance, and how both modern day governments continued to work on that powerful friendship despite the childishness of the UK Government.

"I am," the Adonis said, allowing more of his Scottish accent to come through. "And we are both here to kill the Russians I take it, so why don't we crack on with it instead of standing around?"

Pierre had to admit this man was so hot and he was from MI6 probably so he was highly trained, hot and Pierre really did want to spend more time with him.

"Fine," Pierre said. "I'm invoking the Auld Alliance,"

"I'm Luca and I'm pretty sure you cannot just invoke the Auld Alliance and it was an alliance between our countries to protect us against English invasions,"

Pierre shrugged. "These are modern times my friend and treaties that were never revoked have to evolve. What do you say?"

Pierre loved it how sexy Luca laughed and nodded his head and both of them started walking quickly to the beach where the Russians were meant to be.

And Pierre was seriously looking forward to getting to know this hottie a lot more.

All they had to do first was survive dealing with some Russians.

***

Luca couldn't believe how amazing Pierre was. He was so hot, clever and just flat out amazing, and the past thirty minutes, the length of time it had taken them to get to the beach had been simply magic. Luca felt like he really, really knew Pierre a lot better now and he really liked what he knew.

And it also helped that Pierre had an amazing ass and Pierre had jokingly lifted up his great-looking white t-shirt earlier and revealed his sensational abs to Luca, so at least he also knew that Pierre had a great body underneath his touristic look.

And thankfully the mission wasn't over yet so Luca didn't have to say goodbye.

Yet.

Luca and Pierre knelt down on some hard orange rock on the road that leant down to the large sandy beach in front of them. There was a rather steep rocky ridge lining the semi-circular beech with its dirty yellow sand so that would give them a height advantage over the enemy.

There was a group of four Russians in sand-coloured t-shirts, trousers and army boots working on something in the middle of the beach. Every so often the Russians looked up to see if anyone was around but thankfully they hadn't spotted them just yet.

The air smelt wonderful of sea salt, tea and lamb kebabs but that really troubled Luca a lot more than he wanted to admit because none of the Russians had any kebabs on them.

Luca felt the icy cold barrel of a gun against the back of his head.

"Get up," a woman said in a harsh Russian accent.

Luca and Pierre slowly stood up and his entire stomach twisted into a painful knot at the very idea that something could happen to the stunning Frenchman next to him.

Luca turned around and frowned at the very tall Russian with high cheekbones, black sunglasses and a burnt cheek. She was definitely the leader judging by her military medals hanging off her t-shirt and Luca really didn't want to underestimate her.

If these Russians were arrogant enough not to wear body armour when operating in enemy territory then they were either extremely stupid or they were extremely deadly.

Luca believed in the latter.

Luca and Pierre followed the stupid Russian woman over to the other four Russians who were all men and the Russians just smiled at them like Luca and Pierre were nothing more than toys to play with.

And toys to kill.

Luca just wished he could have saved Pierre from this, but it was probably Pierre's beauty that had made Luca lose focus long enough for the Russian woman to sneak up behind him.

"What are you doing?" the Russian woman asked. "No one is stupid enough to interfere with our plan and the Greek government seems to be okay,"

"How the hell did you figure out that? It was the Greeks that sent us," Luca said.

The Russian woman laughed. "A Scot pretending to be a Brit, that's funny even now as the English prepares to finish off Scotland,"

Luca just ignored the crazy Russian woman. He didn't doubt for a second she was telling the truth but this wasn't a time to get passionate about his belief in Scottish Independence.

All four Russians took out their own pistols and pointed them at Luca and Pierre.

Luca had to figure out a plan to save themselves. There were four highly trained Russians that were all armed and there was only two of them and the woman had taken their guns away.

So the only solution here was psychological warfare because at the end of the day these were Russians and Russian men hated taking orders from a so-called mere woman.

"Who's daughter is she?" Luca asked the Russian men. "You can't tell me a Russian woman actually *earned* the right to lead a mission,"

The men said nothing.

The woman punched Luca in the throat.

"Do you know most of the Russian prisoners in France are all women? It seems if a woman leads a mission then it is doomed," Pierre said.

Luca was seriously starting to fall for this hot sexy man.

The woman kicked Luca in the balls. Crippling pain filled him but it was worth the prize if it kept Europe safe.

"See hows she slashes out to prove how weak she is," Luca said.

"Shut up! Shut up!" the woman shouted.

Luca just looked at her as the woman aimed her pistol at his head but her hands were shaking so much that any bullet would miss him.

A shot went off.

The woman's head popped.

All four Russian men pointed their guns at Pierre and Luca as he quickly realised that it just might have been safer to keep the woman alive because she might have been saner that the men.

Because that was almost a universal truth. Women were a lot saner than men most of the time.

"Now then English," a Russian said, "you will help us open this box or the Frog as you say dies,"

Luca absolutely hated this Russian git. He had no problem with the English but he was Scottish, not English, and he had no problem with the French so he didn't need to call them foul names.

All Luca wanted to do was protect Pierre so that meant playing along a little longer and just hoping that he couldn't get them killed in the process.

Not a very tall order at all.

***

As one of the four Russian men placed Pierre in a very weak headlock, Pierre wanted nothing more than to simply slaughter these little Russian boys. Not because they were threatening him, or because they were threatening sexy Luca, but because of their sheer stinky smell.

It was disgusting.

"Unlock the box," the Russian man said with an eye that didn't work properly.

Pierre hadn't really looked at what foul thing the Russians were working on throughout all of this. He had been focusing way too much on the sexy Scot next to him and then focusing on that dumb Russian woman.

Now Pierre just frowned at the very high-tech looking metal briefcase that seemed to have some kind of biometric lock on the front of it requiring someone to place their fingerprint and a DNA sample on the lock to open it.

It was strange that such an item would be found here but it was a well-kept secret amongst the British intelligence agencies that Pierre had hacked his way into, that they did scatter a series of boxes throughout Europe before Brexit to act as caches for their agents in case they were ever in trouble.

This was clearly one of them.

And Pierre guessed that it was probably hard enough to get the boxes into these European countries let alone retrieve them after Brexit.

So the boxes were simply abandoned. But why did the Russians want this one?

"I can't," Luca said. "It won't open for me,"

The headlock around Pierre got a lot tighter. He was still sure he could break it but he needed the other three Russians distracted first.

"Fine," Luca said, "I'll try it but it won't end well,"

Pierre hated it as Luca knelt down on the hot orange sand, pressed his finger against the biometric lock and even spat on it too.

The box hissed a little and it seemed like it was going to refuse being opened. Pierre had no idea how it worked but right now he just needed to kill the Russians and escape.

And as much as he loved France he knew they would want him to retrieve whatever was in the English box but he couldn't do that to Luca.

The box buzzed open.

A Russian kicked Luca out the way.

All three Russians rushed over to the box and the man with the bad eye smiled as he held up a thick paper folder and just glared at Luca.

"You see," the man said. "This folder contains all the information you would need to blackmail the UK Government. It exposes their corruption, their illegal ops and even an assassination on French soil,"

Pierre felt his stomach twist in pain. He had heard the rumours of MI6 using Europe as its wild west background but it was impossible to believe it was true.

It clearly was.

"This would allow you to blackmail the UK Government into giving the Scottish people a choice about your future. Become an independent country or not. This folder is the key to your future," the Russian said.

Luca just laughed.

Pierre noticed the man holding him wasn't steady on his feet and thankfully it wouldn't take much to knock him over. Pierre just needed to feel where the man kept his gun. On the left or right side.

"Scotland will be free through legal means. No blackmail. No corruption. No nothing," Luca said. "And we would never work with the Russians,"

The Russians shook their heads.

"Fine. It was worth a shot. Kill them," the man said.

There wasn't time to find the gun.

Pierre jumped backwards.

Knocking the man over. The man opened his arms.

Pierre rolled away. Climbing on top of the Russian. Snapping his neck.

Pierre grabbed his gun. Rolled forward. Jumped up.

A Russian flew at him.

Pierre shot him in the head.

Another Russian tackled Pierre.

The man threw sand at Pierre.

The sand caught in his eyes.

Pierre was blinded.

The man slammed his fists into Pierre.

The man whacked Pierre around the face.

Pierre tried to block. He couldn't see the punches.

Blood gushed out of Pierre's mouth.

His vision cleared.

Pierre ducked.

The man didn't expect that. He overshot the punch. Giving Pierre an opening.

He took it.

Slamming his fists on the man's chin.

Teeth shattered.

The man leapt forward.

Pierre's head landed on the sand.

The man pushed him down.

Pierre started sinking. His head sunk into the sand.

Pierre struggled.

Pierre felt the man. He felt his fingers go into the man's mouth. Between his cheek and teeth.

Pierre pulled as hard as he could.

Ripping the man's cheek from his mouth.

The man screamed.

Pierre pushed himself up.

He slammed his fists into the man. The man fell over.

The man threw sand again.

Pierre dodged it.

The man slammed Pierre in the balls.

Pierre collapsed in crippling pain.

The man kicked Pierre in the head.

Pierre lost two teeth.

More blood gushed out his mouth.

Pierre was in agony.

The man whipped out a knife.

He charged at Pierre.

Pierre rolled over.

The man didn't expect that.

Pierre tripped him over.

The man screamed.

He fell on the knife.

The knife slashed the man's throat.

A bullet shot went off and Pierre shot up and froze. He couldn't have his sexy Luca dead. Luca just couldn't be dead. He couldn't lose him.

Pierre spun around and sunk to his knees again in sheer relief that his strong, beautiful, perfect Luca was standing a few metres away with a few marks and cuts and bruises with a dead Russian at his feet.

All the Russians were dead now and finally Pierre understood exactly what they had come for and as much as Pierre wanted to know what exactly was in that folder, Pierre just knew that him and Luca had to decide together.

Partly because of the Auld Alliance but also because it meant spending just a little or wee more time with such a hot Adonis.

A man that Pierre seriously wanted to get to know a lot, lot better.

***

Luca just held Pierre's strong sexy and very firm body as they both sat on the orange sand, staring out over the oddly peacefully Aegean sea with four Russian corpses behind him. Luca really loved the amazing coolness, refreshing and sheer heat of the air and there had to be some sea salt in the delightful air that made the taste of fish and chips form on his tongue like he used to have with his family when they holidayed to England once or twice.

There was something so peaceful, relaxing and simply brilliant about sitting here on a Cretan beach with no one else for miles around and with a hot sexy Frenchman in his arms.

Luca hadn't exactly known what to expect when he had first hugged and held Pierre, but he really was perfect. His body was firm, he had a great six-pack and his skin was smooth, silky and tasted perfect as Luca had kissed his injuries gently earlier.

Something they had both laughed about for a little while before they just silently agreed to enjoy the moments they had left together.

It was a sad truth that all those boxes were fitted with trackers so when one of them was opened, MI6 was notified so Luca just knew that sooner or later some British commandos would show up to "help" him so Pierre had to be gone by then.

Yet until then the two sexy men just wanted to spend a tiny bit more time together, and Luca just looked at the beautiful, injured Frenchman in his arms.

"Do want to take anything?" Luca asked, grinning.

Pierre smiled. "Oh believe me the DGSE would love me for any intelligence for blackmail against the English but I respect you too much for that,"

Luca just shook his head because Pierre really did care about him. "Just take it. Scotland will be fine without illegal blackmail and committing crimes. The British Empire has fallen all over the world. So much of the Empire is free and many former colonies are more successful than the UK. So Scotland will follow in time,"

Luca loved it when Pierre looked at him and Luca got to stare into his stunning eyes.

"Let the English take the folders when they come for you," Pierre said. "France doesn't need it, but I can't say I won't need you. It hardly seems fair we only have a few minutes together,"

Luca wasn't sure what he was talking about there then he noticed there was a little black speedboat coming across the horizon and Luca just frowned and rolled his eyes.

"We will meet again and if you're ever in Scotland or the UK. Find me and I'll show you a great time,"

Pierre laughed as they both stood up. "You have clearly never had sex with a Frenchman. We can beat you Scots at sex any day,"

Luca just kissed Pierre and savoured every single precious second of that hot passionate kiss, and the flavour of his soft silky lips and the sheer electricity that was flowing between them with such intensity that Luca was wondering if they would both be electrocuted.

A fate that Luca might have preferred instead of being apart from him.

"We will meet again my Adonis," Perrie said.

"As you said, my *adore*," Luca said, "the Auld Alliance demands it,"

As Pierre ran off and the sound of the speedboat got louder and louder, Luca just loved listening to the sweet lyrical laughter of Perrie. Not just an intelligence officer for a foreign power, not just an intelligence rival that was apparently a threat to UK national security but a beautiful sexy and clever potential boyfriend that Luca seriously looked forward to meeting again.

And it was just amazing to Luca that it was all only possible because some Alliance made hundreds of years ago. Now that really was a beautiful thing.

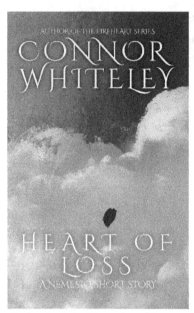

GET YOUR FREE AND EXCLUSIVE SHORT STORY NOW!
LEARN ABOUT NEMESIO'S PAST!

https://www.subscribepage.com/fireheart

About the author:

Connor Whiteley is the author of over 60 books in the sci-fi fantasy, nonfiction psychology and books for writer's genre and he is a Human Branding Speaker and Consultant.

He is a passionate warhammer 40,000 reader, psychology student and author.

Who narrates his own audiobooks and he hosts The Psychology World Podcast.

All whilst studying Psychology at the University of Kent, England.

Also, he was a former Explorer Scout where he gave a speech to the Maltese President in August 2018 and he attended Prince Charles' 70th Birthday Party at Buckingham Palace in May 2018.

Plus, he is a self-confessed coffee lover!

OTHER SHORT STORIES BY CONNOR WHITELEY

Mystery Short Story Collections

Criminally Good Stories Volume 1: 20 Detective Mystery Short Stories

Criminally Good Stories Volume 2: 20 Private Investigator Short Stories

Criminally Good Stories Volume 3: 20 Crime Fiction Short Stories

Criminally Good Stories Volume 4: 20 Science Fiction and Fantasy Mystery Short Stories

Criminally Good Stories Volume 5: 20 Romantic Suspense Short Stories

Mystery Short Stories:

Protecting The Woman She Hated

Finding A Royal Friend

Our Woman In Paris

Corrupt Driving

A Prime Assassination

Jubilee Thief

Jubilee, Terror, Celebrations

Negative Jubilation

Ghostly Jubilation

Killing For Womenkind

A Snowy Death

Miracle Of Death

A Spy In Rome

The 12:30 To St Pancreas

A Country In Trouble

A Smokey Way To Go

A Spicy Way To GO

A Marketing Way To Go

A Missing Way To Go

A Showering Way To Go

Poison In The Candy Cane

Christmas Innocence
You Better Watch Out
Christmas Theft
Trouble In Christmas
Smell of The Lake
Problem In A Car
Theft, Past and Team
Embezzler In The Room
A Strange Way To Go
A Horrible Way To Go
Ann Awful Way To Go
An Old Way To Go
A Fishy Way To Go
A Pointy Way To Go
A High Way To Go
A Fiery Way To Go
A Glassy Way To Go
A Chocolatey Way To Go
Kendra Detective Mystery Collection Volume 1
Kendra Detective Mystery Collection Volume 2
Stealing A Chance At Freedom
Glassblowing and Death
Theft of Independence
Cookie Thief
Marble Thief
Book Thief
Art Thief
Mated At The Morgue
The Big Five Whoopee Moments
Stealing An Election
Mystery Short Story Collection Volume 1
Mystery Short Story Collection Volume 2
Criminal Performance
Candy Detectives

Key To Birth In The Past

Escape In The Hesitation
Inspiration In Need
Singing Warriors
Knowledge is Power
Killer of Polluters
Climate of Death
The Family Mailing Affair
Defining Criminality
The Martian Affair
A Cheating Affair
The Little Café Affair
Mountain of Death
Prisoner's Fight
Claws of Death
Bitter Air
Honey Hunt
Blade On A Train
Fantasy Short Stories:
City of Snow
City of Light
City of Vengeance
Dragons, Goats and Kingdom
Smog The Pathetic Dragon
Don't Go In The Shed
The Tomato Saver
The Remarkable Way She Died
The Bloodied Rose
Asmodia's Wrath
Heart of A Killer
Emissary of Blood
Dragon Coins
Dragon Tea
Dragon Rider
Sacrifice of the Soul

Heart of The Flesheater
Heart of The Regent
Heart of The Standing
Feline of The Lost
Heart of The Story
City of Fire
Awaiting Death

Other books by Connor Whiteley:

Bettie English Private Eye Series
A Very Private Woman
The Russian Case
A Very Urgent Matter
A Case Most Personal
Trains, Scots and Private Eyes
The Federation Protects

Lord of War Origin Trilogy:
Not Scared Of The Dark
Madness
Burn Them All

The Fireheart Fantasy Series
Heart of Fire
Heart of Lies
Heart of Prophecy
Heart of Bones
Heart of Fate

City of Assassins (Urban Fantasy)
City of Death
City of Marytrs
City of Pleasure
City of Power

Agents of The Emperor
Return of The Ancient Ones
Vigilance
Angels of Fire
Kingmaker
The Eight
The Lost Generation
Lord Of War Trilogy (Agents of The Emperor)
Not Scared Of The Dark
Madness
Burn It All Down

The Garro Series- Fantasy/Sci-fi
GARRO: GALAXY'S END
GARRO: RISE OF THE ORDER
GARRO: END TIMES
GARRO: SHORT STORIES
GARRO: COLLECTION
GARRO: HERESY
GARRO: FAITHLESS
GARRO: DESTROYER OF WORLDS
GARRO: COLLECTIONS BOOK 4-6
GARRO: MISTRESS OF BLOOD
GARRO: BEACON OF HOPE
GARRO: END OF DAYS

Winter Series- Fantasy Trilogy Books
WINTER'S COMING
WINTER'S HUNT
WINTER'S REVENGE
WINTER'S DISSENSION

Miscellaneous:
RETURN
FREEDOM
SALVATION
Reflection of Mount Flame
The Masked One
The Great Deer

Gay Romance Novellas
Breaking, Nursing, Repairing A Broken Heart
Jacob And Daniel
Fallen For A Lie
Spying And Weddings

All books in 'An Introductory Series':
Careers In Psychology
Psychology of Suicide
Dementia Psychology
Forensic Psychology of Terrorism And Hostage-Taking
Forensic Psychology of False Allegations
Year In Psychology
BIOLOGICAL PSYCHOLOGY 3RD EDITION
COGNITIVE PSYCHOLOGY THIRD EDITION
SOCIAL PSYCHOLOGY- 3RD EDITION
ABNORMAL PSYCHOLOGY 3RD EDITION
PSYCHOLOGY OF RELATIONSHIPS- 3RD EDITION
DEVELOPMENTAL PSYCHOLOGY 3RD EDITION
HEALTH PSYCHOLOGY
RESEARCH IN PSYCHOLOGY
A GUIDE TO MENTAL HEALTH AND TREATMENT
AROUND THE WORLD- A GLOBAL LOOK AT
DEPRESSION
FORENSIC PSYCHOLOGY
THE FORENSIC PSYCHOLOGY OF THEFT, BURGLARY

CPSIA information can be obtained
at www.ICGtesting.com
Printed in the USA
LVHW041828290323
742975LV00030B/921